"Gripping stories of the web we create from our twisted choices—Blauveldt's writing is swift and engaging. Intriguing and intense, these characters will stay with you long after their stories end."

Lania Knight, Writer, Lecturer, and Tutor

"Once I started reading the second novella in this collection, *Ask Gloria*, I couldn't stop! Did you ever hit the wall over and over? Jennifer did. Her moving story, unfolding in the time of COVID, vividly relates her struggles with alcohol and the specter of her daughter's abuse at the hands of her partner. Is there a way forward for Jennifer? To find out, read *Ask Gloria*, it's worth it."

Suzanne Gagnon
Author of *Passeport Rouge*

TO PLAY AT GOD

Two Novellas

by Anna Blauveldt

PUBLERATI

This book is a work of fiction. Names, characters, businesses, organizations, places, events, and incidents are either the product of the author's imagination or are used fictitiously. Any resemblance to actual persons, living or dead, events, or locales is entirely coincidental.

Cover design by William Oleszczuk

Trade Paperback ISBN: 978-1-7350273-9-5
Ebook ISBN: 978-0-9979137-7-4

Publerati donates a portion of all sales to help spread literacy. Please learn more at www.publerati.com

Dedicated to John, who has unreservedly encouraged my aspirations to become an author.

TO PLAY AT GOD

Two Novellas

"You don't choose your own family. They are God's gift to you, as you are to them."

—Archbishop Desmond Tutu

"Most especially, must I tread with care in matters of life and death. . . . Above all, I must not play at God."

—Excerpt from the Modern Hippocratic Oath

1990s

Chapter One

He'd done it before—countless times—when he wasn't rushed and when nobody on the other side of the door was waiting for the results.

Neither was the case this time.

On his side of the door, the cheerless space (called the Jerkoff Room by clinic staff when they thought he wasn't listening) was pretty much what he expected. Equipped with just the bare essentials to get the job done. Tired white walls with no windows and no pictures. A brown pleather recliner that had clearly suffered the furtive motions of a thousand handjobs. Fortunately, it was covered by a fresh paper shield.

Porn magazines on a side table were supposed to arouse. *Stag* and *Swank* and half a dozen lesser-knowns. Greg Evans was skeptical. He was no germaphobe, but if he actually had to resort to them, he'd avoid the grungy ones with curled-back pages and shadows of too many fingerprints where the ink had rubbed off.

And if the magazines didn't do the trick, a TV and VCR were set up in the corner. Beside them, a stack of old movie cassettes with titles like "My Bare Lady" and "King Dong." It would be way too charitable to call them classics. Couldn't they spend a few bucks to update the viewing pleasure? It was the 1990s, for God's sake.

If he weren't so turned off by the whole scene, he'd find it laughable. But all he could manage was a smirk. How pathetic was this? It was as if the clinic was taunting him and all the others sent here. In this sad little place created just for people like you, we *dare* you to produce the goods.

And produce he did. It only took a few minutes fantasizing about Sharon Stone. In a swanky hotel room. With whipped cream. It wasn't that difficult at all.

He'd risen to the challenge before. At fifty-two, he'd already fathered two daughters with his first wife—Fiona and Sarah, now adults. To him, this was clear evidence that his "boys" were healthy and active. Or at least they used to be. As a result, he'd shown up at the clinic that morning with a certain complacency. At the same time, he was just a little annoyed he had to go through this whole rigmarole to prove the problem wasn't with him.

For two years, his wife, Karen, had tried to get pregnant. She was now forty-one, and the odds were dwindling. He was okay if it didn't happen. He'd already done his paternal duties and would be quite happy to forego the diapers-and-sleepless-nights routine all over again.

But Karen was a driven woman. A successful lawyer and proud workaholic throughout her twenties and thirties, she'd suddenly become broody at thirty-nine. Obsessively broody. Since then, she withered when each passing month, each unwelcome period, robbed her of yet another chance to conceive. She was getting desperate.

So, being Karen, she did something about it. Got them an appointment at a leading fertility clinic with Dr. Alan Wilcross. Dr. Wilcross was universally acclaimed as a miracle worker for the child-hungry well-to-do who flocked to his office.

It didn't go unnoticed by Greg that, in the occasional media feature on the doctor, he made sure people knew he also treated the not-so-well-to-do on a pro bono basis. Greg was cynical about Wilcross and his self-promotion. Conspicuous benevolence gave the specialist's reputation a boost, no doubt. Still, to his credit, he was very good at his chosen profession.

Greg went along with Karen. He felt he had little choice but to support her in her quest. Who was he to deny her something he already had? Besides, their life as a couple might crater if he balked.

First came the physical examination for them both. Nothing seemed amiss there. Then various tests were run. For him, it meant presenting his sperm for analysis. If they were viable, then a whole array of other possible hurdles would have to be explored, one by one. Don't think about that, Greg told himself. Don't think about the irksome and potentially futile procedures. The emotional toll on poor Karen and the expenses piling up. Just take it one step at a time.

So there he was, ejaculating into a small plastic container just like the ones they used for urine specimens. Marching it back to Dr Wilcross' office suite and handing it over to Marjorie the receptionist. Mission accomplished, for that day at least.

He didn't wait for the results.

As he put on his jacket, Greg glanced at other patients in the pink-and-blue waiting area. One woman sat there on her own leafing through *Family Circle,* a magazine not at all like the nasty ones in the little white room. Across from her, a youngish couple perched on the edge of their seats in the corner, holding hands and staring at dozens of baby photos covering the wall to the left. Those babies were the happy endings. Dr. Wilcross' version of gold medals.

Greg turned to leave, and another couple entered. They nodded at him, rushed over to the receptionist, and declared they were Jason and Megan Murray, here for their ten o'clock appointment. He hoped things worked out for them. They both looked so damned eager.

He made a quick exit to the clinic parking lot, jumped into his vintage Volvo and gunned it for the campus. Students would already be assembling for his first lecture of the day. As he sped off, he had only one thought about his little romp in the Jerkoff Room: he was too old for this.

As Greg had suspected, the semen analysis showed all was normal with good sperm shape and count, and they were wiggling around exactly the way they were supposed to.

Next, it was Karen's turn. It didn't take long to find out the apparent culprit: a benign fibroid tumor in her uterus, picked up by ultrasound. That meant an operation to remove it.

It appeared to be a success, but still, after three more months, nothing was happening and Karen was heartbroken. Again. It was almost as difficult for Greg, being around her and trying to provide comfort. He would have been quite happy to give up at that point, but there was no stopping Karen.

Plan B was in vitro fertilization. Not the most romantic way of starting a new life, but to Greg's mind, there was little romance in this anyway. Karen's eggs were extracted and brought together with Greg's sperm in the lab. That first time, three fertilized eggs were implanted in Karen's uterus. Then they waited.

Yes, it was invasive. It was expensive. But after two cycles, it worked. Karen was going to have her baby. She was beyond ecstatic, and Greg had to admit he was getting used to the idea, too.

6

Chapter Two

"Can we talk about a baby again tonight, Lennie?"

Joan Martin and Helen Stewart had been celebrating two decades together by candlelight, over pasta and a nice Cabernet Sauvignon. They were both on the edge of tipsy by the time they reached dessert.

"Like I keep saying, we're not getting any younger. I see more and more gray hairs in the mirror every morning . . . and another cat won't do it for me. Just think, we could have a little boy or girl with your gorgeous blue eyes. Let's go for it, hon!"

It was the first time that evening Joan raised the topic.

Their earlier conversation had been full of memories. Mainly it was about the happy ones, but, inevitably, it also dipped way back to the late 70s when they first came out to their families.

They'd been roomies, secretly shacked up together for six months by that point. For some of their siblings, this came as no surprise. Others, including both sets of parents, found it difficult to accept. They made it known that Joan and Helen were not welcome at family gatherings.

It was tough on both of them.

Gradually, there was reconciliation. Over the past decade, they were invited to all the big events: birthday parties, Christmas dinners, school graduations. They started “borrowing” their nieces and nephews to go to the movies or the circus or the zoo. Fun hours with the kids, then back to the parents for drop-off at the end of the day.

Nevertheless, after all that time as a couple, there was still something missing. At least, as far as Joan was concerned. She didn’t want to borrow their siblings’ kids anymore. She wanted a child of their own. She’d first broached the idea with Helen months earlier. These days, she was pushing for it more fervently.

“Honestly, Joan! Do we have to do this now? You’ve brought it up *so many* times . . .”

Too much wine made Helen blunt. She had doubts about the whole baby thing, and didn’t hide her irritation that she was hearing about it yet again. On their special evening, no less.

“ . . . and I always have the same issues. Are we really up for all the hassle? Not to mention the expense.”

Joan ignored the tone and pressed on.

“Well . . . I am, at least. And you know we can afford it. We’ve almost paid off the mortgage on this place. But tell me, what else is bothering you? Don’t hold back this time. I can take it.”

“What can I say? It’s a lot to think about,” Helen grumbled as she rose and began to clear the table. She organized her thoughts as she removed the plates and blew out the candles. Now she was feeling defensive and had no intention of holding back.

Joan was right. Money wasn't really an issue. Helen was a veterinarian and Joan a university administrator. Neither had reached the six figures mark in their salaries, but pooled together they were doing just fine.

No, there were other things troubling Helen. To start with, how would they go about having a child? Would they adopt? Or try to get pregnant, and with whose sperm? Absurd images of one of their male friends and a turkey baster came to mind. What if that friend wanted access to the child later on, or some other unforeseen entanglement arose? Would it be better to go to a sperm bank? Risk an anonymous donor?

So many questions. Not enough information to go on.

Helen knew they could work their way through the answers, but she also had a much bigger worry. How would it affect the way things were between the two of them? She wanted her life with Joan to stay just as it was. Sweetly cluttered and easygoing, with cherished little rituals that had grown organically over the years. Strolling through the Saturday morning produce market. Sharing the Sunday edition over the breakfast special at the diner. Together, they enjoyed occasional evenings at the repertory theatre and spontaneous road trips south of the border. As far as Helen was concerned, it was pretty much idyllic, the way things were now. Having a baby would change that. Goodbye, spontaneous anything. Hello, diapers, feedings, and car seats. And that would be just the beginning. Later, there would be daycare and playdates and God knows what else. All that planning and paraphernalia would make life *so* complicated, and she preferred things simple. Maybe it was the vet in her, but she could happily settle for another cat instead.

For the first time, she explained all this to Joan.

Joan smiled, walked over to Helen and wrapped her arms around her. Helen was petite. So much so that Joan could rest her chin on the top of Helen's head. They fit together perfectly.

"My poor Lennie!"

Joan rocked her from side to side.

"So many worries . . . we can get through all that. One step at a time. It'll be worth it in the end, don't you think?"

It didn't seem too complicated to Joan. She was the big-picture dreamer of the two. She always figured things would turn out for the best. For her, somehow, they usually did.

"For starters why don't we invite Al over for a beer one of these days? I mean, he's the expert on making babies. He'd help us figure that part out for sure."

Joan and Alan Wilcross had known each other since they were students. They met at one of the early 420 rallies, where they and a dozen others smoking pot in front of the Queen's Park legislative building were briefly detained by the police and then released. After that, they were each other's "date" when they were at loose ends. They comforted each other over failed romances and failed courses. And they indulged in the edgier side of undergrad life, too, going to toga parties, protest demonstrations, and drug-infused rock concerts.

After graduation, though, they drifted apart. Started moving in different circles, especially when Alan began his rise to the top of the fertility business. He "married up" and joined the right clubs. Not Joan's style. To her, he'd changed from socially conscious to socially ambitious. Still, they kept in touch, occasionally meeting for drinks. When it was just the two of them, he seemed like the same old Al. No Dr. Wilcross pretensions and no embellished British accent. Helen wasn't as close to him. She and Joan only got together after Joan graduated, but she knew all about his reputation for successful pregnancies. Everybody did. So she went along with Joan's suggestion to invite him over. Maybe he could make the options clearer for them. But he wouldn't make her feel any better about how a baby would change her life with Joan.

The front door opened and Alan stepped in. This was his first time visiting their home. Even though it was the end of a muggy July workday, he still looked the cool professional in his tailored summer wool blazer, crisp pressed pants, and tasselled Italian loafers. Every strand of his blond hair was perfectly styled to conceal a growing bald spot. There wasn't a hint of perspiration on his forehead or anywhere else.

He put his Louis Vuitton briefcase on the floor in the vestibule before Joan greeted him with her usual bear hug. Helen's embrace that followed was less enthusiastic. Then they led him to their living room.

Alan looked around. The décor, he decided, might kindly be classified as bohemian. Mismatched furniture, likely accumulated from garage sales and a couple of trips to IKEA. A framed Miles Davis concert poster from 1959 hung at a slight angle above the fireplace mantel. The rugs were good quality hand-knotted Afghans, but were almost worn through in places. Probably passed down and now decades beyond their prime. Matchstick blinds, the kind hard-up students buy when they finally upgrade from flags in the windows, did nothing to hold back the summer heat. No air conditioning, of course.

They continued through the dining room and past the kitchen to a covered porch. There, they settled in wicker chairs facing the backyard. A cat seemed to be stalking unseen prey in an overgrown vegetable garden on the left. The rest of the parched yard needed mowing.

The whole scene was reminiscent of Alan's post-grad digs. Except he'd moved on, and they hadn't. Compared to the spectacular residence where he'd dined with colleagues the previous evening—a designer's contemporary masterpiece—this place was totally lacking in style and elegance.

Nevertheless, shabby as it was, there was something about it that reflected the years of deep caring, the taken-for-granted easy affection, between these two women. Alan had to admire that. He almost wished he had the same casual comfort where he lived. Almost.

Over cold beers, he told them it would have to be a short

visit as he had another function to attend that evening.

Joan spoke up.

"So, Al, maybe you wondered why I invited you here this time, instead of the pub?"

He did, but waited to hear more.

"Well . . . we wanted to discuss something with you in private. Kind of a big deal for us, actually. We thought it would be easier to talk about it here."

Easier? Possibly. But Alan could see both Joan and Helen were suddenly fidgety. And they looked everywhere but at him.

Neither of them wanted to go first. Perhaps, Joan thought, she was dreaming in technicolor. Maybe it was presumptuous even to think about doing this at their age, in their circumstances, let alone raise it with Al.

Helen had other concerns. To her, saying the words out loud to him would make it feel real and not just Joan's wistful musings. Like they were starting something that, once it got rolling, couldn't be stopped.

Alan waited a long twenty seconds. Then he made a show of checking his Rolex. Joan saw this, cleared her throat and carried on.

"Lennie and I are thinking we might like to have a baby. And we were wondering if you could help?" She then quickly added " . . . with your expertise, of course. We have lots of questions."

Alan wasn't entirely surprised. It wasn't the first time

he'd been approached by a lesbian couple eager to start a family.

"For sure. What would you like to know?"

His previously relaxed posture snapped into professional mode, and his barely discernable English accent suddenly came on stronger. Joan figured this was how he must look and sound at the clinic.

They asked, and he answered. They covered everything together. The options for finding a sperm donor, and whether a friend or even one of Joan's or Helen's brothers could inseminate his sister's partner. Sperm bank. Artificial insemination. The decision on who would carry the baby. He gave them lots to think about.

It was almost time for Alan to go but before he stood to leave, he surprised them. He surprised himself, too.

"Well, I suppose I could always be the lucky donor . . . "

It was a toss-away line. A weak attempt to lighten things up.

" . . . after all, I don't have two heads, and I'm not a cocaine addict. I can add one and one and get two most of the time. So I qualify on the basics, at least."

Alan stopped himself after that. He realized this might turn serious. Then he proceeded to examine the bottom of his empty beer mug in microscopic detail.

Shit! What was he saying? Was he going to regret this? Maybe he should've thought about it more before opening his mouth.

There were no negatives for Joan and Helen, so far as he could tell. As for him, there was one big drawback: what would his children think if they found out? How would Karoline or Michael feel about a new half-brother or half-sister? What if they hated him for it?

He was less concerned about his wife's reaction. The second Alicia knew, she'd likely dump him in that imperious way of hers. Marriage over, just like that. He'd hear from her lawyer the next day. Alan figured that was going to happen sooner or later anyway. It didn't bother him all that much.

So the big question was, could he trust Joan and Helen not to tell anyone? The answer was yes. He knew Joan and she was solid. For more than twenty years, he and she still kept plenty of secrets from their misspent university years. He was confident nobody else would ever hear about this.

The two women waited for him to continue. Finally he did, but the humor was gone.

"All joking aside, I suppose it really *could* be an option for you . . . and if things worked out, I wouldn't make any claims on the baby. I wouldn't want any involvement at all. In fact, I would need you to keep this just between the three of us. I don't know how Alicia and the kids would react if they knew. Not well, I suspect."

He looked first at Joan, and then at Helen, for some sort of response. None was forthcoming. This was turning awkward.

"So . . . why don't we all think about it a few days? See

how we feel and get back in touch?"

Both women nodded. They needed the extra time. Neither of them was sure how the other was reacting.

Joan tried to hide that she was already excited. But she also worried that Al could easily take back what he was proposing. And she wasn't confident Helen would go for it.

She was right. Helen's first thought was that they were being offered a gift she didn't want.

All three were silent as they rose, carried their mugs back to the kitchen and went to the front door to see him off. Their conversation had taken them far beyond what any of them intended. Maybe it even went too far. Now was not the time to add more.

Alan climbed into his Audi and waved back at them as he left for his board meeting. On the way, he thought about playing one of his AC/DC CDs, but chose Bach's "Goldberg Variations" instead. Classier, he decided, even if he was alone in the car.

He wondered what the hell made him come up with the idea. He'd never done it before. Actually offered his own sperm to a couple.

So why now?

Obviously, he liked to make couples happy by helping them have babies. This time, he could make Joan happy. And this time, she and Helen weren't patients from his clinic roster. It was personal and private. No ethical issues there that he could see.

But there was something else. Something that hadn't

occurred to him before. The idea of fathering another child was appealing to him. A little boy or girl with his genes. His brains. And, according to more than one girlfriend in his single days, his good looks. How could it possibly hurt to pass on some of these advantages? Surely, a couple like Joan and Helen who needed help conceiving would be glad to have his DNA in the mix. He'd be a better candidate than some unknown donor from a sperm bank.

After he was gone, the couple talked about it until Helen shut their conversation down. She pleaded a headache. In fact, she was royally pissed off.

Why would Joan want to go and mess up their lives with a baby? And why was Alan making it *so* easy for her to do so? He had all the answers, didn't he? It was almost like a conspiracy between those two.

What if she just said no to this crazy idea? Would Joan resent her the rest of their lives? Even worse, would it split them up?

That would be unthinkable.

No matter how this turned out, she couldn't win.

After an uncomfortable few hours avoiding each other, Joan raised it again as they went to bed.

"Of course, you're right, Lennie. A baby would complicate things for us," she admitted.

She pulled down the covers on the futon and climbed in.

"Our lives would totally change, just like any other couple who become parents. But I promise you we'd take turns with the diaper duties and midnight feedings and everything else. We'd share the load equally."

Helen got into bed on the other side and peered at Joan. How adamant was she that this was going to happen? She recognized Joan's expression instantly. She'd seen it before. The confidence in her smile, the firm resolve in the lines of her forehead. Joan wasn't going to back off. Things were going to change, no matter what. Not much point trying to resist.

Joan reached over to Helen and stroked her cheek.

"And there's the fun side too, you know. What about the amazing adventures we've had with our nieces and nephews? Don't you just love them to bits? And it would be even better with one of our own."

Helen rolled over on her back and looked up at the ceiling.

Yes, there were positives. She might as well try to focus on that.

"And if anything, hon, my feelings for you would only grow deeper in our little family of three. You *have* to know that, right? It would add so much to our life as a couple."

This appealed to Helen more than anything Joan had said before.

At last, as Joan moved her body close to Helen's and kissed her, she agreed. They would try for a baby. By insemination. With Alan's sperm.

Their conversation started up again over breakfast the next morning. There was a second big decision to make. Which one of them would be inseminated?

At thirty-eight, Helen was younger than Joan. The odds for a healthy pregnancy for her were much higher. But carrying a baby herself was not something Helen had ever wanted. This was Joan's idea. Why shouldn't *she* go through all that? True, she was five years older, but it wasn't impossible.

Eventually, Helen gave in on that, too. It only made sense, after all. If they were going to try to get pregnant, they might as well give themselves the best chance for success.

Joan called Alan a day later. She confirmed it was a "go" with them if he was still offering.

He was.

There wasn't a turkey baster in sight when it happened. It was on a lazy mid-August Saturday morning in his examination room at the clinic. Joan held Helen's hand while Alan inserted the syringe.

Chapter Three

Guests said they'd never seen anything like it. The wedding of the decade, some called it. At least the wedding of 1995. And if you weren't invited, it meant you simply didn't make the list of Who's Who in the city's Spanish and Greek communities.

Cristina Lopez and Alesandro Stephanidis borrowed from the best of both cultural traditions for their big day. Carrying a bouquet of orange blossoms, Cristina strode down the aisle in an elegant designer gown that showed off her svelte figure. Her tanned face and upswept mahogany coiffure were concealed by a lace mantilla veil, the same veil worn by her mother and her grandmother on their wedding days.

At the front of the cathedral, Alesandro turned and smiled back at her. He was slightly taller than his diminutive bride, and had dark good looks inherited from both his parents. With his thick black hair, olive-toned skin, and brown eyes that were almost too pretty for a man, everyone told him he looked just like John Stamos. As the ceremony proceeded and the Stefana crown ritual joined them in marriage, family and friends were sure only wonderful things lay in store for these two.

Afterwards, a Spanish guitarist serenaded the guests as they entered the reception hall. He played with passion and elegance. A feast of paella, lamb with Orzo, baklava, and so much more was served. Ouzo and sangria flowed freely. There was also passion, but no attempt at elegance whatsoever, in the music performed later by the Greek band. The circle dancing and eating and drinking went on for hours. Many of the younger guests partied till the sun came up the next morning.

Following a month-long honeymoon cruise, they settled into married life. Of course, compared to some young couples just starting out, things weren't all that difficult for them. Their wedding gift from Alesandro's parents had been a condo in a gated community. His family owned a successful chain of Greek restaurants and money was no issue for them. Custom furnishings gave their place European flair, and there was a shiny new BMW in their underground parking garage.

Alesandro, the only son, was being groomed to take over the business when his father Ari retired. Cristina's background was less privileged. Still, she had a promising career with the local operations of an international airline. This meant lots of opportunities to fly to all sorts of exotic places. For a while, life was as good as it could get for Cristina and Alesandro.

Six months later, for the first time as a married couple, they joined in the Christmas gatherings of both families. For them, the holiday was celebrated twice—two weeks apart—according to the different Catholic and Greek Orthodox calendars. But they got the same message from both sides. It was time for them to start a family.

They were fully expecting this. Their families tended to be old-country traditional after all. Lots of babies, starting young, was what they wanted for the couple. Cristina and Alesandro easily brushed off the hints.

After the holidays, the pressure continued. Perhaps not surprisingly, Ari pushed the most. He was anxious for them to start the next Stephanidis generation. Cristina's widowed mother Bianca went on about it, too. Still, the young couple wanted a few more years of freedom before being tied down with babies.

Around the time of their first anniversary, the hints started to bite.

"Come on, Alesandro! What the hell are you waiting for? You've had your fun. Now you've got family obligations to think about."

"We have lots of time for babies, Papa. Cristina wants to work a few more years. Things are going really well for her right now with the airline."

"Why is *she* making all the decisions? Aren't you man enough? We're talking about our future, after all. As a family and as a business. Don't let us down!"

It was a stand-off after that.

The two men hadn't spoken in ten days, but Alesandro couldn't stop thinking about what his father had said. Having a child right away wasn't actually such a bad idea. And Ari was making his life *so* difficult about it. Accusing him of being intimidated by Cristina and *her* agenda. Well, he wasn't about to be intimidated by her. Or by anyone else. Ever.

"I've been thinking, Cristina. Let's try for a baby now. Why hold off? We can always hire a nanny so you can go back to work after."

It was twilight. He'd just brought two balloon glasses of cognac to their loveseat in front of the fireplace. His idea of a romantic setting. Maybe she could be seduced into changing her mind.

"Where's this coming from, Alesandro? We agreed to wait a few years. And when it *does* happen, I want to raise our babies by myself. Not leave them with some stranger."

So much for the seduction.

"You know everybody's counting on us. And my parents have been *so* good to you. Why ignore how the rest of us feel?"

"I can't believe you're siding with them against me! Don't try to bully me about this, Alesandro. It won't work. I'm not going to change my mind."

And she didn't.

Two years later, the time was finally right. For both of them. Cristina stopped taking the pill. Then they followed her cycles closely and made extra time for sex when she was ovulating.

But the perfect couple did not get pregnant, even after a full year of trying.

It was twelve months of growing frustration. Everything else in their lives had come to them so easily, why not this? And, of course, they had to cope with the reactions of their families. Cristina found it difficult to deal with her mother's pity. Her mother-in-law's reproaches were even worse. *What was wrong with her anyway?*, was Agnes' message. *Too delicate? Too much for her to handle? So disappointing for everyone. Poor Alesandro!*

It never occurred to any of them that the problem was with him, not her. The couple only discovered this after they were referred to Dr. Alan Wilcross.

At their first appointment, he asked them about their medical histories. Then, he thoroughly examined both Cristina and Alesandro and found no physical anomalies with either of them. Bloodwork and ultrasound and other tests were scheduled, but it was the semen analysis that revealed what was wrong. Alan explained at their second visit that Alesandro had an extremely low sperm count.

Alesandro's reaction was no surprise to him. Alan had seen his type before, and he was not a fan. Right from the beginning, there'd been that alpha male attitude that sprang from extreme privilege. The upfront presumption it was the woman's fault. Then, after learning the truth, the initial disbelief followed by anger and embarrassment.

Alesandro didn't have to say a word. It was all there in the way he puffed up his chest and shook his head in denial, as if doing so would change the diagnosis. Then came the curt statement that they'd go for a second opinion.

Just another entitled asshole, Alan thought. But who said he had to like all his patients?

Alesandro couldn't get out of the clinic fast enough. Cristina drove them home, and he sulked silently beside her all the way.

He let loose as soon as he closed the front door of their condo.

"Jesus Christ! What a disaster! Imagine if my father found out. It's bad enough he insults us about going to see a fertility specialist."

His face was red as he paced back and forth, puffing furiously on a Karelia. Cristina usually made him go onto the balcony to smoke, but not this time. He was too upset. A large ash dropped on the blue silk rug and he ignored it.

"He fucking goes on and on about me not being man enough. Maybe he's right. Maybe I'm not." Alesandro stopped, turned around and looked at her. "Don't tell your mother about this. Don't tell *anyone*! I would be the laughingstock of my whole family if they knew—"

"Seriously? You don't really believe this has anything to do with how manly you are, do you? And why do you give a shit what your father would say? It's none of his business."

Cristina thought Alesandro had a more modern take on being a man. Not this throwback macho crap. Obviously, she wrong. But it was time to calm things down.

"And it's nobody else's business either. So, I'll keep it to myself. But I just *know* your mother will still be pointing her finger at me."

Alesandro stopped his social drinking and even gave up smoking. *Try a healthier lifestyle for a while,* Alan had told him before they'd left his office, and they'd do a second analysis. The problem might be a temporary one.

It wasn't.

Once again, they sat opposite the doctor in his office as he gave them the bad news. The obvious fix was artificial insemination with sperm from a donor. He sent them away with some brochures about the procedure to help them make a decision.

They settled side-by-side on the sofa in the great room when they got back home. Cristina placed the brochures on the coffee table in front of them, but Alesandro wasn't interested. Instead, he lit his first cigarette in months. After two agitated drags, he made his feelings clear. He didn't like it at all.

"I wouldn't be the real father. It wouldn't be my kid."

Cristina stroked his arm. "I totally understand that. But what's the alternative? Adoption? You told me that was out of the question for you."

"It is."

"Then it looks like we either use a donor or we have no

children at all."

Alesandro frowned and forced out another stream of smoke. Cristina went on.

"Look. We both want a baby. I know you want a little Stephanidis to carry on the family name, and as much as I hate to bring it up, that's what your father's been going on about, too. Seems to me this is the only way that can happen."

It took a while for Alesandro to respond.

"Of course, I want a child. For us. Forget about what my father wants."

He stood up, went to the window and looked out over the landscaped gardens.

Why keep fighting it? Cristina was right. And there was no way to get the old man to stop harassing him about it until they popped out an heir. Using someone else's sperm, if they had to. But it had to be their secret.

"Okay, I give up." Alesandro turned around to face her and shrugged his shoulders in defeat. "We'll go with a donor. But if you do get pregnant, we could never let my father—or any of the others—know the baby isn't mine. I don't think they would accept it."

He wasn't sure he could ever fully accept it himself.

In the end, they didn't bother with a second opinion. They saw Alan again and told him they wanted to go ahead. After he reviewed all the procedures and risks, they made a selection from the clinic's sperm donor listings. The one they chose matched

Alesandro physically—his height, his hair color, even his Mediterranean background. Cristina and Alesandro made sure, as much as they possibly could, that a baby conceived with the donor's sperm would stand up to anybody's scrutiny as their own. Like a real Stephanidis. He or she would definitely look the part.

Three months later, to everybody's relief, Cristina and Alesandro proudly announced they were expecting. Their beautiful little boy or girl was due in the spring.

Chapter Four

When he and Megan introduced themselves to Alan Wilcross, Jason Murray's robust build and firm handshake concealed the fact he was seriously ill. That first time, they reviewed Jason's medical history and cancer diagnosis together. Then Alan explained the clinic's services step by step.

"We do a semen analysis. We do sperm freezing and storage. Later, when you want to try for a baby, your sperm can be thawed, and Megan can be inseminated with it. We've done this a million times. Our success rate is excellent. Here's some material that explains it all, with the fee list. You can take it away with you. Think about it and let me know."

Perhaps more than most cancer sufferers, Jason had found his diagnosis difficult to accept. After all, he'd kept himself in top physical shape through extreme exercise and healthy eating.

In his college days, Jason had been a star defensive lineman on the football team. Not the tallest player on the field, but one of the strongest, he had the necessary bulk to be intimidating to opponents and the necessary speed to stand out from the other linemen. A ginger with a ruddy complexion, it was almost inevitable that his teammates called him Red Bull.

Jason knew he wasn't professional football material. According to feedback from league scouts, he had ninety-five percent of what it took to make it. To be so damn close and then be rejected made him crazy. But he stayed in shape anyway after he graduated, landing a job as the manager of an athletic club. Jason aspired to become the owner when the opportunity presented itself.

Megan had been his perfect match. They met in Jason's senior year at the wedding of their mutual friends Brian and Julia, and he was immediately attracted to her. She had curves and wheat-blonde hair and a wicked sense of humor. Just his type.

As for Megan, she'd been hearing about Red Bull from Julia for a while. After all, he was a varsity football MVP. Big man on campus. She'd even watched him play once or twice. When they were introduced by the bride and groom, she knew he was between girlfriends and she aimed to be next.

It wasn't long before they moved in together.

Megan worked hard at keeping her curves. She was into yoga and jogging and the Atkins diet. But the blonde hair didn't last long. A stylist at a beauty salon where the furniture was red plastic and the techno audio track played way too loud, she liked to experiment with new colors just about every month.

It was in her auburn phase that they decided to get married.

They didn't want an elaborate affair, but it had to be somewhere tropical. With just two friends and Megan's mother Lola witnessing the sunset ceremony on a St. Lucia beach, it was more like a destination elopement than a destination wedding. They stayed there for a weeklong honeymoon, then it was back to work at the club and the salon.

They were both in their mid-twenties, with no immediate plans for children.

A few months later, Jason started having problems. He had to pee all the time. It was worse at night, with hourly trips between their bedroom and the toilet. After a couple of weeks of this, a sleep-starved Megan urged him to see their primary care doctor. Jason kept putting it off until he thought he saw faint traces of blood in his urine. He knew this was a really bad sign.

The doctor sent him for a blood test, and the analysis came back showing elevated levels of prostate-specific antigen. No need for concern at this point, the doctor reassured him. Could be any number of things causing this, most of them benign. They'd run further tests. So, Jason didn't worry about it. Until they found out what it was.

He had prostate cancer.

"Isn't that something old men get? I'm only twenty-six, for Christ's sake. I'm healthy. I eat right and I exercise. It's got to be a mistake."

Jason sat in the specialist's office, staring first at her and then down at the papers on her desk. Maybe she had the wrong file. Either that or somebody fucked up the lab analysis.

"That's usually the case. But, unfortunately, younger men can have it, too. I'm sorry to say that's what's happening with you."

She told Jason the prognosis was good. After treatment, the odds were in his favor that he could be totally cancer-free. Then he could carry on with his life as if he'd never had cancer in the first place.

There was just one big hitch. The recommended treatment for Jason was radiation, which could potentially kill his stem cells that produce sperm. If that happened, he would be sterile. She suggested Jason consider banking his sperm before he started the sessions. Later, the stored sperm could be used if he and Megan wanted to start a family.

Back home after their first meeting with Alan Wilcross, they had to admit he was a pretty good salesman. But the fees were steep. Too steep, in fact, for Jason and Megan. It would cost thousands of dollars, depending on how long Jason's sperm was stored, for the chance to have kids in the future. How could a hairstylist and an athletic club manager, their home heavily mortgaged and saving to buy the club, afford to pay that much?

Alan had already picked up on this. The minute they walked in, he could tell they weren't like his usual designer-decked clientele. So sad, what was happening to Jason. Such a crushing diagnosis and treatment regime for this superbly fit man.

And virtually no time before radiation for them to find the means to cover his fees.

He knew all too well about their dilemma. For a long time, he himself had barely managed to get by. He wasn't sure that, even if they did make arrangements to borrow the money, they would ever get out of their tight situation the way he did. So he made an exception for them. Jason and Megan became one of his pro bono couples.

They were both thirty when they decided it was time for a baby. Life was better for them now. Jason had fully recovered from his cancer, and he'd scraped together enough money to become part-owner of the athletic club. Even though the club wasn't doing all that well, he was confident he and his business partner could turn things around.

After too many years as a stylist, Megan was fed up with catering to the whims of salon clients. Catering to members of her husband's newly-acquired business made more financial sense for them anyway. So, she quit the salon and started working the club's front desk at minimum wage. She also gave the occasional Pilates class and planned to continue until, fingers crossed, a baby was on its way.

For four years, since just before Jason's radiation treatment, they had their doubts that all those complicated scientific procedures described by Dr. Wilcross would actually work. The intervening time seemed way too long for Jason's sperm to be frozen and stored, and then thawed and put inside Megan. And still be capable of creating a baby.

They were excited the morning of the insemination. And nervous. What if the clinic screwed up? What if something went wrong with Jason's frozen sperm and the poor little buggers didn't make it after all? Then he could never become a father.

"Don't get your hopes up too high," was what Megan's mother said on the phone just before they left for the clinic. Lola didn't put much stock in all that high-tech medical stuff. "And that way you won't be disappointed."

"Wet blanket as usual," Jason muttered under his breath as they went out the door.

On the way, he got stopped for speeding. Then they couldn't find a parking spot. They barely made it in time for their ten o'clock appointment. But the procedure was a success after all. Megan got pregnant immediately. Jason was more than happy to announce to his mother-in-law she was wrong.

Chapter Five

For the rest of his life, Freddy Wilcross could pinpoint the exact moment things changed for him. Or, more accurately, when he decided to make things change for himself.

It was the morning of Christmas Eve, 1970. He was seventeen, a tall skinny school kid from a blue-collar family in Catford, England, working part-time as a shop assistant and delivery boy for the local greengrocer. It was the shop's busiest time of the year. Housewives were waiting for their fruit and vegetable orders for Christmas lunch the next day.

There were two reasons he was glad to make deliveries that morning.

The first was he knew the tips were going to be good. And sure enough, right up until the very last customer, he was greeted at each door with a smile, a "Happy Christmas!" and an extra half a crown.

The second reason was it took him away from home, where there was no such thing as a happy Christmas. Just more of the misery he lived with the other 364 days of the year. His father, a carpenter by trade, was on the dole—and on the bottle—since his accident two years earlier. His mother was a waitress at the local pub who tried to spend as many hours there as possible. She knew what was likely waiting for her when she got home. Freddy's younger brother George and sister Anne had to fend for themselves when he wasn't there to intervene. There was violence and there was deprivation, and Freddy was fed up with it.

His last delivery of the day was going to be his best, he just knew it. It was the biggest order, going to one of the greengrocer's more prosperous clients. Broccoli, brussels sprouts, apples, oranges, nuts, and a large Christmas bouquet of flowers. It was quite a way to the large Edwardian home on the other side of the heath, where Mr. Styles, the proprietor of several men's clothing shops, lived with his family. Rumor had it he was the younger son of some lord or other nobility. So even though the load was heavy and the distance from the road to their residence was far, Freddy was eager to make the trip. He had every reason to expect his most generous tip of the day.

It was a good sign to see Mrs. Styles, rather than the housekeeper, come to the side door herself. Maybe she could pull that little bit more out of her pocket for him.

Freddy gave her his best smile and used his most deferential voice.

"Happy Christmas, Mrs. Styles!"

Being obsequious usually had the intended effect on her.

She smiled, asked him to take the groceries to the kitchen, and afterwards walked him back to the service entrance. As he stepped outside, she wished him his eighth "Happy Christmas!" of the day. Then she closed the door.

"That's it?" Freddy complained out loud to nobody. "Happy Bloody Christmas! What good is that to me?"

He turned and stomped back down the long path to the delivery truck. Along the way, he kicked a stone so far it left a hole in the sculpted yew hedge on the side.

That was the moment he decided he'd had enough. Enough of his shitty existence. And enough of the miserable future that awaited him here. Why? Because he was on the wrong side of the class divide, with little hope of reaching a level of living that was even remotely comfortable.

He knew he was smart. He was making top grades at his grammar school. The teachers liked him. Or pitied him. He wasn't sure which. Maybe both. They kept telling him he had a "good head on his shoulders," that he could go far if things were different. Too bad about his dreadful circumstances.

In fact, he was likely a lot smarter than anybody in the Styles family sitting on their fat arses in that big fancy house of theirs.

But so what?

Intelligence alone didn't count for all that much in Catford. Or anywhere else in England, for that matter. He wasn't from the right family, didn't speak with the right accent. He was pegged as working-class the moment he opened his mouth. He resented the social pecking order holding him down. That would *always* keep him down.

And to top it all off, after he'd made his last delivery that Christmas Eve, he had to go home to a decaying row house where he lived with an abusive drunk and three other victims.

Surely, he deserved better. It was time he did something about it. Starting right then and there.

The final step in his transformation took place eight months later, somewhere over the mid-Atlantic on the flight to Canada.

"Freddy" disappeared. How could his parents have called him that in the first place? To everybody he met, his name alone told them he was hopelessly common, down there with all the "Ronnies" and "Micks" and countless others reconciled to low expectations. So, sitting in Seat 19E, after the economy-class meal trays were cleared, Freddy became Alan. It was his middle name, after all. A much better fit, as far as he was concerned.

In the intervening months, he'd managed to shrug off the unfortunate accent, too, replacing it with something the North American ear would hear as vaguely respectable. He'd practiced his new voice over and over again, emulating BBC announcers and schoolmates who came from homes of better means. There was the occasional slip back to his dropped "h's" and twisted vowels, but people on the other side of the Atlantic wouldn't likely pick up on those fleeting lapses the way his fellow Brits would.

Of course, his goal was to shed all evidence of his rough beginnings and start the climb up to a life of priviledge. The kind of life the Styles family had. He called it The Plan.

And there was much more to The Plan.

The most important part was leaving England and the limited opportunities he saw for himself there. To do this, he'd used his only possessions—his brains and an appealing veneer—to get out.

Alan had just graduated at the top of his class, excelling in biology. Encouraged by his teachers, he had applied to study overseas. Alan was accepted by universities in Halifax, Montreal, and Toronto, and chose the latter, which also offered a world-class medical school. Of course, he needed a full scholarship to be able to afford college, and he received one.

He was not naïve. Not everybody was equal in Canada, either. But at least there, people seemed to be judged more on professional success and wealth than on their family tree. This was just fine with him. Alan knew he had everything it took to acquire status and wealth. At last, he would show the elite on both sides of the Atlantic that he was at least as good as any of them.

Alan did have one regret leaving England. He could no longer defend his mother and younger siblings against the violence of his father.

He arrived on campus with a pair of jeans, a denim jacket from the Salvation Army Thrift Store, and a couple of sweatshirts, but his limited wardrobe was no different than that of other students. And like them, he found a part-time job for extra cash and embarked on the neverending quest to get laid. Weed and drugs were everywhere. If he wanted, Alan could just walk down the dorm hall and buy the best Acapulco Gold on campus. And he did so as often as his bank account allowed. The same as everybody else.

Then there were the sit-ins. The midnight skinny dips at Beechgrove Beach. The off-campus parties at student digs that were pretty much trashed by the time neighbors called in the police. Alan indulged in all these things with his dissolute gang of friends.

Still, there were two qualities that distinguished him from the rest.

First, even though he fully engaged in the riskier side of student life, he was deadly serious about his studies. High marks were the ticket to maintaining his scholarship, and, as a consequence, to securing his future success. Nothing was going to stop him from that.

And he enjoyed the unexpected attention he got from girls. Maybe it was the British accent, together with his long fair hair and Bowie-esque features. All in all, an exotic package by Toronto standards. Or maybe it was because he was an expert at ingratiating himself with them, a skill he'd honed with teachers and shop customers back in Catford. Whatever it was, he had no trouble finding female companionship. And when the occasional relationship ended badly, someone else always came along soon afterwards.

He met Alicia in his final year of medical school. She conformed exactly to his vision of the way life should be. The daughter of a judge, with a bloodline stretching all the way back to the first European settlers in New England, Alicia had no clue about the meaning of hardship. A product of private schools, riding lessons, and the most exclusive summer camps, she was accustomed to, and expected, the best. And like a dozen girls before her, she was attracted to the future Dr. Wilcross.

Alan was attracted to her, too, with her long copper-colored hair and hazel eyes. Alicia was no beauty, but she moved with graceful confidence in a way that showed others she came from quality stock. Alan liked this about Alicia, and liked being seen with her.

It wasn't until after they were married, and he started his practice, that Alan had to admit to himself they had virtually nothing in common. Apart from enjoying and displaying their affluence, that is. But when Karoline and Michael came along, Alan decided to stick with The Plan. After all, he'd achieved everything he'd set out to do. He was a respected physician in a lucrative practice. He had a wife with the right pedigree. He had two happy, healthy kids whom he absolutely adored. There was no way he would walk away from any of that.

But there were traces of Freddy not far beneath the surface. And every so often, it all crept back. The way Freddy felt that one Christmas decades earlier, when he'd stormed away from the Styles' residence, full of rage at all the people who thought they were better than him. Alan had used that resentment to propel himself towards his new life. He didn't really need it anymore. The Plan had been a success. But Freddy wasn't leaving anytime soon.

Chapter Six

"How come we never visit your relatives, Dad, instead of going to camp every summer?" For once, Alan was at a loss for words. And it wasn't as if he could change the topic or walk away. He was driving Karoline and Michael to Smoke Lake Camp in Algonquin Park. The trip took close to four hours and they were only halfway there.

It was a fair question. Karoline was ten and Michael was eight and they had yet to meet his family in England.

He would happily take them to just about any other place on Earth—Rome, Hong Kong, Bora Bora. They'd already visited Disney World. Twice. And that time they went to Iceland? Unforgettable. But he'd rather drop them off in the middle of the Sahara Desert than fly them to London.

Alan looked back at his daughter in the rear-view mirror. "Why do you ask, Karo?"

"Oh, I don't know. Just seems funny is all."

"Funny?"

"Well, we've met everybody on Mom's side. But not yours. Is it because of what Mom said about them?"

Alan bristled. What the *hell* did Alicia tell the kids about his side of the family? Likely nothing good. There wasn't much good to say. But Karoline and Michael didn't need to know the truth. He'd have words with Alicia when he got back.

"I'm not sure what you heard, my darling. I haven't been in touch with them myself for quite a while, so I don't really know how things are with them these days."

"Why haven't you been in touch?"

Another good question. Alan had the answer, but there was no way he was going to tell his children.

His father had died in 1994 from cirrhosis of the liver and heart failure due to excessive drinking. Alan never once considered going to the old bastard's funeral.

Now in her early sixties, his mother still worked part-time at a pub and lived in a third-floor flat in Tottenham. Alan sent her money every now and then, but she didn't use it to improve her circumstances. Maybe she felt she deserved her shabby surroundings.

His sister Anne, recently divorced, was a nurse who seemed content living an endlessly unremarkable existence.

And then there was George, his brother. Nobody knew where George wound up or even if he was alive. Like Alan, he'd left their toxic home as soon as he could. Unlike Alan, however, he had no desire for self-improvement. He went the other way instead. A low-level drug dealer and petty thief, he'd taken off to points unknown fifteen years earlier. So much wasted potential.

Alan still felt guilty he'd left his mother and siblings behind all those years ago to make their own way with so few skills and resources. But for him, staying was not an option. Neither was going back now. "It's a long story. Let's just say I doubt we have much in common anymore. But maybe some day I'll take you over for a visit."

They were empty words. That visit would never take place. It was time to steer the conversation in another direction.

"Now, tell me, what's your favorite thing you want to do at camp this year?"

"Archery. Last year, the instructor told me I could get my second-class award if I tried real hard this summer."

"Great, Michael. And you, Karo?"

"Horseback riding . . . you already *know* that, Dad!"

Of course I do, thought Alan.

He'd spent the better part of the previous Sunday buying Karoline the exact right riding equipment to take to camp. Starting with a Samshield helmet at five hundred bucks, the whole kit set him back considerably more. But he was okay with that.

Nobody could call Smoke Lake Camp a run-of-the-mill kids' summer camp. It was a private enclave of faux-rustic log cabins on a picture postcard lake in protected woodlands. Wealthy parents from Toronto and Ottawa and abroad sent their privileged children there to engage in elite activities with other privileged children. Alicia had gone there as a girl and insisted that Karoline and Michael do the same. Alan readily agreed. He wanted them to have the kind of childhood he could only have dreamt of when he was their age. As far as he was concerned, they'd always get the best of everything.

Alan adored his children more than he ever thought possible. He wasn't used to such intense emotion. He never had strong feelings like that for Alicia. And the closest he'd ever come before was with his brother and sister, or at least the younger versions of them. The versions he abandoned when he fled to Canada. He knew himself well enough to realize that indulging his own children was a feeble attempt to make up for that.

Alan loved Karoline just a little bit more than he loved Michael. Parents weren't supposed to have favorites when it came to their children, were they? But he couldn't help it and hoped it didn't show.

It wasn't just because she took after him physically. A slender strawberry blonde, already tall for her age, she had his eyes and ivory complexion. It was more than that. Karoline was a go-getter, just like him. Smart and competitive, the feedback about her from school was always glowing. A "future leader" her teachers called her. She made Alan proud.

Michael was the exact opposite. Passive, especially for a boy his age, and exhibiting almost no sense of adventure, he wanted everybody else to keep him entertained. And because he was such a cute kid, blonde with a double dose of freckles, they usually obliged. Alan saw early signs of attitude in his son. Already a hint of the kind of entitlement on display in many of his upper-crust patients. He blamed Alicia for spoiling Michael, even though he likely pampered him too much himself.

Two hours later, Alan turned off the highway onto six miles of dirt road ending at the camp's main lodge. The parking area in the field beside it was a scene of barely controlled chaos, with dozens of other families unloading their offspring at the same time.

Leaving Karoline and Michael in the hands of the irritatingly perky camp counsellors for a whole month was hard, but Alan was anxious to get on the road again. He and Alicia were overdue for a reckoning.

He stormed into their residence after the long drive back from camp and confronted Alicia in the master bedroom.

"What the FUCK did you tell the kids about my family, Alicia?"

Alicia was resting. She'd spent her day sorting used books for the charity book sale at the cathedral and was tired. She didn't need Alan, with that annoying, prickly voice he sometimes used, to disturb her nap. She pulled down her eye mask and sat up on the bed.

"*Really*, Alan! I was sleeping. Can't it wait, whatever is bothering you?"

"No. It can't wait. I want to know what you said to Karo and Michael about my family."

"I don't remember. It would have been quite a while ago."

"Then why did Karo mention it on the drive to camp?"

"I have no idea. Anyway, whenever it was, I would have told them the truth." Alicia paused for dramatic effect and put on her trademark condescending smile. "Does the truth bother you?"

Of course, it bothered him. It bothered him a lot. And she knew it.

"You should have had the decency to talk with me first. We could have agreed on what to say to them. Better yet, you should have left it up to me."

"If it was up to you, they'd never know."

Alan couldn't deny it. She was right.

"Look . . . I understand you're touchy about this, Alan. But I can't help it if you come from . . . shall we say . . . modest origins."

"I don't give a shit what *you* think about my origins, Alicia. I'm more concerned about how you described them to our children. I left the UK to get away from that snotty attitude people like you have towards people like me. And now I see it all over again. In my own family!"

"Aren't you being just a *little* bit paranoid?"

"Maybe. But I know you. You'd get a big kick out of putting me down, just because my family didn't come over on the goddamn Mayflower."

"You can think what you like, Alan. I don't really care. What's done is done."

Alicia sighed, pulled the mask back up over her eyes and

lay back on the pillow.

"I see I'm duly dismissed, your *majesty*!"

Alan kicked one of Alicia's slippers to the side and stomped out of the room.

For half an hour, Alan sat in his Audi in the clinic's staff parking lot. He was tired after a full day of appointments, but he was in no hurry to head home.

Almost two weeks had passed since his fight with Alicia, although it felt much longer. Neither of them had made a serious attempt to patch things up. They'd gone from barely acknowledging each other's existence to coldly cordial conversations at dinner. Otherwise, there was silence.

Was he overreacting about whatever Alicia had told their children? Possibly. But she knew he was hypersensitive about his family. He'd warned her almost from the beginning of their relationship to avoid the topic, either with him or with anyone else. Alicia should have known better than to go behind his back to tell Karoline and Michael.

And once they found out, were they embarrassed to be his kids? Did they think they were better than him? That would be far too hard to endure.

Heat from the August sun shining through the windshield made it stuffy in the car. Alan turned on the ignition to start up the air conditioning but left the stick shift in Park. There was something else he needed to work through in his mind before leaving.

This afternoon, he did something he'd never done before. He wasn't sure he could actually go through with it. But he was beyond provoked.

Maybe it wouldn't have happened had Alesandro Stephanidis not swaggered into the examining room, so pompous and full of himself, just as he'd been in previous visits. He and Cristina had come in for insemination with their selected donor sperm. And Alan was ready.

He knew where the idea came from. Last Saturday, he'd used his own sperm with Joan's partner Helen. It was his present to them. He was glad to give it, and they were glad to receive it.

Today, he did the same thing with the Stephanidises. Only they had no inkling it was his sperm that he used, and the odds were virtually nil they'd ever find out.

As they were leaving, it gave Alan extreme pleasure to look Alesandro squarely in the eye and shake his hand. The prick was screwed. And boy, did he have it coming.

Why did he feel so good about what he did? Probably because it wasn't only about the Stephanidises. It was bigger than that. It was his payback to the Styles, the Stephanidises, and everybody else who looked down on him. And now, even his wife.

Finally, he shifted the Audi into reverse and backed out of his parking spot. By the time he got home, he decided he was ready to make up with Alicia. He poured her a drink as a peace offering and carried it out to where she was on the terrace.

Two weeks later, as he neared the turnoff for Smoke Lake Camp, Alan was getting more and more excited to see the kids. He'd brought a bag of their favorite treats with him so they could celebrate the reunion on the way home.

He missed having the children around the house. While they were gone, there was no noisy welcome when he walked in the door from the clinic. No outings for ice cream or blockbuster movies or Frisbee in the park.

It was a matter of days before school started up again. The way he planned it, Karoline, Michael, and he would make the most of them.

And even though it was too early to know, there were now two other couples who might someday enjoy being with their kids— his biological kids—as much as he enjoyed being with Michael and Karoline.

Would it be such a bad thing if there were even more?

2017

Chapter Seven

Cristina sat for a while in her Mercedes, watching Pete join his friends near the front entrance of Oak Hill Academy. Then she shifted the car into gear and pulled away from the curb.

He had no idea where she was going now. Just as well. He'd find out soon enough.

As she did every school day, Cristina dropped Pete off at OHA before heading to the city center. But her next stop was not part of the daily routine. Instead of going to the office, she had a nine o'clock appointment with a divorce lawyer. Cristina and Alesandro had been separated for ten months, and she was ready to take the next step.

Their marriage had been volatile from the beginning. In the early years, when disagreements arose, they'd shout at each other for a while and make up soon after. No big deal. Over time, the grievances grew, and neither side was prepared to give in.

Alesandro's explosive temper was bad enough. What made things worse for Cristina was his meddling family, who never hesitated to back him up each time the two of them clashed. In their eyes, everything was always her fault.

Eventually, they stopped talking altogether. The cold silence that followed was just as oppressive as the fighting, especially for Pete. When he wasn't in school, he spent all his time in the refuge of his bedroom, avoiding them both. It was almost a relief when Alesandro moved to a nearby condo.

At first, they reassured Pete that things would get better, that they were only taking a break until they sorted things out. Later, it became obvious that neither of them had any intent to reconcile.

What they wouldn't tell Pete was that he, himself, was a major source of their conflict. Of course, that wasn't the case when he was born seventeen years earlier.

Back then, Petros was everybody's darling. He had the most delightful toothless grin, bright eyes and dimples, just like the baby in the Gerber ads. Later, Cristina boasted he was a good sleeper and an early walker. And he was smart, too. At eighteen months, he already knew fifty words. Strange that, unlike his parents, he was so pale and so blond. They figured that would change when he got older.

Alesandro and his father both doted on the newest Stephanidis. Because of Petros, the only son of an only son, the two of them got along better than they had in years. In an unexpected way, he was their shared project. When he was old enough, Alesandro and Ari took him to museums and swimming lessons and movies. At the neighborhood park, they kicked a soccer ball around with him in the summer and laced up his skates rinkside in the winter. Even Agnes was genial, if not exactly affectionate, when Cristina and Alesandro brought her favorite grandchild over for a visit. Such a shame, though, that they didn't seem to want another baby.

Through his grade school years, Pete—as he eventually chose to be called—continued to bring the family together. There were hockey tournaments and school plays and yearly graduation ceremonies. A small contingent always showed up at his events to cheer him on.

At thirteen, Pete showed the usual signs of puberty: the ghost of a mustache, the squeaky voice, and a sudden growth spurt. But his fair skin and sandy hair weren't getting any darker. This puzzled Cristina and Alesandro, and likely the rest of his family, but nobody said anything about it at that point.

When he reached fifteen, he was close to six feet in height, towering over Alesandro by four inches. That's when the questions started.

"Just look at him, Alesandro. He's such a tall boy now. And he doesn't look much like you at all. Are you sure he's yours?"

Ari and Alesandro were in the school gym, watching Pete's basketball team play in the semi-finals. He'd just stretched up to score with a jump hook.

Alesandro looked sideways at his father. He hadn't seen that condescending smirk in a long time. He didn't know whether to respond or ignore him. He chose the latter. Then it got worse.

"Maybe Cristina had eyes for someone else way back when? What d'you think?"

Alesandro turned sharply to face Ari. This had to stop. But he didn't want to get sucked into arguing about it because what his father said was true. Pete didn't resemble him at all. And he couldn't explain why.

"I think we should just watch the game, Papa."

The two men didn't say much to each other the rest of the afternoon.

That night, after Pete went to bed, Alesandro told Cristina about the exchange. He was still pissed off.

"Why does he say shit like that? The S.O.B. thinks he can spout whatever he wants and everybody else just has to take it. Well, FUCK that!"

Cristina was worried Pete might overhear them.

"Calm down, Alesandro! Just ignore him when he goes on like that. It doesn't matter to me in the slightest."

She was lying. It really did matter to her.

After all, they weren't blind. Pete had Cristina's smile and her slender hands. Otherwise, he didn't take after either of them. And Ari was suspicious. Like it or not, his opinions counted when it came to family matters.

So, what went wrong with Pete?

They decided there was only one explanation: some kind of sperm donor mix-up when Cristina was inseminated. Years ago, they'd been *so* careful to choose the perfect donor match.

Background, coloring, height. Everything the same as Alesandro. That way, only the two of them would ever know how their child was conceived. And everybody would be happy with the result.

Too bad that's not how things were turning out. Almost sixteen years later, Pete's appearance was raising doubts.

Alesandro was concerned his family might decide Pete was not a real Stephanidis and cut him off. Cristina was more worried about Pete himself. They'd never told him the truth. As far as he knew, he was Alesandro's biological son. How would he react to accusations that he wasn't?

There wasn't much they could do about it, except try to find out more about the sperm donor. And if their theory was right, tell Dr. Wilcross exactly how they felt about his screw-up all those years earlier.

Their first step was testing Pete's DNA.

They'd seen the TV ads about companies helping people discover their genetic roots and connecting them with newly-found distant cousins. The scenes of al fresco dinners beside Italian vineyards and swimming in Scandinavian fjords showed the glamorous side of exploring one's origins.

There were other things people could find out, too. Things that weren't glamorous at all. Like inherited health risks. And who their father was not.

It sounded easy to do. No mess, no fuss. No blood samples needed. Just mail in your spit.

Alesandro and Cristina ordered a testing kit from AncestryDNA. When they gave Pete the saliva sample collection tube, he was only mildly curious why. Their vague answer about tracing his ancestors' path through Europe wasn't exactly a lie, and it seemed to satisfy him. He'd seen the TV ads, too.

Eight weeks later, an email came back letting them know they could see Pete's heritage report online through a confidential link. When they opened the link, it showed Pete's ancestry was 100% European. There was his Spanish ethnicity from Cristina's side, but 47% of his heritage came from Northern Europe, specifically, the British Isles. Wrong donor. Just as they suspected.

They'd been worried earlier. Now they were angry. And now they had the evidence they needed to face Alan Wilcross.

They saw him the following week.

"Remember us, doctor?"

"Of course, I do. So nice to see you both again."

Alan led them into his office.

Hundreds of couples had sought his help over the years. Alan didn't have a clear recollection of most of the earlier ones, but Alesandro stood out. And not in a positive way.

"How are you doing? And how is your son? He must be all grown up by now."

"We're fine, thank you."

Empty pleasantries out of the way, Alan motioned for

Cristina and Alesandro to sit opposite him on the other side of his desk.

"So, what brings you here today? How can I help you?"

Alan had reviewed their file, retrieved from the clinic archives, earlier in the afternoon.

Their pregnancy was just another of his many successes. Years ago, their baby son's photo would have been one of dozens posted on his waiting room wall. Did they want to try again, after all this time? Cristina was in her early forties. It wasn't too late, but it might not be so easy this go around.

"Well, actually doctor, we have a problem. A big problem. With our son. And we hope you can help us find out what happened."

"I don't understand."

Alesandro opened his briefcase, pulled out a photo and placed it on the desk in front of Alan.

"This is him. Pete. You can tell from the picture he has light brown hair. Pale skin. What you can't tell is that he's now six-feet tall, and he might get even taller. He's not like me at all."

Alan picked up the photo. Alesandro wasn't exaggerating. There was no resemblance.

"Yes, I can see that."

Alan's tone was neutral. His face showed no reaction whatsoever, masking his sudden unease. He knew where this conversation was heading.

To Alesandro, it looked like Alan couldn't care less. He leaned over the desk and glared at him.

"Well, that's just WRONG! When we wanted a baby, you told us we needed a sperm donor. We specifically chose one who matched me EXACTLY. So, Pete should look more like me, right? But he DOESN'T. Someone screwed up. We want to know what happened. You must have it in your records."

Inwardly, Alan bristled at this small man's tantrum. But he was determined to play the sage physician, coolly responding to a distressed patient. His façade was calm, his voice steady.

"I have your file here. But it doesn't have every detail. There's no information on the donor. After all, it was such a long time ago—"

"Well, that's just GREAT, isn't it! You don't know about the donor! And you don't give a damn either, do you?!"

Alesandro reached into his briefcase. "We've got something else to show you, doctor. We've done some research. We had Pete's DNA tested and here are the results."

Alesandro tossed the heritage report, full-color pie chart face up, on the desk beside Pete's photo. Alan didn't pick it up. He barely glanced at it.

"They show his Spanish DNA from Cristina. But the rest is from the UK, not Southern Europe like we wanted. Can you explain that?"

"No. And I'm not convinced these commercial reports are reliable. But as I just said, we have no way of knowing who the donor was. I suppose there's a remote chance there could have been some kind of mix-up. Unfortunate if that actually happened—"

"You're goddamn right it's unfortunate. And it's more than that. It's a TRAGEDY!"

"But surely you love your son, one way or the other. He appears to be healthy. Nice-looking boy, too—"

"You have no idea what this will do to our family!"

"Clearly, you're upset about all this. On behalf of the clinic, I—"

Alesandro jumped up and pounded his fist on the desk.

"ENOUGH!"

Alan pushed his chair back as far as he could in case Alesandro lunged at him.

"We came here today to find out what happened. You haven't helped in the slightest. Nice for you to play God, isn't it? And then hide behind the clinic when you fuck up."

Before anything else could happen, Cristina stood up and grabbed Pete's photo and the DNA report. Then she linked her arm through Alesandro's, tugging him away from the desk and out the door.

"YOU HAVEN'T HEARD THE LAST OF THIS!"

Alesandro's threat was loud enough to startle Marjorie the receptionist, and the two remaining patients in the waiting room.

For ten minutes after they departed, Alan sat quietly in his office.

Despite the intervening years, he still recalled how things went with those two. Alesandro's posturing and Cristina's coping with the awkward fallout. Just like today.

Should he feel guilty about what happened back then? Yes. In theory.

And did he? No. He had no remorse whatsoever.

The prick's attitude put him off the first time he walked into his office. From the day he was born, Alesandro had it all. Built-in wealth from the family business and a gorgeous wife. He enjoyed all the perks his overindulgent existence offered, and he strutted around, putting it all on display.

Alan had too much history with people like Alesandro. He despised their unearned privilege and their utter indifference to him when life was tough, especially back in the UK. How could anybody blame him for his little transgression with the sperm? Alesandro certainly had it coming. At worst, it was a simple act of redress.

Maybe he should have given more thought to the possibility they'd find out.

If Pete had taken after his mother, he would be shorter and darker. More like Alesandro, too. Then there would've been no blow-up today.

And who knew back in the nineties that all these DNA testing companies would pop up? Nothing like that existed at the time. Now, people were discovering things about themselves they were never meant to know.

Even so, why should he feel the slightest bit sorry for giving the boy a better start than some anonymous donor would? Why was *that* such a terrible thing? He'd actually like to meet his son someday. See how he turned out.

Alan closed their file and put it in his out-basket. He stood up, walked over to the mirror near the door and straightened his bias-cut silk tie. Then he went out to invite the last couple of the day into his office.

"Pete's staying after school for soccer practice. He won't be back till five. So, we might as well deal with this now—"

Alesandro was still furious when they got home. He went straight to the liquor cabinet and poured himself a scotch while Cristina reheated leftover morning coffee in the microwave. Then they both sat at the granite breakfast bar.

"How far do you really want to take this, Alesandro?"

"All the way. Hire a lawyer and sue Wilcross' ass off."

"I know how you feel. And he'd deserve it. But how could we prove it was his fault?"

"That's where a lawyer would help us."

"Maybe. But you're not thinking this all the way through, Alesandro. Just ask yourself what would happen if we did this. Pretty soon, Pete would find out you're not his biological father. It's inevitable. And God only knows how Ari and Agnes would react if they knew we used a sperm donor. It could get ugly. Is that what you want?"

"No, of course not. But—"

Pete stepped into the kitchen doorway from the hall. He'd skipped soccer practice. He'd been home all along.

He stared at Cristina and then at Alesandro.

They stared back, both reluctant to say anything at first. Had he overheard them?

"Pete, darling! You're home early from school! I thought you had soccer?"

Cristina knew she sounded pathetic. But it was the best she could do. And Alesandro didn't help at all. He sat there looking embarrassed.

"I . . . I heard what you just said—"

Pete's half-whisper was raspy, forced from the throat. He slumped against the door frame.

"Oh God! Pete!"

Cristina rushed over to comfort him, but he pushed her away. Then he ran to his bedroom and locked the door.

For an hour, Pete ignored their attempts to get him to come out and talk. Instead, he lay on his bed and stared up at the ceiling, earbuds in and tunes turned up full blast. He thought the music would stop the pain. It didn't.

Alesandro wasn't his father after all. They took somebody else's cum and put it in his mom . . . how gross was that? What kind of people did that anyway?

And why did it have to happen like that? His father couldn't get it up. That had to be it. And he was embarrassed. Otherwise, why the big secret?

So, here *he* was, the result of their pervy little experiment. Some kind of weirdo mutant freak. Now he knew why he didn't look anything like his father. Did they think he wouldn't notice? Well, he did. But it didn't bother him. Until now. Now, he felt like a fucking moron.

Did anybody else know? He'd be so pissed if they told other people and not him and he'd been walking around totally clueless and they'd all been laughing at him behind his back.

And who the hell was his real father? Did his mom and dad even know? Jesus. Maybe he was a fucking psychopath serial killer or something.

Fuck!

Pete wanted answers. And an apology. He figured he deserved sympathy, too, even though they couldn't possibly understand how shitty he felt. Because of what they did.

Eventually, he came out of his room and found them sitting in the den. He held his head high as he strode over to his usual place on the sofa and sat down facing them. Cristina tried to stop crying, dabbing at her eyes with a tissue. Alesandro gripped the arms of his chair, barely holding himself back from bolting out of the room. They both saw an angry fifteen-year-old trying to be brave, and waited for him to speak first.

"This sucks. This sucks BIG time. You've been lying to me my whole life. So, why didn't you tell me? Feel dirty about it? Think I couldn't handle it? Or what? And . . . like . . . who *am* I really?"

Cristina wanted to move to the sofa beside him and comfort him, but she held back.

"We're *so* sorry, my darling. Sorry you found out this way. And that we didn't tell you earlier. When you were younger, it was too complicated for you to understand. And I guess we let it slide instead of doing the right thing."

It was difficult for Alesandro to talk to Pete about it. No way this conversation should even be taking place. The whole damn thing was just so humiliating. But thanks to Wilcross screwing up, he had no choice.

"The truth is, before you were born, we tried to start a family on our own. For a long time, nothing happened. So, we went to a specialist and found out the problem is with me. I can't have children. I . . . I have a low sperm count. We used an anonymous donor."

"Anonymous? You don't know who my real father is?"

Alesandro flinched. How could Pete say he wasn't his real father?

Cristina was afraid hurtful words might follow that couldn't be taken back. She had to steer them away from that.

"If you mean who your biological father is, then, no, we don't know. And for us, that's okay. It doesn't matter who the donor was. We love you regardless."

It worked. Alesandro managed to hold on to his composure.

"You're my son. I'm your father. That's how I see it. That's how I'll always see it. And I hope you'll still see it that way too."

Cristina was surprised. For once, Alesandro came through. She wasn't used to hearing humble words—the exact right words—from her husband. Pete was surprised, too. He didn't reply, but his expression softened from outrage to exasperation. It was the look he always gave when he thought they were being total idiots. Usually, they found it irritating. This time, it was almost a relief.

Alesandro had more to say.

"Can you make us a promise, Pete? We need you to keep this to yourself. Nobody in the family knows what we did to have you—not your grandparents or anybody else. And we don't want that to change."

"Why not?"

"Because . . . because they might not understand. For whatever reasons. And they don't need to know anyway. So, it's just between the three of us, right?"

"Okay. But I still feel totally weird. Like this isn't really real."

Cristina nodded.

"I'm sure, darling. It's a lot to take in. We can always talk some more about it. Anytime you want. Even go to counselling, if it might help. Just let us know, okay?"

It wasn't right, of course, how Pete found out, but now he knew his whole story. They didn't have to hide it from him anymore. Cristina felt lighter. She suspected Alesandro did too.

This time, when she went over to embrace Pete, he let her.

Cristina was self-conscious about the loud clicking sounds her stilettos made as she walked across the marble lobby of Barrister Place to the elevator. There was marble in the elevator, too, and brass rails. She started to worry that Hirsch, Evans and Wade LLP would bill her at marble-and-brass rates. The mahogany furnishings of their offices on the ninth floor didn't give her much comfort either.

It felt strange for her to think about the cost of things. In two decades of marriage to Alesandro, she never once looked at a price tag in a designer boutique or chose a particular grocery item because it was the weekly special. But life was going to be different when Alesandro found out she wanted a divorce. Their prenup pretty much guaranteed it.

She was a few minutes early for her meeting with Karen Evans, the lawyer referred to her by one of the other school moms. The receptionist offered her coffee and invited her to sit in the waiting area.

If she was ever going to pull back from doing this, it should be now. Before the clock started ticking on billable hours and negotiations got underway.

But the urge to leave disappeared almost immediately. All she had to do was think about the outrageous behavior of her in-laws the previous weekend.

Cristina and Alesandro had agreed to a temporary truce over Easter and went together to his parents' place for brunch. Pete decided not to go with them. He had to study for an exam the next school day.

She tried her best to be friendly. She really did. But that ended when Ari declared over dessert that Pete looked so little like Alesandro, they must have brought the wrong baby home from the hospital. Or maybe Cristina had a better explanation.

How often—since the first time at the basketball game two years earlier—had he prodded them like that? Insinuated she'd had an affair? And how often did Alesandro take the coward's way out and let him get away with it? It was a major reason they were separated today.

Cristina was fed up. As far as she was concerned, this was going to be the last time.

"I know what you're thinking. That I screwed around and Pete isn't Alesandro's. I'm right, aren't I?"

Agnes brought her napkin up to her mouth in an exaggerated show of shock. "Such language!"

Ari just sat there, grinning. Apparently, Cristina's little outburst amused him. And he didn't deny what she said.

Alesandro was silent. He wouldn't risk telling them the truth about Pete.

This wasn't good enough for Cristina. Couldn't he defend her? At least tell the old bully he knew she'd been faithful? Or did he care too much about his precious inheritance?

Obviously, she was on her own. She threw her napkin on the table and stood up.

"Why don't you say something, Alesandro? Why is it okay he keeps insulting me like this? Well, I'm done. With all of you."

And she left.

The next morning, she made the appointment to start divorce proceedings.

Karen Evans appeared precisely at nine and introduced herself to Cristina. Then she led her down the hall, past the gilt-framed portraits of deceased founding partners, to her office.

Chapter Eight

In the darkened school gym, Zach and Erin slow-danced to *Sign of the Times*, their arms wrapped around each other, her head against his chest. They swayed to the beat, but their feet never moved. The Spring Fever Dance was their schools' last big social event of the year, and their first as a couple.

They were crazy about each other.

Erin Evans was in the tenth grade at Somerset School for Girls, situated three blocks from Oak Hill Academy where Zach Murray was in eleventh grade. Four times a year, the two private schools held dances together. Parents of students in both schools approved. The gatherings were a good opportunity for their offspring to mix with others of a similar social status.

As the daughter of a retired professor and a lawyer, Erin easily matched the profile. She exuded good breeding, too, in her style and manner. She was polite to excess and serious about her studies. And Erin had the right look, with pleasant—if not striking—features, sleek dark hair that was never messy and an almost-too-thin frame under her pressed uniform. The other girls liked her because she tried so hard to be nice to them.

In fact, she fit the model student mould so well, the school had just chosen her to be the face of their new promotional campaign. "Inspiring Girls to Succeed in an Ever-Changing

World" was the catchphrase. Photos of her in various school settings would soon appear in newspaper ads, on their website home page, and in their brochures. She was *the* Somerset Girl of her cohort.

Erin hadn't always been this popular.

In grade eight, before she transferred to Somerset School, she was an outsider taunted about her weight by bullies in the senior class clique. Erin was far from heavy, but she reacted in the only way she knew how.

Meal after meal, she would pile her plate high with lettuce and carrots and nothing else. Apples were the occasional indulgence. Soon the teasing stopped, and the new feedback from classmates was exactly what she wanted to hear.

"You look totally awesome!"

"OMG, you could be a model!"

The thinner she got, the more the other girls approved. She was finally getting the kind of attention she craved. So she kept going.

Her parents started to worry. Especially Karen, who blamed herself for what was happening. She'd repeatedly complimented Erin on her slimmed-down profile until she saw her daughter was taking it too far. That was ten pounds ago. Now she looked like a famine victim, with sunken cheeks and a sharp ridge of vertebrae down her spine. Karen should have realized Erin wouldn't know when to stop. Or how.

Finally, one suppertime, Karen had to speak up. She'd stopped counting the number of times Erin consumed yet another plateful of unadorned romaine.

"My darling, you *really* shouldn't lose any more weight. You've got to eat more than that! You need protein. And also carbs. You know that, don't you?"

Erin exploded. "Seriously, Mom? I know what I'm doing. GET OFF MY CASE ALREADY." She pushed away her half-empty dish and stomped out of the room.

Back in her bedroom, she hated what she saw in the full-length mirror. Her thighs were still chubby and no matter what she did, she just couldn't get rid of that double chin. Was her mom blind or what?

Erin couldn't be deterred at school, either, even when the comments from schoolmates turned negative. She got texts asking if she had anorexia. They went unanswered. There were glances and whispers in the lunchroom, where she started sitting by herself so others wouldn't criticize.

She was an outsider again.

When Erin's periods stopped, and clumps of ash brown hair filled her brush, Karen and Greg forced her into counselling. It was their last desperate move before admitting her for in-patient treatment at the Spring Garden Eating Disorders Clinic.

At first, Erin didn't recognize she had a problem. Early therapy sessions were a disaster, with sullen responses and quick exits. Eventually, though, she opened up. About how she desperately wanted to be accepted by the girls at school. About her impossible struggle for the perfect body and the compulsion to control every little bite she ate.

Gradually, with help, Erin seemed to get better. But Greg and Karen were always on guard for signs she might relapse.

Six months later, Erin began classes at Somerset School. She was still fragile. Her parents weren't entirely sure she was ready. But it was a new beginning, and they were hopeful.

Zach was an exception at Oak Hill Academy when it came to the pedigree of his parents. It was true that his father had run his own business for years. Jason Murray had managed to keep the doors of his athletic club open when others folded in the 2008 recession. The place even held its own against competing clubs that had sprung up since. The business provided his family a comfortable living, but it wasn't enough to allow them to enjoy the affluent lifestyle of the other families. It wasn't even enough to cover his son's annual twenty-five-thousand-dollar tuition. Zach attended OHA on a scholarship.

He was a high achiever, the kind of student OHA loved to showcase. Already aiming for a career in biotechnology, he was active in the school's debating club and excelled at volleyball and soccer.

His parents encouraged his sports, although Jason had hoped his son would take up football as he had done. Too bad

Zach didn't have the right build for it. Tall and slender, he was certainly no Red Bull.

There was only one thing that bothered Zach about going to OHA.

"What did you get up to?" he'd inevitably be asked by classmates after reading week or the Christmas holiday or March break. Each time, he had to give the same reply.

"Nothing much. Worked at the club. What about you?"

He was just being polite. He didn't really want to know what they did, because it was always way more exciting.

"Went skiing in Switzerland. It was awesome!" he'd be told, or "Daytona Beach. Parties 24/7."

Lucky shits! he thought, when they described the girls they hooked up with and the substances—legal and otherwise—they consumed.

It wasn't their fault he had to work and they didn't. His parents expected him to help out at the athletic club in his spare time. And for Zach, it was a way to earn spending money.

He simply wasn't part of his schoolmates' cossetted world. They were friendly enough with him, and Zach was friendly back. But he knew, and they knew, he was different.

Erin and Zach had met for the first time at Starbucks, the after-school hangout at the bottom of the hill, two months before the dance.

It started with Erin. She smiled at Zach as they waited for their orders at the pickup counter. He liked that. Whoever she was, she didn't seem to have the same snobby attitude most of the other Somerset girls had. And she looked so classy in her crisp uniform, her long shiny hair pulled back in a smooth ponytail.

Should he say something to her? What if she ignored him? Then he'd have to stand there, pretending to ignore her too, until his coffee came. How humiliating would that be?

He took the chance anyway.

When he said "Hi," his voice broke.

Erin didn't notice the catch in his voice. She noticed the gorgeous guy from the boys' school who was being friendly. To *her*.

She didn't answer him. She was too shy. But she smiled again.

It was just enough for Zach to go on.

"I'm Zach."

"Erin."

Jeez, Zach thought, she even had a pretty name.

"Nice to meet you, Erin. What're you getting?"

How lame was *that*? He was such a loser.

"Iced latte."

Quick. Think of something else to say.

But he had nothing.

Neither did she.

The silence, until their orders arrived, was excruciating. Then they smiled at each other a final time before parting ways.

They didn't actually sit together at the coffee bar until two encounters later. A week after that, Zach's father drove them to see *Guardians of the Galaxy* on their first date.

By the end of April, they were a couple. Going together to the Spring Fever Dance in May made it official.

Zach and Erin slipped away early that evening. They wanted to be alone, and the only place was his parents' Toyota, in the unlit far corner of the school parking lot. Zach had passed his driver's exam just two weeks before. For the first time, he'd picked up Erin on his own and driven her to the dance.

It wasn't their only first that evening. They didn't plan to go all the way in the cramped back seat. But they did.

Chapter Nine

"Hey! It's Zach, isn't it? I'm Pete. Pete Stephanidis."

"Hey, Pete. Glad I'm not the only one stuck in the city this summer."

It was the first practice of the season for the local team of the summer soccer league. Zach was surprised to see someone else from OHA there. He and Pete were in different classes and didn't hang out in the same circles at school. But OHA wasn't all that big. He'd seen Pete around. Occasionally, he was even mistaken for him.

Zach figured most of his schoolmates were spending their vacation just about anywhere else. Touring Europe or sailing in the Thousand Islands or hitting on girls at some all-inclusive resort. And he'd have to hear all about their adventures when school started again in the fall. He had assumed he would be the only one who had to stay in the city and work for his father.

It turned out that's what Pete was doing, too. Alesandro had decided it was time his son learned the restaurant business, starting at the bottom like he did. Pete spent his days helping in one of the kitchens or waiting tables. He wasn't thrilled about it, but Alesandro promised him his first car at the end of the summer if he kept at it.

The soccer team held its practices at a low-lying pitch near the river where they would be hosting matches in the humid evenings throughout the summer. Returning team members already knew they'd be battling swarms of mosquitos in addition to the visiting teams. But Zach and Pete, like the other new players, would have to cope with bug bites on top of sore muscles for the first time.

The school. The summer jobs working for their dads. The team. Even the bugs. They discovered they had a lot in common.

Erin watched the season-opener from the sidelines with Zach's parents. She was the first of the three to notice.

"Don't you think they look alike? Zach and that other guy? Number 15?"

Jason didn't really care, he was following the play.

Megan scanned the boys until she found the one Erin meant.

"Yes, now that you mention it. Know who he is?"

"No . . . but they could almost be twins."

At halftime, the team was losing 2-1. Zach and Pete stood side by side as the players gathered around the coach, drinking Gatorade and talking strategies. That made the comparison easier. From where Erin was standing, they looked to be the same height, with the same long legs and fair skin. The only difference was that Pete had slightly darker hair.

After the match, Zach introduced Pete to his parents and Erin. Up close, the similarities continued in their wide-set eyes and prominent cheekbones. And when they spoke, there was resonance in their young baritone voices.

Six days later, Cristina saw it too. She was on her own that evening. In the weeks since Cristina filed for divorce, she and Alessandro had avoided each other. He'd gone to Pete's previous match, so it was her turn this time. She was watching the team play for the first time.

Just after the starting whistle, Pete chipped the ball to another player. The two advanced together up the pitch towards the opposing goal. Cristina's gaze followed them as they ran. Their strides were smooth and almost perfectly synchronized. She looked closer, first at one, then the other. It was eerie how much alike they were. The silhouettes of their agile bodies. Their posture. Even what she could vaguely see of their faces.

In the car on the way home, Cristina was cautious about raising it with Pete. He was always touchy about any mention of his appearance. He hated dodging questions about why he was so different from everyone else in his family.

"Who were you chatting with just before we left?"

The question was harmless enough. But Pete figured out

what might be coming next, and he was instantly irritated. He'd already been asked *way* too many times that summer whether he and Zach were brothers. He could see it. Sort of. But it was starting to be a drag.

Now he was going to hear it from his mom, too. He decided to get it out of the way up front.

"You mean the dude everybody says looks like me?"

"Yes. That one."

"That's Zach Murray. He goes to OHA too."

"Really? Funny that I don't know his parents."

"I met them after the first game. They're cool."

Pete put in his earbuds, turned his head away, and looked out the passenger-side window.

Conversation over.

But Cristina couldn't stop thinking about it after they got home. Two boys. The same age. From the same community. And they were so much alike. The way they looked. The way they moved. Everything. One of them knew who his father was. The other one— her Pete—had no idea. What were the odds they were related? Likely pretty slim, but not zero.

She had to learn more about Zach's father. Had he ever been a sperm donor? Could he possibly be *Pete's* sperm donor?

Then she scolded herself.

Here she was, doing it again. Obsessing about it. Every so often, a boy would come along who was so much like Pete she thought he might be the same donor's kid, too. It was silly, jumping to conclusions like that.

Still, for Cristina, this time was different. She might actually be able to find out.

Pete introduced Cristina to Jason and Megan just before the next match. Then he joined the team for warm-up exercises.

"Mind if I sit with you?"

Megan smiled and patted the bench beside her.

Cristina tried hard not to stare at Jason but she couldn't resist. Just how much did he resemble the boys? *Her* boy, in particular? She could see he was tallish, with light coloring. Heavier set than Zach and Pete, although it was possible he wasn't so big when he was their age. But there were no specific similarities. Nothing that said to her Jason might be the one. She needed to dig deeper. They sat together for two more matches, sharing a little more about themselves each time.

Cristina liked that Megan was friendly, but she heard enough to know they didn't have a lot in common. Their conversations didn't go much beyond the latest school gossip and the new hot yoga program at Jason's club.

And Megan had mixed feelings about Cristina, too. She was intimidated by the fancy outfits and luxury car. Pete's mom reminded her of the upper-crust clients at the club. The ones with the perfect manicures and serious bling, oozing entitlement. Still, she was flattered that Cristina wanted to sit with her and Jason so often.

Their shallow conversations were frustrating to Cristina. Somehow, she had to get Megan to reveal more about her husband. More than Jason himself would probably share with a casual acquaintance at a soccer match. He didn't strike her as the type to go around telling people he'd been a sperm donor.

She likely wouldn't get very far with Jason sitting right beside them. Cristina waited until Megan showed up one evening without him.

A slow, gradual approach seemed best.

She asked about Zach's plans after OHA. Then it was Cristina's turn to talk about Pete's future. The stories were similar. First thoughts about university. Aspirations to be accepted by Columbia. Or McGill. Or wherever, as long as it was ivy-covered. It was all very predictable. Christina had to push a little more. "You know, we were so lucky to have Pete. We tried and tried for a baby then and nothing happened. We had to go to a specialist."

It was hard for her, after years of hiding the truth from everyone about Pete's origins. But how else could she nudge their conversation in the direction she wanted?

As it turned out, getting Megan to open up was easy. She had her own pregnancy story and she didn't need any more prompting to tell it.

"I know how you feel. Jason and I weren't sure we could have children, either. He had cancer back then. Prostate cancer.

Fortunately, they found it early. Treated it right away. He's been in remission for years."

"It must've been tough on both of you. But it turned out okay, right? You had Zach."

"Yes. That's because, before Jason's radiation, we went to a fertility clinic and had his sperm frozen. When we decided to try for a baby, they thawed it out and we got pregnant right away."

"Really! So, who was your doctor?"

"Dr. Wilcross."

"No kidding! He was our doctor, too."

"Gee, what a coincidence! We must've been seeing him around the same time. He was the best, wasn't he?"

Cristina didn't answer. She didn't think Wilcross was the best. Instead, she had a question. A big awkward one.

Both she and Megan were Wilcross' patients. He'd stored Jason's sperm for Megan. Did he use it with her, too?

Cristina wasn't ready to push further that evening, even though she wanted to. Small steps. She had to take small steps. And it would be better to raise it with Megan when she was feeling more composed. When she could choose her words carefully. Because she would need Megan's help to get the real story.

It was late August. The summer soccer season was almost over. Cristina still hadn't approached Megan with her suspicions, and time was running out.

One thing was clear. She wasn't going to raise it at one of the matches. Not in front of Jason. And more than that, Cristina couldn't be sure how Megan would react. She didn't want to risk causing a scene in front of other people, especially their sons.

Cristina invited Megan over for coffee on a day Pete was working. They sat together at the kitchen bar with their cappuccinos and biscotti.

"I'm *so* glad you came, Megan. There's something I've been wanting to discuss with you all summer."

Megan was puzzled. Cristina waited all this time to say something to *her*?

"Remember when we said we needed help getting pregnant? And we both went to Dr. Wilcross?"

Megan nodded. Yes, she remembered. But that was weeks ago.

"What I didn't mention at the time was that, in the end, my husband and I had to use a sperm donor. We chose one with a specific profile from the clinic's inventory. But there was a screw-up with the samples. We found out later we didn't get the one we selected."

"Wow! How could that happen?"

"Who knows? Wilcross couldn't explain it. But I had a thought. You told me he stored Jason's sperm. This might sound crazy to you, but . . . I . . . wonder . . . if he might have used one of Jason's samples with us by mistake. If Pete might be Jason's biological son."

Megan was shocked. Was this for real? Or some kind of drama-queen delusion?

"You can't be serious, Cristina!?"

"Actually, I am. Pete and Zach look so much alike. Pete tells me everybody thinks they're brothers. Well, maybe they are. Half-brothers."

Megan frowned and shook her head. She didn't want any trouble for Jason. Cristina noticed her reaction.

"I'm sure this whole idea must sound insane to you. And who knows if I'm right or wrong? But I'm hoping you can help me find out."

"So . . . what are you suggesting?"

"I'm suggesting we check Zach's DNA. It's easy to do. We already had Pete's DNA analyzed. You just order a testing kit from the same company we used. I'll pay for it. Then you mail in a sample of his saliva. The results might show if they're related. If they're not, it all ends there. But if they are . . . well . . . at least, Pete's father and I would finally know who the sperm donor was. And don't worry, we wouldn't make a big deal about this. Jason wouldn't need to get involved at all. Our problem has always been with Wilcross."

"But Jason . . . Jason would be really pissed. I know he used to worry about what happened to his leftover sperm."

"We don't have to tell him right away. We may not need to at all, depending on how the test turns out."

"Okay. I suppose there's no harm in getting Zach to give a sample."

In mid-October, Zach's DNA results came back showing he had Polish and UK origins. They confirmed what Megan already knew. She had Polish ancestry on her father's side, and the UK part came from both her and Jason.

Later the same week, a second AncestryDNA email arrived.

"You and another member share DNA. Find out more about this connection. View this DNA Match."

Evidently, it wasn't just a distant match, but a close family one. Megan moved the cursor over the link. Then she hesitated. What if Cristina's right and it's Pete? What the hell happens then?

When she finally clicked on it, it led to Pete Stephanidis.

Cristina also received an email from AncestryDNA with the same message about a match for Pete. It was the first notification she'd received since his DNA test two years earlier. She opened the link right away.

So, her hunch was right! The donor had to be Jason. Thank God *that* mystery was finally solved.

She called Megan.

"Jason's going to freak out about this, you know—"

"I understand. Perhaps we should talk about this in person. The four of us. We can do it here. Without the boys at this point."

"What's the big deal, Cristina? Why all the secrecy?"

Alesandro marched into his former home looking like it was the last place he wanted to be. He was surprised she wanted to see him. He certainly didn't want to see her. Alesandro was quite prepared to make a quick getaway if Cristina tried to corner him about the divorce.

"Just calm down, Alesandro. Something's come up that we need to discuss. It's about Pete. Another couple will be here in half an hour, but I wanted to talk with you alone first."

They moved to the great room, where Alesandro took a chair closest to the door.

Then she told him.

Cristina expected Alesandro to sound off again about how that dick Wilcross screwed up their lives. Instead, he was quiet. He stared out the window a full minute before speaking.

"So now I'm going to have to talk to this guy . . . what the *fuck* am I supposed to say?"

"You don't have to say anything if you don't want to. But Megan and I thought we should all get together and discuss this. At the very least, we need to decide together about telling Pete and Zach."

When Jason arrived with Megan, it was clear he was upset, too. He couldn't bring himself to look directly at either Cristina or Alesandro. The introductions were stiff and the handshakes, hurried. There was no small talk after they sat down. Instead, Jason got right to the point.

"This is one helluva situation. We had no idea what that doctor did with the rest of my . . . samples. And now we're finding out. All these years later. What can I say? I'm *really* not happy about this."

Jason shrugged as his voice trailed off. He wasn't picking up any signals at all from Alesandro. But why should he be embarrassed? It wasn't his fault. It was the damn doctor.

Cristina looked over at Alesandro. She wanted to give him the first chance to respond.

He didn't. So, it was up to her.

"I'm sorry you folks have been dragged into this. We've known for a couple of years that Wilcross messed up with us. We decided at the time not to pursue it with him. For family reasons."

Cristina was still angry with Alesandro about the "family reasons," but that evening was not the time to show it.

"And now that we know what happened, there are a couple of things we need to discuss. The first is whether we tell the boys. I suppose we could hide it from them. But Pete deserves to know who his biological father is. He's been confused about that ever since he learned we used an unknown sperm donor."

Once again, Cristina waited for Alesandro to say something. She wasn't sure he agreed with her.

Finally, he spoke.

"I want this whole goddamn fiasco to go away. Let's just

tell them and get it over with."

In the car on the way over, Jason and Megan had already talked about telling Zach. Jason answered for both of them.

"I guess it's harder for you than for us. Nothing really changes for Zach except he'll find out he has a half-brother. Someone he's already friends with. And that's not a bad thing. For him, that is."

They decided to do it separately, but at the same time, the following Friday evening. Cristina and Alesandro with Pete; Jason and Megan with Zach. The boys would have the weekend to absorb what they were told before going back to school.

As Jason and Megan stood up to leave, Alesandro had a final request.

"We ask you not to mention this to anybody except Zach. And please, tell Zach to keep it to himself, too. It's a very serious situation for my family. It would cause a lot of trouble for us if this got around."

"Holy shit! You sure he's my father? I mean, my biological father. Not like you, Dad."

Pete couldn't believe it.

"That's what the DNA tests say."

Cristina had done all the talking while Alesandro paced the floor, jiggling his silver lighter in his pants pocket. He was desperate for a smoke and too agitated to sit. The cigarette would have to wait. Cristina told him he'd have to go outside and this conversation was too important to miss.

Alesandro was worried how Pete would react when he found out about Jason. Would he want to get closer to him? And if he did, where would that leave Alesandro?

"So tell us how you're feeling?"

Pete didn't know how to answer. How *did* he feel about it? He wasn't exactly sure. But at least he wasn't the son of some psychopath creep.

"It's okay, I guess. I need to think about it. For sure, it's gonna be strange when I see Jason again. Hey, does Zach know?"

"His parents are telling him tonight, too. So, yes, he'll know by now. And he'll know he has to keep it a secret."

Pete could hardly wait to text Zach, but first he got up and went over to embrace Alesandro.

"I love you, Dad."

"Love you too, son."

Hey, bro! ☺

Hey!

Awesome news, dude

4 sure

They made plans to hang out together the next day.

Zach called Erin later that evening. It was part of their daily routine. They spoke every night before going to sleep.

"Hey, babe, you're not gonna believe what I just learned about Pete Stephanidis and me. But before I say anything, you gotta promise you'll keep it to yourself."

He couldn't resist. He *had* to tell her. It was way too big to keep it to himself.

"Of course, babe. You know you can trust me."

An hour later, they hung up.

Erin was usually good with secrets. She had a few of her own. But confiding in her parents didn't really count. And besides, they wouldn't tell anyone else. She was convinced of that.

Greg and Karen heard the whole story over breakfast the next morning.

Chapter Ten

"And so, fellow graduates, I encourage you to follow your passions. I guarantee you will wake up every morning with energy and enthusiasm. And you will go to sleep every night with a gratifying sense of personal accomplishment.

But more than that, I encourage you to look outside yourselves. Find out how you can make a real difference in your communities. If you do that, you will not only enrich your own lives, but help your generation build a better world for your children.

I say all this from personal experience. Throughout my career as a physician, I have been fortunate to be able to do both these things. I am immeasurably thankful for the opportunity I had to pursue my professional passion for medicine, and humbled to have contributed in a small way to the lives of many deserving families in this city.

I wish the same career satisfaction for you.

Congratulations to all of you on this momentous day. And best of luck as you step confidently into the future!"

It was a crisp Saturday afternoon in late October. Alan had just been awarded an honorary degree for his "distinguished contributions in the field of human reproductive science and humanitarian service to the community," at the university's fall convocation.

He tipped his mortarboard ever so slightly as the audience of black-gowned graduates and their guests applauded his address, a few even rising in a standing ovation. Alan had been working towards this recognition his whole life. He felt he deserved it. And now he savored it.

At the reception afterwards, Joan Martin was one of the first to congratulate him. After all, they were old friends. And he was India's father.

As a rule, Joan didn't enjoy going to these celebrations anymore. Now a senior program director at the university, she'd had to attend dozens of graduation ceremonies over the decades. To her, they'd become a too-precious combination of pomp and tedium. Helen stopped coming with her years ago.

This time, however, was different. She was feeling sentimental, and not only because of Alan. Joan had just turned sixty-one. She was retiring early in the new year and this convocation was likely to be her last. Nostalgia was already starting to set in.

"It's been a long time coming, Al. And much deserved. I hope you're enjoying every second of this . . . where's Alicia?"

"Oh, she's off in the crowd somewhere. Probably chatting up someone on the board of governors. She knows them all, of course. And Helen? Is she here today?"

"No. Too busy at the clinic, unfortunately."

“So, tell me all about India. I haven’t seen her in years. I think about her a lot, you know—”

It was a white lie. He had other priorities. But people always liked to be asked about their children. Alan smiled as he finished his second glass of a rather pedestrian red wine.

“What can I say? She’s a real dynamo. And she’s doing so well in school. I’m pretty sure she’ll be graduating near the top of her class next spring. After that, she wants to go to veterinary college. Follow in Helen’s footsteps.”

India Martin-Stewart attended Gladstone High School. The decision to send her there, rather than enroll her in a private academy, finally seemed to be paying off. She was thriving in the school’s science program, and was active in its charity events and theatre productions.

Her teenage years hadn’t always been easy. There were a few rocky periods early on. In grade ten, she was caught smoking dope in the graveyard beside the school grounds. Later that year, she surprised Joan and Helen with a mandala tattoo on her left wrist. And for a while they worried that she seemed a little too popular with the boys. India still showed her rebellious side on occasion, but, overall, the wild-child phase seemed to be passing.

Joan and Helen had never told India who her father was. All she knew was that he was a doctor. She didn’t seem interested in finding out more.

Eventually, Alan wandered off in the crowd to look for Alicia. Joan put her glass down and turned to go. She saw Greg

Evans moving in the same direction and went over to greet him. They left the reception hall together.

"Greg! It's been a while . . . how's Karen these days?"

"Nice to see you again, Joan. She's fine. We're both fine. You still keeping this old ship afloat?"

"Trying to, but our best professors keep retiring. Like you."

"I'm almost seventy, you know. It was time—"

"But now you can't stay away from us?"

"Oh, I have no problem at all staying away. Today is an exception. I came to see Alan Wilcross get his degree. He was our doctor years ago. Karen and I wouldn't have had our Erin without him."

Small world, Joan thought. But then, Alan has helped so many people in this city.

"I have a personal connection with him, too. We were students together way back when. Up to no good most of the time, to be honest. We've kept in touch over the years."

And Alan was her daughter's father, but she couldn't talk about that.

They collected their coats and exited the building together. When they reached the sidewalk, Greg turned to face Joan. He frowned and hesitated before speaking.

"You know, at the risk of being indiscreet, I heard something very curious about Alan's clinic the other day. According to Erin, her boyfriend Zach just learned one of his friends is actually his half-brother. Evidently, years ago, both boys' parents were patients at the clinic. The two couples went the artificial insemination route and it seems sperm samples from Zach's father were accidentally used for both."

"Really? And they only found out recently?"

"Yes. Erin says they decided to check out the boys' DNA this summer when they saw how much they looked alike."

"What a surprise . . . for both families—"

"I'm sure it would have been. But I'm taking all this with a grain of salt. Second-hand gossip from Erin, you know. Still, if it's true, it makes one wonder whether something like that might have happened with other patients, too."

Of course, Greg thought, it didn't happen with Karen and him when they were seeing Alan. They didn't need another donor. The problem had been with Karen, not him.

He paused. He'd probably said too much. Greg usually didn't comment on the dramas in other peoples' lives. Still, he wasn't unduly worried. This was Joan, after all. Discreet to a fault.

"I'm sure I don't need to tell you to keep this to yourself."

Joan nodded.

She had no words. It was unthinkable that a mistake like this could happen. How could Alan have used the wrong sperm with even one couple?

"Anyway, Joan, I've got to dash. By the way, Karen and I plan to invite a bunch of people over one evening for pre-Christmas drinks. We'll send you an invitation."

"Lennie, you won't believe what I heard this afternoon at the convocation."

"Okay, shoot. I'm listening."

Helen was lying on the sofa with her feet up. She was exhausted after a long day at the clinic. Her last appointment had been particularly difficult. She'd had to put down a beloved pet cat and the entire family was in tears. After all these years, it still got to her, too. She was glad for the distraction.

Joan dropped into the easy chair beside her.

"I almost can't believe it myself." As Joan told her about the conversation with Greg Evans, Helen sat up.

She didn't have the same warm feelings about Alan that Joan did. Still, he was the widely acclaimed specialist with a gift for creating babies. The papers loved running stories about him. But this was a serious accusation. A huge scandal, if it ever got out. Alan's reputation and practice would likely be destroyed. The papers would love running this story even more.

"Do you think it was a mistake? Or could it have been intentional?"

"Really, Lennie! You honestly think Alan would do something like that on purpose? He might be arrogant, but he's not some kind of evil scientist!"

"Then what you're saying is he's careless—"

"No . . . no . . . I'm not sure *what* I'm saying . . . but I doubt it would make any difference to either family one way or the other. The damage is done."

At the end of November, Joan and Helen received an invitation to a reception at the residence of Greg, Karen, and Erin Evans on Sunday, December 17th.

They were among the first to arrive that evening. After Erin answered the door and took their coats, Greg and Karen greeted them in the living room. The scene was picture-perfect festive, with logs burning in the fireplace next to the Christmas tree and holiday music by Nat King Cole playing in the background. Eventually, Joan and Helen made their way to the dining room where they were served mulled wine from a crystal punch bowl.

More guests started to show up. Greg's older daughters and their partners. Neighbors. Lawyers from Karen's firm and a few professors Joan recognized from the university. She was happy to linger and catch up with them, but Helen wanted to leave. The reception was getting way too crowded for her.

Joan went to the front hall to get their coats. Erin was there too, opening the door to another guest. Joan tried to look busy as they embraced and kissed. Erin's boyfriend, of course. Likely the one Greg talked about at the convocation. Zach, if she remembered correctly.

Erin took Zach's hand and turned to lead him to the living room. He smiled and greeted Joan as he passed. The gesture only took a couple of seconds, but that was long enough. Joan didn't see Zach, she saw Alan. Alan of forty years ago. Tall, with a gaunt face and intelligent eyes. Hair that was long and straight and dirty blonde, just like Alan's used to be. And when Zach spoke to her, she recognized the voice. She'd been hearing Alan's version of it for decades.

Joan didn't sleep at all that night.

What had Alan done? And how many patients had he done it to?

He'd been happy to offer his own sperm when Helen and she wanted to have a baby. And they were grateful to him for it. India was their best gift ever.

But that was one thing. This was another.

According to Greg, Zach was conceived at Alan's clinic. By artificial insemination. And Zach was the image of Alan in his student days.

He was Alan's son. She just *knew* it.

Even worse, Zach had a friend who turned out to be his half-brother. If Zach was Alan's son, then so was his friend.

Clearly, what happened with these boys was no accident. And who knows? Alan might even have used his own sperm with other couples, too.

Joan had nightmarish visions of countless identical young people filing down the steps of the fertility clinic, like clones from some apocalyptic science fiction movie. *All of them, children of Alan.*

She stopped herself. She was getting carried away. She could be wrong about this. Joan didn't know Zach's parents. Maybe one of them had the same features as Alan, and Zach took after him or her instead. She really wanted to believe it. But she didn't.

Should she get involved? None of this had anything to do with her. And it was dangerous, meddling in other peoples' lives. Making accusations that could cause so much grief, not just to Alan but to everyone involved.

Did the families need to know what actually happened? They'd already had to deal with the discovery about the boys' shared paternity. Imagine if they found out who the real father was.

For the next three days, Joan struggled. Maybe she should just leave it alone. But what if he were still doing it today, creating more little Alans without their parents' consent?

The families deserved the truth. And he had to be stopped.

Joan called Greg and they agreed to meet at the café on the edge of the Christmas market.

"Helen and I really enjoyed your reception, Greg."

"It was nice to see you both. And I was pleasantly surprised when you suggested we have coffee today—"

Actually, Greg thought it was strange Joan wanted to get together again so soon. They didn't usually socialize all that often. Once or twice a year at the most.

Joan took a long sip from her dark roast before speaking.

"Well, I always enjoy chatting with you, Greg. But today, there's something serious I need to discuss."

Another sip. Greg waited.

"Just as I was leaving your place the other evening, your daughter's boyfriend arrived. Zach, isn't it?"

Greg nodded.

"We passed each other in the hall. From what I saw, he reminded me of . . . a very young Alan Wilcross."

"Really? I guess you have a point. There is some similarity. So you're saying what, exactly?"

"I'm saying that, when we met at the convocation in October, you told me Zach's parents had been patients of Alan way back when. You heard he might have used their sperm sample with another couple at the time. And you wondered whether this happened with his other patients, too."

"Yes, I remember saying that. But I also said I wasn't sure how true it all was."

Greg started picking at the edge of his paper napkin. He was feeling distinctly uneasy. Why did he ever tell Joan about this in the first place?

"Well, after seeing Zach on Sunday, I think there was more than one mix-up. I'm wondering if Alan used the wrong samples with the other couple *and* with Zach's parents, too . . . and . . . I suspect it was his own sperm he used. For both."

Greg sat back in his seat and frowned.

"That's quite an accusation, Joan."

"I know. And I don't want to cause any trouble if I'm wrong about this. But if I'm right, something needs to be done."

"I can understand why you think Alan and Zach bear some resemblance to each other. But not enough to start pointing fingers."

"There's more than a faint resemblance, Greg. I knew Alan when he was a student. Just a bit older than Zach is now. I remember how he looked back then. Thirty pounds lighter and rough around the edges. I also remember how his younger voice sounded. And Zach is exactly like all of that."

Joan swallowed the last of her coffee and pushed her empty mug to one side.

"But don't worry. You *know* I'm not going to take this any further unless there's something solid to base it on."

"What do you mean by taking it further, Joan? And what do you call *something solid*?"

"Okay, so now I have to tell you a secret I swore I would never reveal to anyone. Our India is Alan's biological daughter. Eighteen years ago, when Helen and I decided we wanted to have a baby, we went to Alan for advice. He volunteered to be our sperm donor and we accepted. So, we know for sure that India is his . . . I'm thinking if India's DNA could somehow be compared to Zach's or the other boy's, then we could tell for sure whether Alan is their father too."

"You're full of surprises today, Joan. It's a lot to take in. And you're telling me all this because?"

"Because I'm hoping you can help me find out what's really going on. Maybe you could ask Erin where the boys' DNA was tested? Then I could get a sample from India and send it to the same place. See what the results are. If it turns out they're different for India than for the boys, I'll stop there. No harm done. But if they're the same . . . well . . . I'll have to deal with it somehow."

"I guess that's easy enough for me to do. Let me get back to you after Christmas."

"Sure, Greg. But please keep in mind that, if it turns out I'm right, I'll need to act quickly. I don't want Alan to do this even one more time."

Greg called Joan in the first week of January with the testing details.

When the kit arrived, Joan collected a sample from India and mailed it back the same day.

Then she waited.

Chapter Eleven

"Who the hell is India Martin-Stewart?" Jason was furious. Megan had just told him there was a message from AncestryDNA. Another match. A girl this time. "Enough is enough! What the fuck did Wilcross think he was doing with my sperm? How many kids do I have out there anyway? He can't get away with this! I'll take him to court, if I have to—"

"Hold on, Jason! We need to be careful. There're three families involved at this point. Let's not start anything that'll upset the others. And make things embarrassing for us."

"But I have to do something! I'm the one who's got children popping up all over the place."

"Don't exaggerate. There're only two others so far. But I get your point. Maybe we should begin by contacting this girl's parents. Let them know what we think happened."

"Okay. And then we *all* go after Wilcross."

"Not all of us. Cristina and Alesandro won't want to. They told us that themselves."

Megan sent a message intended for India through the AncestryDNA website. Joan picked it up.

She'd also received confirmation of India's matches with Zach and Pete. But Joan wasn't ready to reply to Megan right away, or deal with Pete's family. There was something else she had to do first. She called Alan, and he agreed to drop by her home the following evening.

India opened the door.

"Hi. I'm Alan Wilcross. Your mom's expecting me . . . India, isn't it? Nice to meet you."

Alan stared at his daughter as they shook hands. He hadn't seen her since a chance encounter with Joan and Helen when India was a toddler. She certainly didn't take after him physically. Average height at most. Dark brown hair, so short it almost looked shaved. A tiny diamond stud on the left side of her nose. Something about the way she looked at him was familiar, though. Her eyes were bright and probing and just this side of defiant. All signs of a budding rebel. He pictured her on the frontlines of student demonstrations, protesting the issues du jour. Climate change. Abortion rights. #MeToo. When he was young, he used to get involved in things like that.

Joan came down the stairs and stopped in front of Alan. There was no embrace this time, just a sweep of her arm directing him to the living room.

"India, love, do you mind if I ask you to leave us on our own? We need to talk in private."

India did mind. She'd heard a lot about her mom's friend and wanted to stick around to see if he really was all that awesome. But she disappeared up the stairs.

Alan settled in an armchair near the window.

"So, Joan, it's been a while since the convocation. And Helen, do I get to see her this time? How're things with you two?"

Joan sat in the rocking chair on the opposite side of the living room. She wasn't in the mood to be sociable. She was dreading this conversation.

"Helen's fine. She's out. And I have a lot on my mind tonight."

She pushed her chair into action, rocking back and forth. The movements were rough and rapid, and she made no attempt at eye contact.

To Alan, it looked like she didn't want to share the same space with him. And this after no hug, no offer of coffee, and no sign of Helen. Joan was upset about something. They weren't about to have a pleasant fireside chat. So, what was up?

"I can see you're not happy. Is it about me? Something I've said or done? Why don't you just spit it out? We know each other well enough, don't we?"

"Yes, we do. Or at least I thought we did. Until recently. I've discovered something very disturbing about what's happened at your clinic. I'm hoping you can give me a rational explanation. One that will exonerate you."

Alan frowned. Exonerate him? From what? What the hell was she talking about?

"Do you remember the Murrays, Al? They were your

patients some eighteen years ago. Their son's name is Zach. And the Stephanidis couple? Also eighteen years ago. Their son is Pete."

"Yes. Barely. So much time has passed . . . so many patients."

Alan was deliberately evasive. He remembered the Stephanidis' too well. Alesandro's hissy fit at the clinic wasn't all that long ago. And the Murrays? He seemed to recall they were one of his pro bono couples. Otherwise, utterly unremarkable. How did Joan know these people?

"Well, to get right to the point, the two boys discovered last fall they're half-brothers."

Fuck! How did they find *that* out? he wondered.

"Go on—"

"And not only are they half-brothers, but it turns out India is their half-sister. So that tells me you're the biological father of all three of them, and God knows how many more!"

Joan rocked forward in her chair and glared at him.

"Al, how could you *do* this?"

It was his turn to look away.

Alan felt cornered, but it didn't show. Instead, he assumed his most convincing professional pose with legs crossed, hands steepled, and head cocked to one side. He had to take control of this conversation.

"Whoa! Let's back up a bit, Joan! Where are you getting

your information?"

"I'm getting it from DNA tests that show they're all related. Right now, I'm the only one who knows you're the father. The other two families think you used Murray's sperm. But that needs to change. They have to be told the truth."

"So where were they tested?"

Alan remembered the DNA charts Alesandro tossed on his desk. Joan and the Murrays likely used the same company. He objected to it then and he'd do the same now. "If it was one of those companies with do-it-yourself, mail-in kits, I question their results. Genetics shouldn't be a hobby for the amusement of the general public, you know. Drawing the wrong conclusions could cause trouble for lots of people."

Joan noticed that Alan's British accent—the blue-collar version, not the carefully cultivated one—came on stronger with each sentence. Despite the calm exterior, Alan was nervous.

"In this case, you mean trouble for you, don't you, Al? But I don't hear you denying it. Aren't you going to tell me I'm wrong? That you didn't deliberately use your own sperm with them? Or do you admit it's true?"

"My point is, there's insufficient proof for you or anybody else to conclude anything—"

"Okay. You don't think there's proof. So that leads to my next question. Are you prepared to have your DNA tested by a lab you *do* consider reliable? I could arrange to send the boys' DNA samples there, too. Then we'd know for sure."

Alan wanted to get out of there. Fast.

“This is crazy. How could you think I would intentionally do such a thing? I’m truly offended. The answer is *no*.”

He stood up.

“Just hold on a minute, Al. I don’t understand why you wouldn’t get tested. If you’re *not* their father, the test would prove that, too.”

Alan was already on his way to the front door. Joan went after him.

“Leave if you want. But I’ll give you one week to do something about this. And then let me know. Either you arrange for a DNA test or you tell the families what you’ve done. One or the other. If you don’t, I’ll tell them myself.”

Alan turned and glared at her.

“You and your accusations! You realize what this would do to me? IT WOULD RUIN ME! After all these years, Joan! This is *such* a betrayal!”

There was contempt in his voice, but she wasn’t intimidated.

“What about those families? They trusted you. And you screwed them around. *That’s* what I call betrayal.”

Alan’s hand shot up, ready to strike.

Joan stepped back.

“GET OUT! …NOW!”

“FUCK YOU, JOAN!”

He turned and charged out, slamming the door behind him.

India, perched at the top of the stairs, came running down.

"Mom! Are you okay?"

Joan was shaking.

"I'm fine, love. Don't worry. I just need to calm down a bit. Such an ugly conversation. I'm afraid things got way out of hand."

India took her mother's arm and steered her back into the living room where they sat together on the sofa. India waited to speak until Joan managed a weak smile.

"So, he's my father . . . I always thought he might be, the way you talked about him."

"India! You were listening! But, yes. He is. He wanted to keep it a secret. That's why we didn't tell you."

"And I have brothers . . . half-brothers."

"Two that I know of, not counting his son and daughter with his wife. There may be others."

"Wow! How could he *do* shit like that?"

"Who knows? There's no rational explanation. What happened to those couples is simply unacceptable. Maybe even a crime, for all I know. And he likely thought he'd never get caught."

"So, are you really going to do what you said?"

"I'll wait a week. If he won't deal with this, then he leaves me no choice . . . and in the meantime, can I rely on you not to talk about this with anyone? We need to keep this quiet for the time being."

"I won't tell anyone, Mom."

A week passed. Joan heard nothing from Alan.

Chapter Twelve

The Ides of March. Outside, it was sunny but windchill frigid, a perfectly appropriate day to stab someone in the heart. At least, that's how Joan felt about what she had to do now.

She forced herself to get into her car and drive to the Murrays' home, cursing Alan the whole way. Then she circled the block a couple of times, rehearsing the speech she'd carefully constructed in her head, before parking in their driveway.

Joan hesitated in front of the ice-covered path to the steps. This visit was already going to be difficult. Why did she have to deal with an obstacle course too?

She made it without falling. But after she climbed the steps and rang the bell, all she wanted to do was turn around and leave before the door opened.

Joan was no coward. She'd held her own in clashes with rogue professors and prima donnas on the university's board of governors. This was worse. Introducing herself to total strangers and telling them their son was the product of someone else's sperm. Explaining that the "someone else" was the doctor who helped them have that son in the first place.

She felt like an invader, barging into this couple's lives and exposing an intimate deception she had no right to know. But what choice did she have? Obviously, Alan wasn't going to do it himself.

His silence after their confrontation was a serious miscalculation. He must have thought she was bluffing, that she would never tell them what he did. He should have known better.

Megan opened the door and they shook hands.

"Nice to meet you, Joan. Come in. I'll get my husband."

She took Joan's coat, led her to the living room and disappeared down a hall.

Joan sat at one end of the green leather sofa, rehearsing in her head what she wanted to say to them.

Megan returned with Jason. First came the introductions, then the offer of coffee. Joan declined. How could she accept their hospitality when she was about to give them such bad news?

It was Megan who spoke up first.

"This must be *so* difficult for you, Joan . . . I can tell you, we already went through this with the Stephanidises several months ago. We were all shocked when we found out Dr. Wilcross used Jason's sperm with them . . . and now here we are with you. Same story all over again!"

She was trying her best to be sympathetic. She thought it would make things easier. It just made Joan feel even guiltier.

"That's . . . that's not exactly why I'm here, Megan. And Jason. There's something I need to tell you. And the Stephanidis couple too, later this afternoon. What happened with your boys is not what you thought. I'm afraid it's worse."

Joan paused. Her tidy little monologue suddenly eluded her. She'd have to improvise.

Jason shook his head. What now? He thought. He really didn't need this stranger coming into his home with some disturbing variation on what Wilcross did.

"The first thing I have to explain to you is that my partner Helen and I decided almost two decades ago that we wanted a child. So, of course, we had to find someone who would donate his sperm. We approached Alan Wilcross because he was my friend, and because he knew all about helping couples like us have children . . . and as it turned out, he offered his own sperm to us."

She held off a few seconds. This next part was going to crush them.

"We accepted. Helen got pregnant and we had India. She is Alan's daughter. We're one hundred percent certain."

Joan stopped. They could figure out the rest.

Megan looked over at Jason, then back to Joan. "So, you're saying your India is Dr. Wilcross' daughter, and that means Zach is his son. If we go by the DNA tests. Have I got that right?"

"I'm sorry, but, yes, that's what I'm saying."

Jason sprang up out of his chair and started pacing.

"THE FUCKER! After all we went through! He made such a big deal about freezing my sperm for us . . . and then he uses his own shit instead . . . and that high and mighty attitude of his! *Look what I'm doing for this poor couple.* Like he was the goddamn Pope or something. It was just one big power trip for him, wasn't it!?"

He smashed his fist on the fireplace mantel.

"And Zach? He's *my* son! I don't give a DAMN about the DNA!"

He turned to Megan.

"I'm done with holding back, Megs. I'm taking that asshole to court whether or not the others want to join us."

Jason sat down again and put his head in his hands.

Megan was confused. Was this for real, what they were hearing? Why would the doctor do this to them?

Then she went to comfort Jason.

It was as bad as Joan thought it would be. And she didn't blame them. Did they really have to know what Alan did? Originally, she thought it was important. Today, she wasn't so sure. But she couldn't take it back now.

"I'm really sorry."

They ignored her.

Joan quickly got her coat out of the hall closet and left. Then she sat in the car for a while, steeling herself for her next encounter. Alan had caused so much misery. And there was more to come. Now she had to go through this all over again with the Stephanidis family.

" . . . so you see, the DNA results show that Alan Wilcross is the biological father of your son and the Murrays' son and our daughter . . ."

It was an hour later at Cristina's condo. Joan finished talking and waited for their reaction.

Alesandro shook his head in disgust. He wasn't surprised at all. He'd known for years that Wilcross was a smart-ass fraud. What Joan just told them merely confirmed that.

"How many times do we have to hear about this? First, he uses sperm we didn't choose. Gives us no explanation. Tries to brush it off. Says it's okay, when it really isn't. Then, we hear it came from a guy who never gave his consent. Oh, but *that's* not right either. It's Wilcross' sperm! All these years, he's been playing us. Laughing at us. And the Murrays, too. Who the *hell* does he think he is, anyway?"

"Alesandro's right, Joan. We've had to live with this situation for several years. And I can tell you it's taken a huge toll on us."

Cristina frowned at Alesandro. Joan guessed this was a sore point between them. And Cristina didn't stop there.

"You know, it's frustrating because—no matter who gave the sperm—Wilcross is still getting away with messing up our lives. Isn't he, Alesandro?"

He scowled back at her and they both went silent. The only noise was the irritating tapping sound of Alesandro's Ferragamo Oxford on the hardwood floor. Joan sensed these were the first words of an argument they'd already had many times before. They were waiting for her to leave so they could continue. She was quick to oblige.

What was *that* all about? she wondered as she backed out of the visitor parking spot. Obviously, this wasn't a happy couple to begin with, and her news just made matters worse.

As soon as she got home, Joan went to her laptop and opened her email inbox. Still nothing from Alan. She didn't think there would be. It would have been too late anyway. Then she took a deep breath. This was going to be so difficult but she was determined to go through with it. She knew what she had to say to Alan. She also knew he would never understand she'd done the right thing by revealing to the parents what happened all those years ago.

Al,
I spoke with the Murray and Stephanidis couples today. I told them the truth about what you did to them. I didn't want to. I didn't want to be involved at all. But you left me no choice.
Joan

Then she clicked the SEND button.

After forty years of friendship, it was likely the last time she would ever contact him.

"This just never goes away, does it?"

Cristina, Alesandro, Megan, and Jason sat in Cristina's great room that evening. Before Joan's revelations, none of them thought they'd ever have to meet again like this.

"No. And we don't want it to. Not until the bastard pays for what he's done to us."

Jason's face was red and his voice hard. He wanted revenge. His first instinct was to find Wilcross, wherever he was, and pound him to a pulp. And maybe he'd get to do that someday. But for now, the best route—the one that would hurt the most—was slightly more civilized. They'd take legal action. Was it a crime, what Wilcross did? Could he be charged and tried in court? Or would they have to sue him? Either way, he'd be finished. No more honorary degrees and fancy cars and country clubs for him. No more pro bono cases like theirs that turn out to be self-serving instead.

"You really have to wonder what goes on in a mind like that," Megan said, "I mean, what was he thinking?"

There was no good answer to her question, but Cristina tried anyway.

"Who knows? Maybe he's got some kind of God complex. Trying to populate the world with his own offspring. If that's the case, he could have dozens of children out there—"

"Let's get back on topic," Jason was impatient. He wanted to talk about their next steps. He didn't care what variety of crazy Alan Wilcross was. "We intend to consult a lawyer. Find out what our options are. Then, we'll take this to the limit. So, my question to you folks is: will you join us in this?"

Cristina looked over at Alesandro. She'd let him answer. He was the one who'd been holding back.

"I'm just as pissed off as you are, Jason. But given our circumstances, we'll have to pass on legal action."

Jason was disappointed. What was the problem with this Stephanidis couple? They got screwed by Wilcross just like he and Megan did. And they have plenty of bucks to hire a big expensive law firm to take this on. But no. He and Megan would have to do this on their own. He'd have to mortgage the house again if it came to that.

"Okay, then, we'll go it alone. Let us know if you change your minds."

He got up to leave.

Cristina was annoyed, too. Still the same old story from Alesandro. Still afraid of his father.

"Hold on for a minute, Jason. I can give you the number of my lawyer, if that'll help."

Alesandro looked sharply at Cristina. Was she really going to do this? Refer them to her divorce lawyer? In front of him?

Cristina left the room and returned with a hand-scribbled note. "Here. Her name is Karen Evans. She's very good. And if she can't take you on, maybe she can suggest someone else from her firm who will."

Megan took the note.

"Karen? She's the mother of Zach's girlfriend. I'm not comfortable approaching her on this."

Jason shrugged. He was beyond feeling embarrassed.

"But let's start with her, Megs, and see where it takes us."

There was only one thing they all agreed on before the Murrays left. They would tell Pete and Zach about their biological father after school the next day.

Chapter Thirteen

Inside the front entrance of Cristina's condo building, Alesandro entered the code for her unit and she buzzed him in. As far as he was concerned, they were spending way too much time together lately. And it was always about the same damn thing: Wilcross' big ego trip two decades ago and the trouble it was causing them today. This is the last time I come here for this, Alesandro promised himself in the elevator going up to her floor. The last time I come here for anything.

Cristina opened the door. Alesandro walked past her and continued to the kitchen where Pete was waiting. They embraced and then all three sat at the table in the breakfast nook.

"Mom told me you were coming over tonight, Dad. Must be serious."

Given what was going on between his parents, there was no way his father would show up for a casual visit.

"It is."

Alesandro was ready to take the lead this time. He wasn't worried about Pete getting too close to some other so-called father. It didn't happen with Jason. For sure, it would never happen with Wilcross.

"I'll get right to the point. There's been a development about who donated the sperm the clinic used when we were trying for you. Turns out it wasn't Jason Murray after all."

Pete slouched in his seat. "This again?"

"It was actually the doctor who ran the clinic. Alan Wilcross. I think he switched the samples on purpose. And he obviously did the same thing with Zach's parents. They're telling him about this tonight, too."

"Jeez, Dad! Is this for *real*? Are you sure you got the right story this time?"

Cristina answered.

"We found out yesterday. There's a girl whose parents agreed to use Wilcross' sperm for their insemination. Her DNA was tested recently and it matches yours and Zach's."

"So, now I have a half-sister, too?"

"Yes. And I suppose there could be others."

"No shit!"

Pete started to have the same weird feeling as when he learned Alesandro wasn't his biological father. But he'd already had two years to reconcile himself to that, so the feeling passed quickly. Then he decided it might actually be better in one way. He'd felt awkward around Jason ever since he was told he was his son. No need to feel awkward with him anymore.

"At least nothing changes for me and Zach . . . we're still half-brothers, right? What's this doctor like, anyway?"

Alesandro snorted.

“Wilcross? Never liked the arrogant son of a bitch. Even before we found out what he did.”

“Wow! I’m not sure I’d like him much either. Can I go now?”

Pete pushed his chair back and stood up.

“Okay. But remember, you still need to keep this to yourself.”

Pete went to his bedroom and thought about what he’d just heard. So, it was his parents’ doctor. At least it wasn’t some kind of homicidal dirtbag. But he was curious. Someday, he might just go and check this dude out. Face to face. See the one who was responsible for all the embarrassing questions he got about his looks.

Pete played *Grand Theft Auto V* the rest of the evening.

Zach’s reaction was entirely different. That morning, before he left for school, his parents had been acting strange. His mom was over-the-top cheerful, almost manic, for no obvious reason. And his dad was the exact opposite: sour-faced and wordless. His body language said stay out of my way. Zach thought they must have had a massive fight they didn’t want him to know about. Or they were hiding something else.

It wasn’t any better when he got home later in the day.

When they finally sat down with him that evening, he could tell his mom had already been crying. She had a box of tissues beside her now, just in case. Jason was still surly, but no longer holding back. He did all the talking.

When he finished, Zach sat for a moment trying to understand.

"I don't get it, Dad. Why would he *do* something like that?"

"I think he was playing some kind of sick game with us. *Look how great I am! I'm offering you poor people my services for free!* Well, we got more of his services than we bargained for. Condescending prick. And who knows? Maybe he just threw my samples away. He didn't give a shit whether or not I had my own kids."

These last words hit Zach hard, but Jason was oblivious.

"I remember how excited we were the morning we went to his office," Megan added. "Your dad and I had waited so long to have a baby and it was finally going to happen. Afterwards, when we found out I was pregnant, we were *so* happy."

Her tone was wistful at the end, as if she wasn't happy about this situation anymore. Megan grabbed a tissue and dried her wet eyes.

I'm not who they thought I was, was all Zach could think. *I'm not the one they wanted.*

He hadn't cried in front of anybody since he was a child. But now, tears spilled down his cheeks.

"Zach . . . Zach! Please don't cry. You know we love you more than anything. That won't ever change, no matter what."

The story hadn't come out quite the way they wanted. Megan and Jason did their best to make it better. They told him how proud they were of him. How they couldn't have hoped for a better son.

Zach eventually stopped crying. And then he got angry, even angrier than Jason, at Alan Wilcross. Someday, he'd pay that shithead back for what he did to his parents. And to him.

Jason had to wait until after the weekend to go to the clinic. He wanted to talk to Alan alone, after all his patients were gone.

It was late Monday afternoon when he walked into the empty waiting room and looked around. Not much had changed over the years. Still the pink-and-blue color scheme, the wall covered with baby photos. This time, Jason wondered how many of those babies were Wilcross'.

Marjorie was surprised to see him.

"Your name, please?"

"Jason Murray."

"I'm very sorry, Mr. Murray, there must be some misunderstanding. We don't have an appointment for you today. Perhaps we can fit you in another time?"

"No. I'd like to see the doctor now. It won't take long—"

"But we're finished for the day."

Alan opened the door to his office and came out to the waiting room. Burberry trench coat on and briefcase in hand, he was ready to leave. He pulled up short when he saw Jason.

"Dr. Wilcross. I'm Jason Murray. You may or may not remember me. I don't much care either way. My wife and I were patients of yours almost nineteen years ago. I'd like a word with you. In private."

"Yes, of course I remember you. How are you?"

Jason didn't answer.

The face was only vaguely familiar to Alan. But the name. He'd heard it recently. Oh *fuck*. It was at Joan's. Murray is here because of the DNA results.

Alan walked over to shake Jason's hand, but Jason refused.

"Marjorie, Mr. Murray and I will be having a short chat in my office. Could I ask you to stay until we're done?"

"Yes, of course, doctor."

Alan didn't explain why he wanted her to stay, but it was so she could call security, if it came to that.

He led Jason back to his office and gestured for him to sit. Alan took off his coat and sat down opposite him.

"So, Mr. Murray . . . Jason. What brings you here today?"

Jason felt strong. Even invincible. But this wasn't going to turn into a fight or even angry words. He had a much better way to get even. And he was here because he wanted to see the look on Alan's face when he told him about it.

"I've come to let you know I intend to take legal action against you. We both know what you did to my wife and me years ago. And I plan to make sure everybody else knows, too."

"I have no idea what you're talking about."

"Don't pretend you're innocent. We've just learned our son has your DNA, based on tests that show a match with a girl we understand is your daughter. You had my sperm . . . you stored it for four years. But when we wanted to use it, you substituted yours instead. You did *not* have our consent to do so. And then you lied to us about it. It's as simple as that."

"That's pure speculation. But I certainly won't discuss this any further with you now. I suggest any future communications should be through our lawyers."

"Agreed."

Jason stood up to leave. When he reached the door, he turned around.

"Pleasure to see you again, Doctor. And you can kiss your fat-ass life goodbye."

It was only at these last words that Alan showed any reaction at all. Jason could see it in his eyes. First there was outrage. Then there was fear.

Chapter Fourteen

When Jason called Karen Evans and explained they wanted legal advice on a personal issue, she suggested an off-the-record chat at her home. No booked appointment at the distinguished offices of Hirsch, Evans and Wade LLP meant no premium billing.

And the invitation didn't come too soon from a personal perspective, either. Even though Zach and Erin had been dating for a year, it was the first time the Murrays were welcomed to the Evans' residence.

Greg greeted them at the door and left for his daily jog. He had planned it that way. It was better if he stayed out of Karen's dealings with potential clients, no matter who they were.

Karen served coffee, and they talked about their children. How Zach and Erin were *so* good for each other. According to Karen, Erin seemed more confident, more outgoing, since she'd started seeing Zach. And Megan said Erin was like the daughter she and Jason never had.

A few minutes of this were enough for Jason. He wanted to talk about the real reason they were there.

"Let's cut to the chase, Karen. We'd like to take legal action against a fertility clinic. Specifically, the specialist there,

Alan Wilcross. For malpractice. We were hoping you could give us some advice on how to proceed."

Karen wasn't entirely surprised.

"We know Alan Wilcross. We used to be patients, too, and as for your situation, Erin told us something about it last fall. Zach has a half-brother. A biological son you never knew about, Jason. Sounds like there was a screw-up with the insemination. Have I got that right?"

From what Erin had said, Karen knew the other boy was Pete Stephanidis. But she'd kept that to herself. Cristina had never mentioned it when they discussed the divorce.

Jason and Megan weren't happy to hear how much Karen knew. They'd asked Zach not to tell anybody. That's what they'd promised Cristina and Alesandro.

"You're partly right. Zach does have a half-brother. But we were wrong about who the father is. We've just learned that Wilcross used his own sperm and not mine for both boys. There's been a new DNA match with Wilcross' daughter."

"Really?!"

"Yes, really . . . and we're convinced this was no accident. The fact that it happened twice tells us it was intentional. We want to know if Wilcross broke the law. And what our legal options are. He shouldn't get away with this."

Karen was shocked. Maybe this wasn't just a one-off fumbling of sperm samples. Maybe there was something more sinister going on at the clinic.

"I practice family law, Jason. So, I can't tell you right now whether what he did was a crime. But someone else in the firm could take a look at this. If it falls under the criminal code, the police could press charges. If it doesn't, I suppose you might consider litigation. What about the other boy's parents? Are they thinking of pursuing this, too?"

"No. They've declined. They want to stay anonymous. So, it's just us."

"Okay, I'll talk with my colleagues and get back to you as soon as possible."

"You remember when Erin told us last fall about Zach and his friend Pete? That they found out they were half-brothers?"

Greg, back from his run, was in the shower. Karen stood just outside the glass stall. She couldn't wait till he came out.

"Yes, of course I remember. Is that what the Murrays wanted to talk about today?"

"Yes. And it seems Erin was right. The boys *are* half-brothers. But it's not what they thought at first. Jason's not their father after all."

Greg turned off the faucet and opened the shower door. Karen handed him a towel.

"Well, don't you want to hear more?"

"Okay. So tell me while I'm getting dressed."

And she did. But even before she started, he already knew what she was going to say. The boys were Wilcross' sons. Joan must have followed through with her daughter's DNA test to confirm it.

After she finished, Greg turned and faced her.

"And you're saying this to me right now because?"

"Because I'm beginning to wonder how many times Wilcross did the same thing with other patients."

"Yes? And?"

"And I wonder if he did it with us. Used his own sperm, I mean."

Her voice was shrill at the end.

"Really, Karen? That's what you're thinking? It's a bit of a leap, isn't it?'

"I know . . . I know . . . but a few months ago, it was just teenage gossip. Now, it turns out to be true. And even worse. Should we be worried?"

Karen sat on the edge of their bed and Greg sat down beside her.

"Go ahead. Tell me I'm crazy . . . please!"

"You know I won't do that. But let's take a day or two to think about this. If it's still bothering you, we can check it out. Have Erin's DNA tested. In fact, let's do that anyway, just to ease our minds. But I'm pretty sure there's absolutely nothing to worry about. My sperm was tested at the time, remember? And it was totally healthy. Wilcross told us that himself. And I was right there when our embryos were transferred to you."

They both stood up and Karen gave Greg a hug. She was already feeling better. But now Greg wasn't so sure. He hadn't actually witnessed the in vitro fertilization with his own semen.

"Hi, Joan. It's Greg Evans. I wonder if you have a minute."

He hadn't spoken to Joan since January, when he told her where Zach and Pete's DNA had been tested.

"Sure. I always have time for you, Greg."

"I'm calling about this DNA business again. Your daughter's results, and the match with the boys."

"Oh? You know about that?"

"Yes, we heard about it from the Murrays."

"Really? Why did they tell you?"

"They spoke to Karen. They're thinking of taking legal action against Alan. They wanted her advice."

"So?"

"I'm calling you because, after hearing their story, Karen is starting to wonder whether Alan used his sperm with us, too. We're thinking of having Erin's DNA tested. But before we do, I thought I would touch base with you to get confirmation. If there's any chance the Murrays got it wrong, then there's a lot less for Karen to worry about."

"Well . . . I'm afraid it's true. There was a match between the three kids."

"I see."

"I . . . I don't know what else to say, Greg. Except I hope things turn out the right way for you."

"I'm pretty sure they will, Joan. Karen may be worried about this, but I'm convinced that Erin is totally ours."

He was trying to sound confident. But right after their call, Greg opened up his laptop and ordered the DNA kit.

As they entered Phil Hirsch's law office and shook his hand, Jason looked around. Antique barrister bookcases, original artwork, and burgundy leather club chairs. Just what one might expect for a senior partner. Maybe they should have gone for a storefront lawyer instead. It'd be a lot easier on the bank account. But Karen said Hirsch was the best.

"Mr. Murray, Mrs. Murray, very nice to meet you. Have a seat. Karen has filled me in a bit on your situation, but maybe you can tell me yourself why you've come in today."

Five minutes were enough for Jason to tell the whole story, starting with his cancer diagnosis more than two decades earlier.

When he finished, Phil Hirsch put down his Mont Blanc pen and looked up from the notes he'd been taking.

"I must say, yours is the first case of this type I've encountered myself, although I know this kind of thing has happened elsewhere."

"So, can you help us?"

"I believe I can. But let me give you some context first.

What this doctor allegedly did to you is certainly reprehensible. But it wasn't a crime."

"Really? That's hard to believe."

"I know. But it simply isn't covered anywhere in the Criminal Code. First, we looked at the provisions for assault and sexual assault. It doesn't fit there. Even though you might now feel an assault of some kind took place, there was no actual physical force involved. The other possibility was fraud. But that involves the loss of property or money. There was certainly deception here . . . an unforgivable deception. But not for financial purposes."

"Where does that leave us, then?"

"Well, since criminal charges can't be filed, you're looking at a civil suit. In the very least, we could pursue negligence as the basis for your claim."

"Negligence?! It's *way* more than that. He did this on purpose!"

"I understand why you feel that way. Let me assure you that, once all the evidence is assembled, we will certainly go over the facts and allegations you might include in your Statement of Claim. You'll also need to think about the damages you are seeking."

"Mr. Hirsch, as I mentioned, we're not the only people Wilcross did this to. Right now, there is at least one other family. Unfortunately, they're not interested in taking legal action. But there could be others. Is some kind of class action suit a possibility?"

"It might be. We could investigate that. Use the media to reach out to other patients. That would take a bit of time. Then there's a process of certification, and the court would have to decide if the suit can proceed as a class action. Is that how you want to proceed with this?"

"Yes. If Wilcross hurt other families the way he's hurt us, I think they should be able to get involved too."

"Fine. I'm happy to work with you to get this launched. One of the first things I would suggest is that Zach and Wilcross' daughter submit DNA samples again, this time to a genetics testing laboratory. We want to be absolutely sure of the evidence we use for the claim."

They were in good hands with Hirsch, Jason decided, as they exited the underground parking garage of Barrister Place. He no longer cared about the expense. Whatever the bottom line was, it would be worth it to bring Alan Wilcross—defendant Alan Wilcross—to court.

Chapter Fifteen

"Can I make you a drink, Alicia?"

"Sure. I'll have the usual, please. A double this time. I've just spent two interminable hours with those dreary Foundation people."

Alicia went to change while Alan made her a gin and tonic. Then he poured himself a scotch. They were both doubles. Alan needed a strong drink, too.

When she returned, they took their glasses out to the terrace overlooking the lake and sat in the chaise lounges near the fire pit. As they watched the occasional cloud drift over the copse of trees on the far side, Alicia described in excessive detail the latest power struggle between board members of the Chapel Grove Charitable Foundation.

She'd been on the Foundation's board for only six months, but had known most of the members for decades, ever since she and Alan moved to the gated community after their marriage. Alicia knew everything about their grubby little affairs, their feuds, their shifting self-serving alliances. All of that ugliness was on display at the Foundation meeting that afternoon. And even though Alicia shared their pretentious attitudes about living in the city's richest enclave, she'd had enough of the endless local soap opera.

Alan didn't take in a single word Alicia said. He had other things on his mind. How the reflection of the early evening sun glinted off the rippling lake waters. How the only sound, other than Alicia's whining voice, was the faint tinkling of a distant wind chime. And how his elegant, accomplished existence was about to be shattered.

That morning, Alan's lawyer told him he'd been contacted by Phil Hirsch. Jason Murray was going ahead with his plans to sue him. What's more, Hirsch was starting to look into the possibility of a class action lawsuit.

Should it proceed, the media would undoubtedly get involved. This wouldn't be one of those dry legal disputes that came and went without the public taking notice. If similar cases were any indication, there could be extensive, and sensationalized, press coverage. A feeding frenzy of speculation. Whether or not the suit was successful, his reputation might never recover.

Alan was deeply resentful. Was it really so terrible that he gave the Murray kid the benefit of his good genes? Moreover, he'd done so *much* for the people of this city over the years. And this was the thanks he got.

Now he had to decide how to deal with it. Starting with Alicia. It was probably best to ease her into the situation gently, a little at a time. That way, there was a slim chance she might be convinced to stay with him, at least until the case made headlines. Anything to delay the extra hassle of a divorce on top of a lawsuit.

He waited until she'd finished her first drink and was well into her second.

"Alicia, darling, I'm afraid I got a bit of bad news this morning."

"Really? Must you tell me now? Is this going to spoil my evening? I was just starting to feel relaxed."

Alan had been noticing that Alicia felt "relaxed" a lot more often lately. He thought "sloshed" was the more appropriate word.

"Nothing for you to worry about. Seems that a couple I treated at the clinic years ago has some kind of complaint against me. I'll let my lawyer handle it. I doubt it will go anywhere."

"Good. You've had so many patients over the years. I suppose it was inev'table that some of them might be troublemakers."

"Exactly . . . and not only that, but they were one of my pro bono couples, too—"

"How ungrateful of them."

Time to change the topic. He'd gone far enough for this evening. He'd wait for another occasion to tell her more. When she was feeling "relaxed" again.

The opportunity came a week later. Alicia had spent the day at a spa with friends and was feeling mellow even before they sat down to dinner. By the end of the meal, her mood was positively amorous. Alan figured it was due to the fine burgundy he'd picked up at the vintage wine shop on the way home.

It was a shame to waste the occasion. They hadn't had that many intimate moments in recent years. But Alan wanted to take advantage of her mood to slip in just a few more details about his trouble with the Murrays. Maybe Alicia would take it in stride and the evening could continue.

Unfortunately, that's not how it turned out.

"Darling, I'd like to get something off my chest before we umm . . . get friendly?"

"Really. Must you? Right now? You know what I've got in mind—"

"It's no big deal, I promise. Then you'll have my undivided attention and I can focus on making you feel good."

"Okay. If you insist."

"It's about the complaint I received from my former patients. You remember I mentioned it last week? I've just found out more from my lawyer."

Alicia nodded.

"Well, it seems it's all about something that happened almost twenty years ago. They—the Murrays—consulted me originally because they needed to have his sperm frozen. They planned to use it later. But now they think there was a problem with the insemination procedure."

"What kind of problem?"

"They're saying there was a mix-up and the wrong sperm was used."

"Why would they think that?"

"Who knows? But I guess they must have had some kind of DNA testing done."

"And?"

"And it's possible that their child's father might not have been Murray after all."

This was starting to go further than Alan planned. But he couldn't think of a way to shut it down.

Alicia was visibly annoyed.

"Alan, you're not giving me full answers. Don't make me keep asking. Just *tell* me. What's going on?!"

Damn it. He should never have started this in the first place. But she had to find out sometime. If she didn't hear it from him, she'd get it from someplace else. And soon.

"Alicia. I can't explain it, but it seems they think I'm the biological father."

In an instant, Alicia went from annoyed to furious.

"WHAT!? Are you serious!? Are you telling me you fucked one of your patients?"

"No, Alicia, of course not. Nothing like that. I've never done that."

"So, how could you possibly be the father? Unless you jerked off and used *that* with them? Did you actually do *that*?"

"I have no idea how it could've happened. I mean, twenty years is a long time. I can't remember everything I did back then. But what I *can* say is that, so far, they haven't proven anything."

Alicia slapped her napkin on the table.

"What if this gets out, Alan? WHAT IF THIS GETS OUT?! We'd be the laughingstock of the whole community . . . the whole goddamn city! They'd feast on us for months. And—oh my God—the Foundation board . . . those pathetic busybodies would *love* hearing all about this! It's just *too* fucking much, Alan."

Alicia stood up abruptly and swayed slightly as she stepped back from the table.

"You're overreacting, Alicia. PLEASE! Let's not get too upset. Let's just wait and see how this plays out . . . it may come to nothing. ALICIA!"

By the time Alan finished, Alicia had staggered out of the room.

The next morning, she moved everything—her clothes, her shoes, her jewelry, her toiletries and cosmetics—into the south wing of their residence. She avoided him as much as possible, and when they happened to be in the same room, she ignored him. Alan kept looking for Alicia to give him some kind of signal that he could approach her again and try to make peace, but that never happened.

Five days later, as Alan was leaving for the clinic, she confronted him at the door.

"I won't be here when you get back, Alan. I'm flying to Europe. This afternoon. I'll be gone at least a month. And while I'm there, I've instructed my lawyer to start divorce proceedings."

Alan froze.

"Alicia! Don't *do* this! Can't we talk about it? Try to work it out?"

"I'm not interested in talking. Ever again. And when *your* shit hits the fan, I want to be somewhere else . . . how could I possibly show my face around here?"

Alan searched for calming words, but none were coming to him. He gave up and walked out.

Alicia slammed the door behind him, then immediately opened it again.

"Oh, and by the way, Alan . . . Michael and Karoline know all about your sleazy little tricks. I told them myself last evening . . . just in case you were wondering."

She smiled at him. Alan hated that version of her smile. It was more like a sneer. Alicia only used it with people she considered inferior.

Then she slammed the door a final time.

Alan got in his Lexus, jammed the key in the ignition and floored the gas pedal. The tires screeched as he pulled away.

How could she be so cruel? Trying to turn his children against him? He'd have to call them himself with an explanation. Something convincing.

"Hello?"

A female voice. An unfamiliar one. Alan couldn't keep track of the women in his son's life. They came and went all the time.

"Is Michael there?"

"Who's calling?"

"It's his father."

"Just a minute."

Alan didn't wait long, but it was the woman's voice he heard again, not Michael's.

"Mike can't come to the phone. He says don't bother to call again."

Then she giggled and hung up the phone.

What the fuck? Michael wouldn't speak to *him*? And he got some strange woman to *tell* him that? What the hell did Alicia say to him anyway? He'd have to go to Michael's place to talk to him face-to-face. Soon. But not while one of his girlfriends was there.

Karoline answered the phone herself.

"Hi, my darling. How are you?"

"I'm not sure I want to speak to you right now, Dad."

"Why not?"

"Because I'm totally pissed at you. And after what Mom told me, I realize I don't really know you. Or like you."

"Why are you saying these terrible things, Karoline? I don't deserve this!"

"No? Well, what am I supposed to say? 'Jeez, thank you, Dad, for giving me a brother or sister I've never heard of before.'? Or maybe 'Thank you for embarrassing us when your little scandal goes public!'"

"Hold on, Karoline—"

"Okay. I'll try to be fair . . . I've heard Mom's side of it. You can give me yours. So explain to me why what you did is okay."

"That's exactly what I want to do, Karoline. But I'd rather talk to you in person. Can I drop by?"

"No. The kids are still up. They shouldn't hear any of this. We can do it right now, over the phone. Or not at all."

"Okay . . . well . . . I'm not sure what your mother told you, but I can promise you I've not knowingly done anything wrong. I was never unfaithful to Alicia. Never. And it was so long ago, I can only guess what might have happened. At the time, I had samples of my own sperm frozen. Just like the husband's samples were. It's possible that mine somehow got switched with his. And then used with his wife. Most unfortunate, of course, but not something I would ever do on purpose."

"Really, Dad!? That's your best explanation? Why in God's name would you have frozen *your* sperm? And it's hard to believe you wouldn't have been extra careful about keeping the samples separated—"

"Like I said, Karoline, I just don't know. Can't you give me the benefit of the doubt?"

"I don't want to take sides on this. But Mom is *really* upset. So am I. I think we should stop communicating for a while. Till we see how this all turns out."

"You're breaking my heart, darling!"

"Sorry, Dad, I have to go."

Then she hung up.

Chapter Sixteen

Erin sat alone near the back of the Number 6 bus, staring out the window. It was smudged all over with kids' fingerprints and other grimy streaks of dubious origin. Someone had written "FUCK U JEREMY" in coral lipstick in one corner. It was partially rubbed off again, but you could still see the words through the smears.

She'd never been on this bus before. In fact, this was only the third time in her life she'd ever travelled on a public bus. Same as her friends. When they needed to go somewhere else in the city, outside the boundaries of their safe, upscale neighborhoods, their parents chauffeured them.

Because of this, Erin was sure she wouldn't run into anyone she recognized, either on the bus or later when she got off on the other side of the city. And that's exactly the way she wanted it.

Erin knew precisely where she was going. She'd Googled earlier to find the Shoppers Drug Mart that was the farthest from her home. And from her school. And from all the other places she and her friends usually went. The one she chose was attached to a strip mall in a blue-collar community in the south end.

The bus, drawing nearer to her destination, passed through a neighborhood of neglected brick row houses. At the stop before hers, it picked up a young mother and her toddler, who suddenly emerged from a dingy shelter beside a gas station. Maybe because it was raining, there was nobody else in the street. But there were other signs of life. Plastic lawn chairs and rusty Bar-B-Qs and kids' toys littered grassless front yards. One house still had Christmas icicle lights drooping along the edge of its roof. This neighborhood was only a few miles away from her home, but it might as well have been on the other side of the planet. Perfect, Erin thought.

The strip mall was across the street from where she got off. Besides the Shoppers Drug Mart, there were a small bank branch, a 7-Eleven convenience store, a laundromat, and an Indian food restaurant advertising an all-you-can-eat lunch buffet. Erin walked past them, entered the drug store and looked around. She hoped it wouldn't be busy. She wanted to get what she came for and leave again as fast as possible. Fortunately, the only other person she saw was an elderly man buying lottery tickets at the kiosk near the front.

Erin headed straight for the Family Planning aisle, picked up a Clearblue Pregnancy Test package and took it to the checkout counter. The cashier looked down at the test and then up at Erin. Was that disapproval or concern in her eyes? Erin wondered. But why should she care? She'd never see her again. Erin paid in cash and hurried out. The return bus was due in ten minutes.

Erin hid the pregnancy test under her mattress for two days. She went to the toilet a dozen times both days, even when she didn't have to pee, hoping to see blood spots on her panties. She imagined she felt faint menstrual cramps a couple of times. But that's all it was. Her imagination.

When she woke up the third morning, there was still no bleeding and no cramps. Even though she wasn't sure, she figured it had been about six weeks since her last period. She'd never gone *this* long before.

That evening, Erin told Greg and Karen she wasn't feeling well and went to her bedroom early. She pulled the Clearblue package out from under the mattress, took it into her bathroom, and sat for a while on the closed lid of the toilet.

They'd always been so careful, Zach and she, hadn't they? There was only that one time they started to make love and discovered his condom had a tiny tear in it. She told him not to worry. She told him it wasn't the dangerous time of the month for her. So they did it anyway.

Turned out she was wrong.

She took the test stick out of its packaging, but even before she used it, Erin knew what the result would be.

For the first time in months, Erin didn't answer when Zach made his nightly call. She wasn't ready to tell him she was pregnant. She wasn't sure how she ever would be. Of course, she could try to pretend everything was okay, but she was never good at faking it with him. He'd probably know there was something wrong just by the sound of her voice. That evening, they texted instead. She told him her throat was sore. It was the easiest way out.

Erin didn't want to go to school the next day, either. She didn't want to do anything at all, except stay in bed and go back to sleep and not wake up until everything was normal again. But she had no choice. The final photo shoot for the Somerset School promotional campaign was scheduled at the end of the afternoon. And it was all about her. The campaign had been launched months earlier, but the website needed to be updated with pictures of Erin in the new school uniform the girls would be wearing in the fall.

The shoot started off well enough, even though the photographer had to keep telling her to smile, but it ended abruptly when Erin ran out of the room in tears.

Why hadn't they chosen someone else to be the Somerset Girl? These days, her face was all over the place. On social networks, in the newspaper, even on the sides of buses like the one she took the other day. Always framed by the words "Inspiring Girls to Succeed in an Ever-Changing World." Now, the Somerset Girl was in trouble. She was *never* going to succeed. They'd have to start a new campaign all over again with somebody else. What's worse, the whole school would be gossiping about her when they found out.

It felt just like her lonely days in middle school.

"Karen, we need to talk."

Greg called out to Karen as she walked in the door from work. His voice sounded serious to her, even disturbed. It wasn't like him to be that emotional.

But Karen was upset these days, too. Something was wrong with Erin. For the past week, she'd hardly spoken to them. She hadn't been eating much. And every day, when she came home after school, she went straight to her room.

Both Karen and Greg had seen behavior like this before. Fortunately, it ended two years ago. Things had changed for the better once Erin started at Somerset School. Still, there was always the chance their daughter's eating disorder might return. They'd never stopped watching for the signs.

But that's not why Greg wanted to speak with Karen now.

She joined him in his office.

"I know what you're going to say, Greg. That we need to find out what's bothering Erin."

"Yes, of course we do. But it's not about that. It's about an email I got this afternoon. Perhaps you should be sitting down when I tell you."

"What *is* it, Greg?"

Greg pulled a second chair up to his desk and motioned for her to sit beside him. "Erin's results came back from AncestryDNA. It's bad news, I'm afraid. There's a match for Erin. Several matches, in fact. But not with anybody on my side."

He opened up his computer monitor to show Karen the message.

"You were right when you said Alan Wilcross might have tricked us like he did the other families. It looks like he's Erin's biological father, too."

Karen scanned the words on the screen in front of her. Then she leaned over and wrapped her arms around his shoulders.

"Oh my God, Greg! This is just terrible. I'm *so* sorry! You must be—"

"Wait! Don't say anything, Karen. I don't want your pity. I've had a few hours to think about this, you know. Right now, I have to admit it feels surreal. But give me time and I'll be okay. Of course, as far as I'm concerned, Erin is just as much mine as Fiona and Sarah. That will never change. My biggest worry now is how she'll react when she finds this out."

Greg sagged in his chair. Then he suddenly straightened up. "And this means she'll have to stop seeing Zach. Immediately. I'm sure she'll agree, once she learns he's her half-brother."

"But how can we tell her *that*? You know what she's like now. She's already depressed about something. I'm afraid this'll push her over the edge."

"We don't really have a choice, do we? And the sooner the better. Tonight."

"Erin, dear, can we talk?"

"Do we *have* to, Mom? I don't feel like it right now."

"It's important, love. This can't wait."

Erin lagged behind as they all went into the den.

She didn't need this. She *really* didn't need this. They probably noticed she was bummed. And they were going to ask a million questions why. Couldn't they just leave her alone?

"I know what you're going to say. That I don't seem happy lately. Well, it's because I have a super heavy exam schedule coming up. Way too many readings and essays. I'm stressed out about it. Same as all my friends. I'll get over it—"

It was true, what she said. Just not the whole truth.

"Well, yes, we've been worried about you. Both your dad and me. We can help you with your studies. We also want you to eat better and get more sleep—"

Oh God, Erin thought, it's the eating thing again. *Will I have to hear about this the rest of my life?*

"But that's not why we need to talk to you tonight."

"Let me try, Karen," her father sounded troubled.

Erin was surprised. Was he *that* upset about her, too?

"Erin, there's something we have to tell you. It's hard for me to even get the words out. And it's going to be hard for you to hear them. You already know part of the story. You told it to us yourself. Zach and his friend discovered they're half-brothers. Their biological father turned out to be their parents' fertility doctor."

"I *know* all that, Dad. But what's that got to do with me?"

"Well, he was our doctor, too."

Greg couldn't continue. He motioned with his hand for Karen to carry on.

"We started to wonder if he might have done to us what he did to them. We wanted to find out for sure, one way or the other. That's why we checked it out with your DNA test. We got the results today. I'm afraid, my darling, that the doctor is your biological father, too."

Erin looked from Karen to Greg.

"NO! You're my Dad . . . you *have* to be."

Erin started sobbing. This was just too much.

Greg finally spoke again.

"Of course, Erin. This doesn't change anything for me. I love you more than ever. We both do. We're still a family . . . and we know this is already a big shock to you, but there's another thing we have to say. Maybe you've just figured this out yourself . . . you need to stop seeing Zach. He's your half-brother."

"NO! NO! I can't do that! I won't!"

Erin was wailing now. She covered her face with her hands and fell sideways on the sofa.

"OH MY GOD OH MY GOD OH MY GOD . . . "

"Erin, we're so sorry, but it has to be like this."

" . . . OH MY GOD OH MY GOD."

Karen went over and kneeled beside her. She tried to smooth Erin's wet tangled hair back from her forehead, but Erin pushed her hand away.

"My poor darling . . . I hate to see you like this."

Karen spoke softly. She hoped her words were soothing. But Erin couldn't be consoled. Her moaning only stopped when she gasped for air.

"Please, love. Please. Calm down. Do your deep breathing. I know this must feel like the end of the world right now, but it isn't. I promise you."

Erin suddenly went silent. Then she sat up again so quickly it startled both Greg and Karen.

When she spoke, her voice was flat.

"It is . . . for . . . me. I'm . . . pregnant."

Chapter Seventeen

"Erin! Babe! You there? What's the matter? Speak to me!" Zach could hear her ragged breath at the other end of the line, but no words.

Erin had been acting strange lately. In the past week, they'd even missed a couple of their nightly calls. He was hoping she'd be over it by now. Whatever *it* was. But no. There was still something wrong.

"Won't you tell me what's bothering you? Should I come over?"

"No! Not tonight. I can't handle it tonight."

Erin's voice was faint. Zach could barely hear her.

"How about tomorrow morning? I can skip my first class. Mom and Dad will both be at work and we can talk here."

It made Erin feel better to know she would see Zach in the morning, but only a little. Maybe she wasn't alone in this nightmare after all. Still, what could he do about it? It was hopeless.

"Okay. Mom always drives me to school. After she drops me off, I'll take an Uber to your place."

"Don't worry, babe. Whatever the problem is, it's gonna be okay."

But Zach wasn't as sure about that as he sounded. In fact, he was scared.

Erin was crying even before she reached the Murrays' front step and rang the doorbell.

When Zach opened the door, she stepped in and wrapped her arms around him, pressing her wet face against his uniform shirt.

"Shhhhhh. Calm down, babe . . . I'm here for you. We can get through it together."

He thought saying this would stop her tears, but it had the opposite effect. Her sobbing grew louder.

Zach led her to the living room and they sat on the couch. Then he reached for her hand and held it in both of his.

"Erin. Talk to me. What's going on?!"

"It's just too *awful*, Zach—"

"What's too awful, babe? Take it slow. Start at the beginning."

"The beginning? I know exactly when *that* was. It was the time a couple of months ago when we were together and there was that problem with your condom."

Zach flinched, but still held on to Erin's hand.

"No, babe . . . don't tell me—"

"I'm pregnant, Zach."

"Jesus! You sure?"

"Yes, I'm sure. I took the test."

"Ahhhh SHIT!"

"Please don't be mad at me, Zach! I thought it was my safe time of the month. I honestly did. I didn't lie to you. Please believe me."

"I believe you . . . but what are we going to do about it? Do your parents know?"

"Yes. I told them last evening before you called. That's one of the reasons I was so upset."

"One of the reasons? There's more?"

"Yes. And it makes it *way* worse."

"How could it get worse?"

"Because we're related. You and me."

"That's bullshit! We're not related—"

"Just listen to me, Zach!"

Erin closed her eyes and inhaled.

"A few months ago, you found out about you and Pete, right? That your parents' doctor is your father? Well, my parents went to him, too. And they got DNA results back for me yesterday. He's *my* father, too."

"Fuck! You're my sister!"

Zach finally let go of Erin's hand.

"They want us to break up, Zach. I know why they're saying that. But it hurts so bad."

"And what about the baby?"

"They want me to get rid of it . . . they want me to have an abortion."

Zach looked up at the ceiling. Tears slid down the sides of his cheeks, and he wiped them with his sleeve.

Why us? was all he could think. Why couldn't this happen to somebody else? Erin didn't deserve this. Neither did he. He thought they'd always be a couple. Even move in together someday. But that was impossible now.

"Maybe they're right."

Then he thought about Wilcross, who caused this fucked-up mess.

"And maybe I'll beat the shit out of that asshole doctor, if I ever meet him. I don't give a *fuck* if he's my father."

Erin and Zach sat for a while, not speaking and not touching, until they agreed it was time to leave. They each booked an Uber and waited at the front door.

"Before I go, Zach, I just want to say I'll always love you. For the rest of my life."

"Love you too, babe. I'll call you later."

They embraced one last time. Then they stepped outside and Zach locked the door behind them.

He went to school and Erin went home.

Greg rushed to the front door when he heard her come in.

"Erin, I've been so *worried* about you. The school called an hour ago. They said you hadn't shown up for class this morning. I tried to reach you—"

She was ready for this.

"Sorry, Dad, I should've texted you. Mom dropped me off, but I was feeling sick, so I sat outside for a while after school started. I was hoping it would get better, but it didn't. I decided to come home again."

"Is there anything I can do to help?"

"Thanks, Dad, but I think I'll just go to my bedroom and lie down for a while."

"Good idea. Take it easy. We'll see how you feel later on. I'll call the school to let them know you're here. And I'll let Mom know not to pick you up on her way home."

Greg watched as Erin slowly climbed the stairs.

They came in lots of shapes and colors and sizes. There were small round white ones and large red oblong ones and capsules that were green and yellow. She knew the capsules were decongestants and the white pills were pain killers. She wasn't exactly sure what all the others were for.

It didn't really matter.

One by one, Erin opened each bottle, emptied the contents into a growing pile beside the sink, screwed the cap back on and returned it to its place in the medicine cabinet.

Then she ran the cold water.

It took her three full glasses to swallow them. It wasn't easy. Her hands trembled the entire time and she gagged on the big red ones. But she managed to down them all.

Erin stared at her reflection in the mirror before turning out the light.

Her eyes were already dead.

Karen usually had lunch at work, but today was different. Greg had called to tell her about Erin and she decided to come home.

"So, how's Erin? She feeling any better now?"

"I'm not sure. She went to bed right after she arrived. I checked on her a while ago, and she was still sleeping. I didn't want to disturb her. She's been through a lot."

"Yes, she has . . . in fact, I was surprised she actually went to school this morning. It must've been too much for her after all."

Karen took off her suit jacket.

"I'll go up and see how she's doing."

"9-1-1. What's your emergency?"

"We need an ambulance! It's our daughter! We think she's taken an overdose of prescription pills—"

"What's the address?"

"353 Manor Road."

"Her name?"

"Erin. Erin Evans."

"How old is your daughter?"

"She's sixteen. Please tell them to hurry!"

"Is your daughter conscious?"

"No! She's not and I can't wake her up! Oh, God—"

“Is she breathing?”

“Yes. But just barely. They need to hurry!”

“Ma’am, an ambulance is on the way. Please stay on the line.”

Greg and Karen huddled together in a small room in one corner of the Emergency Department. They were alone, except for a nervous man in biking gear who paced back and forth and finally disappeared down the hall in search of a coffee.

Outside the door was a constant parade of hospital staff and worried people who’d rather be anywhere else. Again and again, they had to move over to make way for gurneys transporting patients in various degrees of distress. And every few seconds, announcements over the PA system added to the commotion.

Karen’s eyes were closed. She hadn’t prayed since she was a little girl, but she was praying silently now. Greg, his arm around Karen’s shoulders, kept his eyes fixed on the second hand of the clock above the door. He didn’t want to remember anything about this place. Not the speckled brown carpeting, not the orange vinyl armchairs, and not the dreary view of a crumbling brick wall outside the only window.

They’d been there less than an hour, but it felt a hundred times longer.

The door opened and a fortyish woman with a stethoscope around her neck walked in. It was a bad sign she wouldn't look at them until the moment she spoke.

"Mr. and Mrs. Evans?"

They both leaped up.

"Yes?"

"I'm Dr. Lund. I've been with your daughter since she arrived—"

"Yes?"

"I'm afraid I have bad news—"

Karen fell against Greg. He struggled to steady her.

"I'm so sorry. Erin didn't make it . . . we tried our best to save her, but, in the end, we couldn't bring her back."

Chapter Eighteen

The chapel was full. There was a place reserved for Zach and his parents at the front. Eyes red-rimmed from grief and three sleepless nights, he walked slowly toward his seat. Jason and Megan supported him on either side. They were among the last to arrive.

Erin's classmates, in their burgundy school uniforms, already filled several pews behind the Murrays. Many of them held on to each other and wept quietly as the coffin proceeded up the aisle.

The Evans' legal and academic colleagues were there, too, together with their friends and neighbors. Joan, standing near the back with Helen, recognized many of them from the Christmas reception. And here they all were again, five months later. To her, this service was a cruel echo of that earlier time.

Greg and Karen, with his daughters Fiona and Sarah and their families, followed behind the coffin. Karen could feel the somber presence of just about everybody they knew, but she didn't look at any of them. She was afraid she'd break down if she saw the pity in their eyes.

Instead, she stared straight ahead, past the coffin, at the flowers displayed across the transept. There were so *many* of them. Baskets and wreaths. Lilies and roses and orchids. Mainly white arrangements, but there was one with lavender and carnations and Birds of Paradise. Bright tropical colors. Erin would have loved that one, Karen thought.

After they reached their places, the minister welcomed the gathering and introduced the service. His words flowed by Karen as she deliberately examined in extreme detail each blossom in each arrangement. She was trying hard not to hear any of what he was saying.

" . . . We look not to the things that are seen
but to the things that are unseen;
for the things that are seen are transient
but the things that are unseen are eternal.
Today we come together
to remember before God our sister Erin,
to give thanks for her life
and to comfort one another in our grief . . . "

"Amazing Grace" followed, but Karen didn't sing.

Then, Fiona spoke about her fondest memories of her baby sister.

Sarah came after, reciting *If I Should Go*. It was just a short poem of loss, but she struggled to finish.

Nearing the end of the service, the minister read from Ecclesiastes 3. "A time to be born and a time to die . . . ." The words were supposed to bring comfort. It didn't work for either Karen or Greg.

Finally, they endured a closing hymn and prayer.

Simple elements of a very traditional service. Karen and Greg weren't sure that's what Erin would have wanted. They never thought they'd have to make such choices.

At the end, the mourners left to a recording of *Ruin* by Shawn Mendes. It wasn't traditional at all. It wasn't even appropriate. But it had been Erin's favorite song.

Before leaving for the burial, Greg and Karen lingered outside the chapel entrance, thanking all who came and receiving condolences. When Zach and his parents emerged, they embraced.

Greg spoke first.

"We know how hard this must be for you, Zach. You made Erin very happy. We'll always be grateful to you for that."

Zach didn't respond. He was puzzled. Didn't they know Erin was with him that last morning? That she told him *everything*? And here they were, talking to him as if that shit didn't happen. As if that wasn't why she—

Megan broke the silence.

"Erin was a lovely girl. We'll miss her a lot."

Karen took Zach's hand and murmured something. Her voice was so weak, he asked her to say it again and leaned in to hear her.

"Zach, I noticed some potted plants with the floral arrangements at the front of the chapel. I'm going to take one of them home. Would you like to choose one for yourself? To remind you of Erin?"

Zach wasn't really interested in plants. And he'd have no trouble remembering Erin without one. But he didn't want to offend Karen, so he went back inside.

He picked up the first one he saw. Some kind of twisty vine with a white star-shaped flower and a small butterfly decoration stuck in the soil. A card was attached. "With Deepest Sympathy" it read.

The name inscribed below was Dr. Alan Wilcross.

What the hell? How *dare* that fucker send flowers? It was his fault Erin did what she did.

He wanted to stomp on it. Smash it into little pieces. Then he changed his mind. Zach picked it up and carried it out to his parents' car. It sat beside him in the back seat as they drove to the graveyard for the burial.

As soon as they got home, Zach wanted to leave again.

"Can I borrow the car for an hour, Dad?"

"You sure you're okay to drive right now, Zach? It's been a tough day—"

"I'll be fine. I need to get out. Better than just sitting around, feeling sorry for myself. Besides, there's something I have to do."

Jason handed Zach the keys.

Ten minutes later, Zach parked the car in front of the Parkview Medical Building and got out. He opened the rear door, scooped up the plant and carried it inside.

The directory in the lobby listed Dr. Wilcross' clinic on the third floor. Zach couldn't wait for the elevator. Instead, he rushed to the side stairwell and took the steps two at a time.

Zach burst into Alan's reception area and slammed the plant on the counter, startling a couple in the waiting room.

"I want to see Dr. Wilcross. NOW!"

Marjorie pushed her chair back out of Zach's reach.

"I'm afraid he's with a patient. And he's fully booked today. He can't see you."

"I don't give a shit. I WANT HIM OUT HERE. NOW!"

"That's not possible. And if you don't leave immediately, I'll call the police."

Her hand was already hovering over the phone.

"I'M NOT LEAVING TILL I SEE HIM."

Alan came out of his examining room, looking annoyed at the disturbance. He was followed by a patient struggling to adjust the side button of her slacks. That done, she pulled her jacket off the rack near the door and scurried out.

"What's going on here?"

"Hello, doctor. Or should I say DAD!"

"I beg your pardon?"

"I'm Zach Murray. Remember my parents? Jason and Megan Murray?"

"Yes. Of course."

"Well, we *all* know you're my biological father. Because you screwed them around. You used *your* sperm with them. Isn't that right . . . DAD?!"

Alan glanced toward the waiting area, hoping they were alone. They weren't. He recognized Nicole and Mark Price. His next appointment. Artificial insemination.

Mark, cellphone held up, was capturing the scene on video.

"Mr. Price . . . Mark . . . stop! I don't allow recording here!"

He turned back to Zach.

"You need to go!"

"Oh, I'll go. But not just yet. I'm here for a reason. I'm returning your *fucking* plant. The one you sent to Erin Evans' funeral. I'm pretty sure she wouldn't have wanted it. Because, after all, you killed her—"

"That's nonsense—"

"No, asshole. It's *not* nonsense! She found out a few days ago you used your sperm with *her* parents too. We were together a whole year. We loved each other. And she was pregnant. She killed herself because of what YOU did to us!"

Zach grabbed the plant off the counter and threw it at Alan, who dodged to get out of its way. The pot hit the wall behind him and shattered, spraying dirt on the photos of newborns posted there.

"How many kids you got, doc? Ten? Twenty? A *hundred*?"

Zach closed in on Alan and pushed his chest hard with both hands.

"I SAID, JUST HOW MANY OF US *ARE* THERE, DICKHEAD???"

Alan fell back against the wall.

As he slid to the floor, soiled baby photos tumbled down around him.

Seconds later, two police officers rushed in, seized Zach and hustled him out. Marjorie came from behind the counter to help Alan to his feet. And the Prices left after Mark finally put his cellphone away.

"Why'd you do it, Zach? What the hell were you thinking?!"

"I did it because he deserved it!"

"But you *know* I've already started legal proceedings against him, right? Isn't that the best way to handle this?"

Jason was driving Zach home from the police station. Alan had refused to make a formal statement about the incident and Zach was released on an understanding to stay away from him.

"That's not enough. As far as I'm concerned, he's responsible for what happened to Erin."

"That's a pretty strong statement. You're going to have to explain yourself when we get back. To both your mom and me.

Today's been too much for her to handle, you know. First, the funeral. Now this!"

They didn't speak to each other the rest of the way.

It was only after they got home that Zach told Jason and Megan about seeing Erin for the last time on the morning of her overdose. He told them about her pregnancy and the realization they could never be together.

They agreed to keep Erin's story just between the three of them. She would have wanted it that way.

Chapter Nineteen

The 85-second unedited video, at #Waitingroombeatdown, was posted on Twitter the day after the confrontation. It disappeared later that same evening. Mark Price deleted it after a Twitter friend warned him about breaching the privacy of minors.

In those few hours, it didn't exactly go viral. But it was retweeted enough times that the local media noticed and quickly saw the potential for a sensational story.

After all, Alan Wilcross was a minor celebrity in the city. A high-profile physician adored by his patients and honored by his community. And there he was on video, accosted by a young man—apparently, his son—in his own clinic. Accused of duping his patients. Even accused of being responsible for a suicide. If the allegations were true, the tragedy could become front-page material for months to come.

"Mr. Murray, can we ask you a few questions?"

Jason locked the side door of his home and went to his car. He was already late for a supper meeting at the club. Half a dozen reporters and cameramen lined the sidewalk at the end of the drive. It was the third time that day they'd approached him, and he was angry.

"For God's sake, just leave me and my family alone!"

But they persisted.

"Mr. Murray, can you confirm the accusations against Alan Wilcross by Zach?"

"Is it true that Wilcross is his biological father?"

"I said leave us alone. Get the HELL away from us!"

Jason climbed into his Toyota and slammed the door closed. The media types shuffled to the side, and he backed out and drove away. But he knew that, sooner or later, they would return.

And they did, over and over again. Jason gave up a week later. He'd had enough of them waiting outside the house and the club. Megan and Zach—especially Zach—were followed, too. And when they were at home, they all grew tired of hiding behind drawn curtains. Maybe life could go back to normal if they told their story once. On their terms. Jason agreed to an interview with Janice Vaughn, a senior journalist with *The Morning Journal.*

"So, Mr. Murray, can you tell me what led to the incident at Dr. Wilcross' clinic?"

"It really all started a couple of decades ago when we found out I had prostate cancer—"

"I'm sorry to hear that."

"Thank you. It's in remission now. But at the time, we were worried we wouldn't be able to have a family after my treatment so we went to the doctor for help. He stored my sperm samples at his clinic for later. We went back for artificial insemination in 1999 and Zach came along nine months later."

"But things didn't happen quite the way you expected?"

"A couple of months ago, we learned it wasn't my sperm Wilcross used after all, but his own."

"How did you find that out?"

"I can't go into detail, but let's just say we sent a sample of Zach's DNA to AncestryDNA. Eventually, there was a match with the doctor's biological daughter. And Zach's not the only one. There're other victims. But I'm not going to talk about them."

"I understand. Let's just focus on your family. How did you feel when you learned about this?"

"Megan and Zach can speak for themselves, but I felt tricked. Like we were offered one thing, and the doctor gave us something else. Please don't get me wrong. Things aren't any different between me and Zach. I'll always consider him my child, even though he isn't biologically. So it's confusing. And it's raised a lot of other issues, too."

"Other issues?"

"Yes . . . well . . . I have to wonder what actually happened to my stored sperm. If Wilcross switched samples in our case, and didn't use mine for us, then what did he do with it? Throw it away? Use it with other patients? Do I have children out there I don't even know about?"

"I see—"

"And that's not all. We're worried about how this will affect Zach."

"Yes. Go on."

"Well . . . for example . . . each time Zach gets serious with somebody, will he have to ask her to get a DNA test? Just to be sure they're not related? It's outrageous, what Wilcross has done to us. Makes zero difference if he's incompetent or just plain nuts. Either way, he's messed up our lives."

Janice Vaughn turned to Megan.

"And Mrs. Murray. Could I ask how you are dealing with this?"

"I've cried a lot. I still cry about it. It's like Jason was saying. My feelings are all mixed up. I love Zach. But the fact that Dr. Wilcross put his own sperm in me . . . well . . . it makes me feel violated. Almost like he raped me."

Megan stopped when she noticed Zach squirming in his chair, looking like he might take off at any second.

Janice noticed, too.

"Zach, I know this must be hard for you. But can I ask you to stay with us? This won't take much longer."

"Okay."

"And maybe you could share how you're feeling right now? Of course, we can stop anytime you want."

Zach nodded. He started slowly, then his words came out fast.

"I'm . . . feeling . . . so many . . . bad things. When I first found out, I was *so* pissed. Like, what's *with* this dude anyway? I mean, was this just some big frickin' joke for him? Am I the result of some kind of crazy experiment in his lab?"

Megan reached over and squeezed Zach's shoulder to reassure him.

"Also . . . I know I don't really look like Dad, but I thought we had *some* things in common. Then I find out half of me comes from that doctor instead. I Googled his name. There's tons of pictures of him. I kind of look like him in some of the earlier ones. And I hate it."

"What made you go to his office, Zach?"

"I'm not supposed to talk about that. But I'll just say it's total crap to be related to the person who did this to me and to other people."

"Thanks, Zach, for being so open with me."

Janice turned back to Jason and Megan.

"Any final comments, Mr. and Mrs. Murray? Where does this go from here?"

Jason had an important message he wanted to make public.

"Well . . . I'm not letting this drop. What happened was unforgivable. We're victims of Dr. Wilcross. We trusted him and he deceived us. And it's hurt our family on so many levels. So, we're taking legal action against him. And if there are other families who find they are in the same situation as us, I want them to let us know. My lawyer is exploring the possibility of a class-action suit."

"Alan, one of the security guards at the front desk just called. There's a lot of reporters hanging around the entrance. He thinks they might be waiting for you."

"I'm not surprised, Marjorie. They're here about what that vicious Murray kid did to me. The whole scene was posted on Twitter."

"So, what are you going to do? Will you talk to them?"

"Absolutely not! They're out to get me . . . they want to make me look like I'm some kind of monster."

Alan stayed in his office a full hour after his last patient left. Then he made his way to the staff parking area through the service door of the cafeteria.

Three reporters finally caught up with him two days later.

"No comment," was all they got.

Chapter Twenty

"Have you seen the papers lately? The piece the other day in *The Morning Journal* about that fertility doctor? What a farce!"

"I haven't been following it, Papa. Too busy at the Wellington location. We've got staff problems there."

"But I seem to recall that Wilcross was your doctor, wasn't he? When you were trying for Pete?"

After an early dinner at the elder Stephanidis' residence, Alesandro and Ari had taken their Mastiha liqueurs out to the patio and were sitting by the pool watching the sun set.

Alesandro didn't want to discuss the Wilcross scandal with Ari. Everybody was talking about it. It was making newspaper headlines and even getting national coverage on TV. Despite what he told his father, Alesandro read and heard it all. And it made him uncomfortable.

Why did the Murrays have to go public? Just how far would the media run with it? And what if they found out about those damn DNA results that linked the Murray boy to Pete?

Ari had a point to make. He went back inside, brought out the front section of *The Morning Journal* from the previous Saturday, and placed it on the glass-top table in front of Alesandro.

"Here it is. Read it for yourself."

Alesandro glanced at the headline.

BAIT AND SWITCH

ONE FAMILY'S NIGHTMARE EXPERIENCE WITH RENOWNED FERTILITY SPECIALIST

by Janice Vaughn, Senior Journalist

Underneath the headline was a close-up photo of Jason, Megan, and Zach, followed by Vaughn's article.

"Actually, Papa, I've seen it already."

"Really? So, what do you think?"

"I think it's a sad story about a backstabbing doctor and his victims. That's what I think. And you're right. Wilcross was our doctor a long time ago. Never did trust him. Superior son of a bitch."

"Take a closer look at the young man in the photo."

"I told you, I already saw it—"

"The same photo was on the national news the other night. Don't you think he looks a lot like your Pete?"

"So, what if he does?"

"It makes me wonder—"

"About *what*?"

"You know what. I've always doubted Pete is your son. Now I'm convinced he's not. Perhaps Cristina wasn't the guilty party after all. Perhaps it was the doctor. Maybe he did the same thing to you as he did to that family. Have you thought about that?"

"What the hell, Papa!? Just leave it alone! You and I will never agree on this."

Alesandro stood up abruptly, tipping over his wicker chair. For years, he'd been avoiding this showdown. Maybe he still could if he got out of there now.

"We need to deal with this once and for all, Alesandro. There's a lot at stake. The future of our family. Our business. Everything I've built up over the years . . . and if Pete is really that man's son . . . well . . . where does this leave us? Unless you show me proof he's yours, then I refuse to acknowledge him. He won't be part of this family, you understand?"

"How could you be so cruel? Pete's a great kid. *My* great kid. This will crush him. Is that what you really want?"

Ari turned his head away. For him, the conversation was over.

"Who the hell do you think you are, anyway? Playing the almighty patriarch all these years! Well . . . I've got news for you. You're really just a bitter old man sitting all alone in your big house. Nobody pays attention to you anymore. And that includes me. I'M THROUGH WITH YOUR BULLSHIT!"

Alesandro kicked his overturned chair to the side and stomped away.

At that moment, Agnes came rushing out. She'd heard the yelling.

Alesandro passed her without speaking and kept going.

"Alesandro, this is a surprise! Why didn't you call first?"

"I've come straight from my parents' place. Is Pete here?"

"No, he's out with friends."

"Good. Can we talk?"

Cristina opened the door wider and Alesandro stepped in. He was clearly agitated. She recognized the signs. Red face. Crazy-looking eyes. Hands clenched in fists. And from the smell of alcohol, she could tell he'd been drinking. Despite his frequent outbursts, Alesandro had never been violent. Still, she was alarmed at the way he was looking now. Was he angry with *her*? Was it about the most recent impasse in their divorce negotiations?

But Alesandro went straight to the great room, flopped down on the sofa and bowed his head. Evidently, this wasn't about the divorce.

"He knows. Papa knows."

"What does he know?"

"He knows about Pete."

"I see . . . well, I always thought it might happen sooner or later."

Cristina sat down in the chair opposite him. "So, how did he find out?"

"He saw all the news coverage about the Murrays. He saw the photos of Zach looking a lot like Pete. And he remembered we went to Wilcross, too. So, he put two and two together. We had a big blow-up this evening about it. Now he says he's disowning Pete—"

"What?! The miserable bastard! How could he *do* that?"

Alesandro looked up at Cristina.

"I don't know how to handle this. Help me . . . please."

He was pleading with her. He even had tears in his eyes. This was a first for him.

"Wait here, I'll be back—"

Cristina went to the kitchen, poured a strong coffee and brought it to him. Maybe it would calm him down.

"If you ask me, Alesandro, the first thing we need to do is keep Pete away from Ari and Agnes. At least until Ari changes his mind."

"I don't think that'll ever happen—"

"Well, then, if he finds out Ari is cutting him off, we have to make sure Pete knows we'll always be on his side. That we love him no matter what."

"That goes without saying—"

"Meanwhile, you should keep trying to convince Ari he's wrong about this."

"Fat chance of *that*. And anyway, after this evening, we're not on speaking terms."

"Alesandro, you asked for my help. My advice is don't give up. Keep trying. You have to resolve this. And maybe you have more leverage than you think. What would Ari do with the business if you told him that he either accepts Pete or you're out of it too? That you would disown *him*?"

"I'm pretty sure the whole thing would fall apart. I'm basically running the show now. He comes in occasionally just to push me around. He wants everybody to think he's still in charge. But he isn't. I doubt it would survive if I left. He has nobody else to replace me."

"Exactly! I know it's not the best way to get him to accept Pete, but maybe it's the only way. Of course, it's a risk for you. If he still won't give in, it might mean walking away from your family and your career. And all that money. Could you do it?"

Alesandro responded instantly. "It's the last thing I'd want to do. But for Pete, yes. I would do it."

Cristina never thought she'd hear Alesandro say words like this.

"We need to talk, Papa."

Ari didn't respond.

It had taken Agnes several days to get him to agree to see his son, and Ari kept telling her the same thing. He had no intention of backing down on what he had said about Pete, so why bother debating it again? When Alesandro finally appeared, he just sat in his easy chair and stared at him.

"Okay . . . I see you're still not speaking to me. So, I'll do the talking . . . and Mama, I want you to hear this too. I'll start back when Cristina and I decided to have a baby. You remember we tried and tried, but nothing happened. We went to Wilcross to find out what was wrong. What we never told you is that the tests showed Cristina was perfectly fine. I was the one who couldn't have children."

This was too much for Agnes. Embarrassed, she looked away.

"At that point, we really had only one option. We decided to use a sperm donor."

Ari frowned and finally spoke. "I was right. Pete isn't yours."

"No, he's not my biological son. But in every other way, I consider him mine. And you would never have known the difference if Wilcross had followed through with the donor we selected. But he didn't. We found that out a couple of years ago. And we only learned this spring that he used his own sperm. So now you have the whole truth about Pete. I should have told you earlier. If I had, Cristina and I might still be together today. But that's another story . . . I've known all along you'd judge us for what we did. That's why we never told you. And our fight the other evening proved me right. You're narrow-minded. Arrogant. And you don't give a shit about me or my son's feelings."

Alesandro paused. It was a big moment. What he intended to say next was as overwhelming to him as it would be to Ari, but he had to say it. "Well, I won't stand by and let you hurt Pete that way. So, I'm giving you a choice. Either you accept him as your grandson, as a full Stephanidis, or if you don't, I won't be part of this family anymore. And I'll walk away from the business. You take both of us or you'll have neither of us. And if you choose the latter, you know as well as I do that'll be the end of your precious Stephanidis empire."

Alesandro stood up to leave. "Think about it. Let me know."

Agnes, weeping by this point, tugged on his sleeve to stop him from going, but he left anyway. Ari closed his eyes as if doing that would erase what he'd just heard.

"I did it, Cristina. I gave him the ultimatum. Like you suggested."

"And how did he react?"

"He didn't. I think he was in shock. Now it's a waiting game. I wonder how long it will take for him to come to his senses?"

It was early evening of the following day. Alesandro and Cristina had met at the front entrance of her complex, then crossed the road to the lakefront, and were now sitting on a bench watching kayakers streak by. Flower beds stretched out pink and yellow alongside them.

Alesandro had visited her condo several times over the past year, but the discussions there had always been acrimonious. For him, this time was different. There'd been a breakthrough. He'd stood up to Ari and felt surprisingly good about it. It deserved a change of scenery.

"You did the right thing, Alesandro."

"Yes. And I should have done it a long time ago. Now, I don't have anything to hide from the old bully anymore. What a relief!"

It was a relief to Cristina, too.

She had no delusions. Alesandro would still be Alesandro. Temperamental. Opinionated. More than a little chauvinistic. None of that would change. But he'd finally faced up to his father and defended Pete. This was the first truly independent stance he'd ever taken against Ari. Cristina knew how difficult it must have been for him.

Nothing was going to stop the divorce proceedings, as far as she was concerned. But maybe now they could deal with it on civil terms. And now they could work better together as parents to their son.

"Well, Alesandro, let's just hope for a good outcome for Pete."

"I've been thinking, Cristina . . . now that my parents know what happened, I see no reason why we can't join in the lawsuit the Murrays started. I'd like nothing better than to see Wilcross pay for what he's done to us. What do you think? Should we do it?"

"Of course, we should . . . but we need to ask Pete about it, too. If he agrees, I'm sure the Murrays will be grateful for our support."

Chapter Twenty-One

India sat under the patio awning outside the Dirty Duck Pub and ordered a draft from the server. It was late Monday afternoon of the long August weekend, and the market was overflowing with people enjoying their remaining hours of freedom before work the next day. In stalls across the street from the pub, aproned produce vendors struggled to keep up with the demand for their tomatoes, peppers, and blueberries. At the corner, folks paused to listen to a busker's Bryan Adams medley, tossed change into his open guitar case and then moved on. And the scent of sandalwood incense wafted over in waves from the busy tie-dye T-shirt kiosk next door.

India enjoyed the music and the smells and the bustle of the crowd, but she was looking for two people in particular. Her half-brothers. She'd never met them, but she already knew what they looked like from recent media coverage. By the time she spotted them approaching the pub, fifteen minutes late, her beer was half-finished.

She stood up and waved.

"Pete . . . Zach . . .over here!"

They came to her table, and after she greeted them they all sat down.

She could tell they were checking her out, and she knew why. The boys wanted to see how much she looked like them. *And him.* But they wouldn't find any trace of Wilcross in her appearance. Unlike Pete and Zach, she didn't take after him at all. India had always been told she was a younger version of her mother Helen.

The waiter returned and took Pete and Zach's orders, too. Then India explained why she contacted them. "I've thought about getting together ever since I learned about you from my mom. Before that, I always thought I was an only child. And I gotta say, it feels freaky meeting you today. Anyway, when I saw all the news coverage on your family, Zach, I decided it had to happen now, while we're still in the same city. I'm leaving next month for veterinary school in Guelph. We might not have the chance after that."

Zach nodded. "You're probably right. I'm heading to university in New Brunswick in a couple of weeks."

"Awesome! What about you, Pete?"

"Commerce at U of T."

India finished her beer and ordered another, with nachos this time.

Over the next forty-five minutes, they tried to catch up on eighteen missed years and discover things they had in common. Traits passed down to them from Alan Wilcross. It turned out they all had widow's peaks and suffered from hay fever, loathed lima beans and claustrophobic spaces and reality TV. They all had high

IQ test scores, too, but recognized that might also have come from their mothers.

Eventually, Pete turned the conversation to Wilcross. "I've never met him. And from what I've heard, I never want to."

"I met him once. He came to our house. Got into a shitfight with my mom. Total asshole—"

"I met him, too. If you can call it a meeting. I went to his clinic and called him out about what he did to us. Maybe you saw the video. It got ugly. But he deserved it."

"I heard about that, and about your parents' lawsuit against him."

Zach looked over at Pete. "Both our parents are involved in it now."

"So, what's the latest with that?"

Pete answered. "My parents only joined in June. But since then, it seems like every week there's another family popping up with some new complaint. They think Wilcross either used his own sperm or he used the wrong sperm from someone else. There must be a dozen families by now."

Zach had more. "And then there're the men like my father who want to know if Dr. Dickhead secretly used their samples with other couples." He wasn't sure he could continue. But he did, with a noticeably shaky voice. "The absolute worst is . . . is . . . what happened to the girl I used to date. She was our half-sister too. She couldn't handle it when she found out. She's gone. Her parents are joining in the lawsuit, too."

"I'm so, so sorry!" India exclaimed.

The three grew quiet. The gap in their conversation was filled by a burst of laughter coming from the next table.

Zach inhaled and spoke again. "So, yes, he fucked us up big time."

India responded immediately. "I bet he thought he'd never get caught. And, up to now, *nobody* has held him accountable—"

"Because who would have thought someone like him would do this?" Zach sipped his beer.

India leaned forward and raised her voice a notch. "But isn't it time that changed? I've been researching this ever since his blow-up with my mom. Wilcross isn't the only one getting found out. There're other cases here in Canada and in the States and Europe. And likely a whole lot more that haven't been uncovered yet. Shouldn't there be rules for these guys? I mean, for starters . . . shouldn't they have to keep donor records? And maybe even make their own sperm samples available so patients can check their DNA against them? What about *our* rights? The daughters and sons. It should be easier to find out who our biological fathers are."

Both Pete and Zach were surprised at India's intensity.

"Wow! You're *so* into this."

"I am, because it's personal for me. It should be for you dudes, too."

"Totally! I agree with everything you're saying. And I think, from what my parents told me, the lawyers are already raising a lot of these questions." Pete added.

"But can't we do more? Like get involved somehow? Speak up on what needs to change? My DNA test result was the only way we found out the truth about what that creep did to you and the others. That sucks!"

The bill arrived and Pete paid for all of them. Then they walked together to the corner. The busker was still there, playing Dylan. India stayed to listen, but the boys had to go.

"Isn't it about time I get my very first hugs from my brothers?"

India embraced them both and watched them weave their way through the crowd until she couldn't see them anymore. Then she flipped a dollar into the busker's guitar case. This is just the beginning, she thought, as she headed for the bus stop to go home.

Three days later, Pete and Zach received a text message.

> *Hey—check out Donor Conceived Alliance of Canada. I'm in. U guys too I hope. GL @ uni.* ☺
> *Talk soon, India*

Chapter Twenty-Two

Alesandro drove through the wrought iron gates and parked the Jaguar near the front entrance of his parents' residence. He sat there for a while, mulling over his mother's voice message from the previous day.

"Your father wants to see you." Agnes had said. "Please come. Tomorrow. Late afternoon is the best time for him." And, almost as an afterthought, "I'd like to see you again, too, Alesandro."

Her tone was pleading, but it gave nothing away.

He was undoubtedly being summoned to hear Ari's response to the ultimatum he gave him in June: either accept Pete as his grandson or forget about both of them. It was an important decision. And given how stubborn his father was, it could go one way or the other.

They had avoided each other all summer. Ari, already in semi-retirement mode, stayed away from day-to-day restaurant operations, leaving Alesandro to manage the entire business on his own. And Alesandro was tired of making excuses to Pete as to why they didn't visit his grandparents anymore.

Alesandro had called back to confirm he would come. Two months were more than long enough for their standoff. He, too, wanted it to be resolved.

He finally got out of the car, passed between the Greek goddess statues at either side of the steps, and climbed up to the arched front door.

Agnes was waiting there for him. She embraced him, and they went arm-in-arm to where Ari sat in the sunroom.

"Hello, Papa."

"Alesandro—"

"How are you?"

"I'm doing okay, all things considered."

All things considered included their feud, Alesandro guessed. But he refused to feel any guilt.

"You wanted to see me?"

"Yes. Sit . . . please."

Alesandro remained standing.

"You've put me in a very bad position, Alesandro—"

"Before you say anything more, Papa, I want you to know that I do not feel the slightest bit responsible for this mess. You created it all by yourself. You and your attitude towards Pete. So, don't go blaming me."

"Alesandro, I didn't ask you here to fight about it again. I'm too tired for that."

"So?"

"So, I give up. You win. And your mother. She's been after me all summer to change my mind. Well, I'm only partly there. I still have problems with this whole sperm donor business. It's just not right, as far as I'm concerned. But I recognize why you did it. And I recognize if you hadn't, it would be the end of the line for our family anyway. So, I'm calling a truce. I will continue to acknowledge Pete as my grandson."

"And you will treat him exactly that way? As your grandson? Like he is your own flesh and blood?"

"Yes. He will never know the difference. Your mother made me promise that, too . . . and maybe someday I might actually get used to the idea."

Alesandro looked over at Agnes and nodded his gratitude. Then he turned back to Ari.

"Let's move on. And I never want to hear about this again. Agreed?"

"Agreed."

Alesandro walked over to Ari and shook his hand.

Agnes invited him to stay for dinner, but Alesandro declined. It was too soon for that.

He phoned Cristina as soon as he returned to his apartment.

"I thought you should know, Cristina. After all this time, Papa has finally decided to accept Pete."

"Thank God for that!"

“And this is due to you. It was your idea for me to play hardball with him in the first place. And it worked.”

“So, tell me how it went.”

Alesandro recounted the entire conversation he had with Ari.

“Kind of a lukewarm concession, isn’t it? ‘He’ll try to get used to it?’”

“You’re right, but he knows I won’t tolerate any bad behavior towards Pete.”

Alesandro paused, then changed the topic. It was a risk, what he planned to say next. But he’d been thinking about it for a while.

“Cristina, would you have time for a coffee one of these days?”

“Maybe . . . why?”

“I thought we might discuss the way things are going between you and me.”

“You mean about the divorce? Shouldn’t we leave that to our lawyers? I understood the terms had pretty well been settled.”

“It’s about the divorce, but not what you’re thinking—”

“Oh? You want to make more changes?”

“I’d rather discuss this in person, Cristina, but I wonder if you might consider putting it on hold.”

“Are you serious, Alesandro!? Whatever for?”

"Well . . . now . . . don't answer me right away on this, Cristina, but we seem to be getting along better these days. For one thing, we're not fighting anymore about my family."

"That's true—"

"And I've been going over things in my mind, doing a lot of thinking lately. Trying to see how things looked from your perspective. I admit I let my parents interfere too much in our marriage. I know they made life difficult for you over the years. And I didn't defend you. At the time, I felt caught in the middle. But what happened was wrong and I'm sorry. It's over now. It would never happen again."

"So what are you suggesting?"

"I'm suggesting we might try counselling. See where that takes us."

"I'm amazed you would even think about going to counselling, Alesandro. It's not like you at all."

"Let's just say I'm trying to get my priorities straight, Cristina. And I wonder if we can give it another try."

"I'm not sure, Alesandro. First, let's see how things go between your father and Pete. Then we can talk about this again. Meanwhile, if you want, I can ask my lawyer to hold off on finalizing things."

Cristina sat in her kitchen after their call ended, thinking about what Alesandro said. Had he really changed that much? Maybe. Maybe not. With time, it would be easier to tell. But there'd been so much bitterness between them for so long, it was difficult for her to believe they could live happily ever after.

Chapter Twenty-Three

Joan knew Alan would be looking at her through the security camera after she rang the doorbell. She wasn't sure he'd let her in once he saw who it was. And who could blame him if he didn't?

She hadn't been in touch with Alan since their confrontation in March. But in the months after he stormed out of her home, she'd followed every development in his very public shaming. The Murray family's interview, first in *The Morning Journal* and then on national television. The launch of the class action lawsuit. And, more recently, the announcement about an investigation into his practice by the College of Physicians and Surgeons. She wasn't sure how this would unfold, but there would likely be some kind of hearing. Evidence might be presented. Victim impact statements, too. And the whole process could very well end in Alan losing his medical licence. More fodder for the scathing media stories about him that seemed to pop up every week.

It was no surprise when Alan closed his clinic months ago. He'd rarely been seen in public since.

None of these things would be happening if she hadn't uncovered the truth about the paternity of Zach and Pete. Joan didn't feel guilty. Alan had brought this on himself. But it was a sad situation for someone she'd been close to for such a long time. And it was about to get worse. Joan had learned from her former colleagues that the university was planning a sanction of its own. She was there because she felt she should warn him it was coming.

Joan rang the bell a second time. Still no response. But just as she turned to leave, Alan opened the door.

His appearance had changed since their last encounter.

He was tanned. Joan had seen his out-of-season tan before, after his annual vacations in Bermuda. Maybe that's where he'd been hiding lately.

What's more, he'd lost weight. He obviously hadn't shaved in days. New lines creased his forehead and there were gaps in his usually perfect comb-over where the bald spot showed through. Alan would never have let anyone see him like that before.

At first, he avoided eye contact, staring down at the flagstone doorstep instead. When he did look up, he scowled at her. Then he forced an unconvincing half-smile that didn't reach up to his eyes.

"Hello, Joan. I guess you might as well come in."

She was close enough to smell alcohol on his breath.

He led her to the den where the last embers of a log glowed in the massive stone fireplace. To the right was an Italian leather recliner. A half-empty bottle of scotch and a glass were on the table beside it. It was 11:30 in the morning.

“Please . . .” Alan gestured for her to sit on the sofa facing the fire. “ . . . something to drink?”

“No thanks.”

He returned to his chair and his scotch.

“I wasn't sure you’d invite me in.”

“I wasn't going to at first. Let’s just say I’m curious to know why you've come. But before we get into that, how is India doing?”

“She's fine. She's been away at veterinary school the past few months. She’ll be home in a couple of weeks for the holidays.”

“How nice for you. I won't be having a family Christmas this year. That’s because I don’t *have* a family anymore. I won't be celebrating at all.”

“I'm sorry to hear that, Al. I suppose you think that’s my fault—”

“I do. And I blame all the others too. Especially the media vultures."

"Yes, they’ve been tough on you."

"Everybody’s *so* quick to judge. They’d never understand my side of the story. And I won't give it to them. They'd just twist my words. Use them against me. So, I keep to myself these days.”

Alan poured himself another couple of ounces and swallowed half of it in one gulp.

“I can tell you’re bitter, Al. But can't you at least try to see things from their viewpoint? All those couples came to you for help. And you gave them babies. But not the babies they thought they were getting."

"And what's wrong with those babies? You can see they've grown up to be bright kids. Attractive kids. They're probably turning out better than if I'd used any old donor's sperm. I don't get why the families are so upset . . . and, by the way, it sounds to me like you're happy with the daughter I gave you and Helen. So why are you taking their side?"

"Of course, we're grateful for India. But we *chose* you to be her father. It's different for the other families. These are peoples' lives you've played with, Al. Their identities. They're human beings, not items on a shopping list, where you can switch brands and it's no big deal." Joan hesitated before speaking her next words, but what happened to Erin was too tragic to let pass. "A girl has died, Al. *Your daughter* has died. Likely because she found out what you did. Have you thought about that?"

"Nobody could have predicted that, Joan! I feel sorry for the family, of course, but there must have been other issues with her."

His deflection disgusted her.

"Is that why you came here today? To pick up where we left off the last time? If so, we're done. I don't need to listen to that shit again. Especially in my own home."

Alan downed the rest of his drink and slammed his glass on the table. Then he started to rise out of his chair. For him, the visit was over.

"No, Alan. That's not why I'm here. There's something else I need to tell you."

Alan sat again. "Go ahead. But nothing you can say now will make any difference to me."

"I get that. I'm giving you a heads-up just the same. I understand the University Senate will be meeting next week. One of the items on the agenda is your honorary degree. I heard they intend to rescind it."

"Well, that's just great, isn' it! Sanct'monious pricks!" Alan was starting to slur his words. "Go ahead, kick a man while 'e's down . . . why not? Ev'rybody else has. Well, fuck'em all!"

Alan was drunk. The maudlin, self-pitying kind of drunk Joan didn't want to be around, old friend or not. "I think it's time I left. I'm sorry for the way things have turned out for you, Al. I hope, when all this is over, you'll be able to make a new start."

"Pffff . . . no chance of that."

Joan stood up. Alan pushed himself up out of his chair and they walked to the front entrance together. By the time he opened the door, his mood had changed.

"Y'know, Joan, you might find this hard to believe, but I've missed you. I miss our good ol' days. I think you're the only real frien' I ever'ad. Th'only one who understood me. Too bad."

"I've missed you too, Al. But I disagree. I don't think I ever really did understand you. I still don't."

"There's an article on Alan in today's *Morning Journal,* Joan. The university decision you were telling me about last week, want me to read it to you?"

It was the last Saturday before Christmas, and Helen and Joan were lingering over a late breakfast before leaving to get India at the train station. Joan looked up from her muesli and nodded. Helen swallowed the last of her coffee and cleared her throat before starting.

"DISGRACED DOCTOR
LOSES HONORARY DEGREE"
by Janice Vaughn, Senior Journalist

> *At their meeting earlier this week, the University Senate unanimously voted to rescind the honorary degree awarded to Dr. Alan Wilcross at its 2017 fall convocation. According to a statement released yesterday, the Senate's decision was taken in view of recent, very serious allegations about disturbing irregularities at the doctor's fertility clinic."*

"You can stop right there, Lennie." Joan didn't want to hear any more. "I imagine the rest of the article is just a rehash of what Alan did. We've already heard it dozens of times before."

"You're right. It is. But why are you being so touchy about it?"

"I'll tell you why. You remember I saw Alan a couple of weeks ago to warn him this was coming? He was in really bad shape, Lennie. There he was, sitting in that mansion of his, working his way through a bottle of scotch. In the morning. All by himself. When you think about it, he's lost just about everything. His family. His work. His reputation. And now he's self-destructing. It was hard to watch."

"And I suppose you're feeling bad about it? That you're somehow to blame?"

"Yes and no. He's responsible for what happened to those families. But it all went public because of what I did."

"Well, he more or less forced you to get involved, didn't he? You had no choice but to uncover his dirty little secrets."

"I guess."

"And if he's reacting by drinking too much . . . well . . . that's not your fault either, is it?"

"No."

"So, go ahead. Feel sorry for him for a while. And then you should get over it."

Joan knew Helen had never liked Alan all that much, and had little sympathy for the trouble he was in. But she was right.

Helen put the front section of the paper to one side.

"Let's save this for India."

“I’m going, Mom. I want to testify, if they’ll let me. You okay with that?”

It was New Year’s Day and Joan was in India’s bedroom, helping her pack. The winter semester at the Ontario Veterinary College was starting in a few days.

Over the Christmas break, they’d learned that the College of Physicians and Surgeons would be holding its hearing on the allegations against Alan on January 24th.

“Of course, love. Do you want me to go with you?”

“Thanks, but I’ll be fine. And besides, I won’t be alone. Zach and his parents’ll be there. He’s going to give an impact statement. Pete’s not sure he’ll go, but I’ll try to convince him.”

“And what would you say at the hearing?”

“Oh, I’d have lots to say! Like, how come it had to take a random test from AncestryDNA for Zach and the others to find out Wilcross is their biological father? And how come it’s okay he threw out the donor records so nobody could access them? There’s just so much that sucks about what happened.”

“But you’re not one of the ones whose parents he tricked—”

“Well, they only found out what he did because of me. They might never have learned the truth otherwise. And that’s totally wrong.”

Joan wasn’t entirely surprised that India would take up a cause like this. Her daughter was always getting involved in one human rights issue or another. She'd been the same at her age. India had her full support.

And it was only logical that Zach and his parents intended to speak out at the hearing. After all, they were already leading the class action suit against Alan. The Stephanidises might very well show up, too. But Joan doubted Greg and Karen would be there. Their daughter was gone. In a formal hearing, surrounded by strangers, it would be excruciating to have to explain why.

Chapter Twenty-Four

Alan's flight to Heathrow wouldn't leave for another ninety minutes. After airport security, he went straight to the Maple Leaf Lounge, poured himself a glass of wine, and picked up a copy of the Globe and Mail. Then he settled into a corner seat, as far away as possible from a pack of dot-com millennials who were clearly in a partying mood. He hoped they weren't going to London.

Alan had booked himself a business class pod and planned to sleep most of the flight. He was exhausted. It hadn't been easy, physically or emotionally, getting everything done before he left Canada. Forever.

In a way, it was fortunate he'd already closed his practice the previous summer. Not that he had many patients left after the unfortunate Murray business went public. He'd referred the few remaining ones to Dr. Gillian Taylor, head reproductive endocrinologist at the city's other major fertility clinic. And Marjorie got a nice little severance package. Moreover, he was still estranged from his family and that wasn't likely to change anytime soon. All communications with Alicia would continue to be handled through their lawyers. And while it hurt that Michael and Karoline hadn't spoken to him in months, there was nothing Alan could do about that.

Dealing with the other complications in his life hadn't been so straightforward.

After being on the market since January, the sale of his residence had only closed the week before. He knew the buyers, Ethan and Tanya Roberts, a nouveau riche couple in the high-end organic food business. He remembered meeting them once, at a gala fundraiser, and he was not impressed. Too much name-dropping and too many references to expensive possessions. Early in his marriage to Alicia, Alan learned that the truly well-bred never talked about those things. But he didn't care who bought the place. They were welcome to it.

Of course, half the money from the sale would go to Alicia. It would be the same split when their art and antiques sold at auction, scheduled for later in the spring. After she got her share of their assets, Alan hoped he'd be left with enough resources to find himself a decent place somewhere on the outskirts of London.

And beyond all the paperwork for the house, there'd been a million other details to attend to: resigning from the remaining board directorships he hadn't already been removed from; cancelling club memberships, insurances, utilities, cable, internet, and newspaper subscriptions. Giving notice to the housekeeper and gardener. Selling his Lexus and remaining furniture. Sorting and giving away clothing.

Too bad there was still one major piece of unsettled business that would follow Alan no matter where he went. The class-action suit. His lawyers would be dealing with that. He'd hired the best. But it would be a constant irritant until it was resolved.

Alan decided to move back to the UK shortly after he lost his medical licence in January. There was no reason for him to stay. Nobody to stay for. And every impetus to escape. To the few who asked, Alan insisted he was leaving of his own free will. Taking an indefinite sabbatical. But in reality, he had little choice. The way everybody was treating him, it felt like he was being forced into exile.

It was the shunning that bothered him the most.

He'd been successful beyond anything he could have imagined when he landed in Canada as a student, with nothing but twenty bucks in his pocket and The Plan in his head. For decades, he'd enjoyed increasing prosperity and status. He'd become a much-photographed celebrity guest at charity galas and opening night performances, was frequently invited to be keynote speaker at medical conventions.

That was then.

These days, he was still recognized in public. But not for the right reasons. Instead of the friendly encounters he once enjoyed with patients and colleagues and neighbors, those same people now avoided him. Each time his photo appeared in the papers or on television—always the same unflattering one with his tie askew and eyes looking furtive—he secluded himself at home until several news cycles had passed. Even then, there were stares and whispers when he emerged again.

Shunned. Everywhere he went.

Alan got up, went to the lounge bar, and poured himself another drink. Then he returned to his corner. The tech types were several rounds ahead of him now and getting rowdy. God, he hoped they were on a different flight.

Was it really so bad what he had done? In hindsight, maybe he *had* made some regrettable decisions.

For years, his patients had been happy with the babies he gave them. Until they learned the truth. But they would have remained childless without his help. And now they have sons and daughters.

Of course, what happened to the Evans girl was a tragedy. Poor thing must have been unstable. A worry to her parents, no doubt. One never knows what's going on in kids' heads at that age. Maybe he *was* partly to blame for that sad situation. But only partly. Certainly not enough to justify what the Murray boy did, attacking him at his clinic.

And those other families. The entitled ones. No way could he feel sorry for them. He never bothered to explain how he felt about them to Joan. Or to anybody else, for that matter. How he hated that their lives were so effortlessly easy, when his had been so hard. How Freddy Wilcross had no future in his own country, just because of the family he was born into. And how he had to move across an ocean and work his ass off to bring himself up to their level.

So, sure, he held a grudge against them. But it was a well-founded grudge. And the way he saw it, he was simply setting things straight. What was the expression? 'Levelling the playing field.' Yes, that's what he was trying to do—level the playing field. Simple as that.

Alan's flight was called. He stood up, gathered his things, and headed for the lounge door. So did the party boys. Damn. They *were* on the same flight. They'd likely be all around him in their own pods. So much for getting any rest on this flight.

As he walked to the gate, Alan thought about his first flight to Canada. How he'd transformed himself on that plane. Discarded the final traces of the origins that had held him down, replacing Freddy with Alan. Could he do it again?

He certainly didn't want the notoriety, so unwelcome and beyond unfair, to follow him to the UK. What he craved was to move himself quietly back into British life at a different level—a more appropriate level—than the one society had imposed on him at birth. He had some money, at least before the lawsuit was settled. He had an interesting mid-Atlantic accent. A carefully cultivated style. He could use these assets to find a comfortable place somewhere and enjoy being anonymous for a change.

So, why not leave Alan and all his shitty baggage behind? Now was the perfect opportunity.

At the gate, he pulled out his UK passport and opened it to the page with his full name. Frederick Alan Wilcross. And his photo. It was taken only five years earlier, but he'd aged a decade since then. He showed it, and his boarding pass, to the gate attendant and proceeded along the enclosed bridge to the aircraft.

He found his pod. As he started to put away his carry-on bag, the man settling in next to him spoke up.

"Excuse me, but haven't we met before? You look very familiar."

No surprise there. The guy was a complete stranger. But that damn unflattering picture had been in the news so many times over the past nine months.

"Perhaps."

They shook hands.

"Name's Hugh Keith."

"Fred—yes—Fred Wilcross."

ASK GLORIA

a Novella

Chapter One

August is the worst month to have a hangover, Jennifer decided. By August, summer has matured to a state of verdant perfection. The days, though growing shorter, still seduce the senses with color and warmth and a certain special quality of light.

And it was the goddamn splendor of August that confronted her when she woke up that morning, judging her deficient in just about every human virtue and forcing her to keep her eyes shut while she tried to assess, without moving, which part of her ached the most.

This time, it was her gut.

Jennifer hadn't eaten anything the day before. Instead, she'd drunk whiskey. Whiskey for breakfast. Whiskey for lunch. Whiskey for dinner. And the previous day? She couldn't remember back that far. All she could think of now was that she needed something solid, something bland, to tame the churn in her stomach. Dry toast might help. If she could keep it down.

She opened her eyes. It took half a minute before they could focus. When they did, it wasn't the cracks in the bedroom ceiling she saw. She'd passed out on the couch. Again.

And she was still wearing the same clothes as yesterday. Her sweatpants, already grimy from being worn for God knows how long, now smelled suspiciously of pee. Her Red Hot Chili Peppers T-shirt had peculiar odors of its own. Sweat mingled with traces of vomit.

It must have been one helluva night.

Jennifer sat up, pulled the T-shirt off over her head and threw it in the corner. Leaning on the coffee table in front of her for balance, she slowly got to her feet. The sweatpants came off and wound up in the corner, too.

Then she lurched to the kitchen looking for bread. She found it. The tail end of a loaf, covered in blue-green fuzz. Jennifer was desperate, but not *that* desperate. Instead, she settled for the single slice of pizza she found in the fridge. It was well past its prime. The cheese was like plastic and the crust had the consistency of the cardboard box it came in, but it was better than nothing. She revived it in the microwave and gnawed on the pointy part as she wandered to the bathroom.

The light, when she switched it on, seemed ten times brighter than usual. Jennifer forced herself to look in the mirror. Just as she expected. That's exactly how she'd look after five years' hard labor in a gulag. Serves me right, she thought, splashing water on her face. Next came an unsuccessful attempt to pull a brush through her matted violet-tinted hair. Her head was hurting now, too.

Jennifer had been wasted on and off for most of the summer. Alcohol was an issue even before, but it took full control in May. And three months later, she'd pretty much hit rock bottom. She knew what was happening to her. She'd been this low before. She just didn't care.

And why should she? Why care about *anything* anymore? She'd fucked up again. Very publicly fucked up. Her biggest, most ambitious project had crashed, just like everything else she'd tried to do in her life. Only it felt worse this time.

Jennifer had mostly good years with *La Casita*, her Mexican hole-in-the-wall restaurant in Ottawa. Opened in 2011, the quirky little establishment had won her numerous culinary awards, and, early on, its five-star reviews meant long lines at the door every night.

Unfortunately for Jennifer, it became *too* successful. At first, she basked in good reviews and the fame brought on by celebrity endorsements. But a couple of years along, she started to sink under the weight of trying to keep up her reputation. Her remedy of choice was self-medication with Famous Grouse, liberally applied every night, as soon as the last patrons left and the neon OPEN sign was turned off. Two ounces followed quickly by another two ounces, building up to even more. After a while, she couldn't hold off till the restaurant closed. The drinking started earlier and earlier. She didn't think the staff would notice, but they did.

And then, one night, everybody noticed. An unhappy customer complained a little too loudly about his scorched nachos. Jennifer, in a combative ugly-drunk mood, confronted him.

"What's yer prob'm with the nachos, dickhead?!" she spat at him.

Before he could answer, the plate wound up overturned in his lap.

What followed was a small out-of-court settlement and an embarrassing article in the back pages of the newspaper.

There were other missteps, too. Jennifer stopped paying close attention to what was going on in the kitchen. The quality of the food suffered as a result and the service got sloppy. Reviews grew more and more negative. People stopped coming and Jennifer was too far along in her alcoholic slide to turn things around again.

La Casita shut its doors for the final time in April of 2019.

For the rest of that spring and into the summer, Jennifer grieved in her own way. After she dealt with the tedious close-down paperwork and disposed of *La Casita's* meagre assets, she hid in her condo, subsisting on scotch, dry corn flakes, and the occasional Uber Eats delivery. She put off seeing anyone she knew except her daughter, Layla Walker, the only human being on earth she absolutely adored. And they got together just once for a quick coffee when Layla came up from Kingston.

The last thing Jennifer wanted was pity. And she didn't need anybody preaching at her about the drinking, either.

Later that afternoon, the condo buzzer sounded. Jennifer had no intention of answering it. Whoever was down in the lobby would give up soon enough.

But they didn't give up. On and off for ten minutes, the noise drilled through her ears and jangled the tender corners of her brain. Not what she needed on top of a hangover.

Then, a long merciful silence.

They're gone, she thought. And thank God for that.

It buzzed again.

What the *hell*?

Jennifer couldn't believe it. This was too much.

"Can't they fucking leave me *alone*?" she snarled.

Jennifer struggled to get up off the couch and staggered to the video intercom monitor in the front hall. By the time she got there, all she could see was the lobby entrance door closing. Someone else must have opened it for them. Either that or whoever it was had their own key. She'd given out a couple.

And now they were on their way up.

"Oh shit!"

Jennifer hurried back to the living room. She grabbed two empty liquor bottles and three dirty glasses off the crowded coffee table and stashed them under the kitchen sink. There was no time to tidy anything else before she heard the knocking. She smoothed back her hair, ran her finger over her teeth, and answered the door.

In front of her were the people she knew, and who knew her, the best. Layla, her friend Rachel Potter, and Eric Nash, her second ex. They were the ones she was closest to until her life fell apart in the spring.

"Hi, guys. Long time no see. To what do I owe the pleasure?" Jennifer tried, but failed, to sound pleasantly surprised. Instead, the words came out as a challenge. So did the irritated look on her face. The three of them stood there, waiting for her to invite them in. Their awkward smiles didn't fool her. It was no coincidence they showed up unannounced together, and it wasn't for coffee and an amiable chit-chat.

Rachel finally spoke. "Can we come in, Jen?"

Jennifer didn't answer. Instead, she reluctantly stepped back and they entered. She followed them to the living room and scanned it for telltale signs of her lost summer. There were plenty.

The place was a wall-to-wall disaster. Every ashtray was overflowing. Used tissues and dirty socks were strewn across a rug that hadn't seen a vacuum since June. Beside the couch, a half-empty can of Heinz beans was perched on top of a stack of newspapers, most still neatly folded and clearly never read. Thick dust coated everything except the circles on the coffee table where the now-hidden whiskey bottles and glasses had been.

Maybe, Jennifer thought, she should feel embarrassed. But she didn't. She was resentful instead. They'd entered her personal space uninvited and they'd have no right to get all judgy about what they saw there. Then she stopped herself. Why be so defensive when they hadn't said one word . . . yet? Still, she had a good idea what was coming.

"Have a seat, guys."

Jennifer decided not to offer them coffee. She'd let them say their piece and then they could go.

Nobody spoke at first. Then Eric cleared his throat and leaned toward her. "How are you doing these days, Jen? Folks are asking about you."

She had to admit he sounded concerned. But so what if he was?

"Don't worry about me. I'm hangin' in—"

"Are you really? No offense, but you look like you're in pretty rough shape to me."

Jennifer bristled. He had *some* nerve, walking into her home and insulting her like that.

"Is it really any of your damn business? We're divorced, remember?"

Rachel and Eric glanced at each other. Layla gasped. The visit was off to a nasty start. The three of them had already discussed what might happen. They knew Jennifer wouldn't welcome what they came to say, but the instant hostility was unexpected.

Eric tried again.

"Come on, girl! We're just here to help."

"Let's get real, Eric. This is your pathetic attempt at an intervention, right? Well, I don't need your help. And I certainly don't *want* it. So let's not even start—"

Rachel interrupted her. "Can't you see you're in trouble again, Jen?"

"I can see you're all ganging up on me. *That's* what I can see."

Jennifer looked over at her daughter. "You too, Layla? You came all this way just to get on my case?"

Jennifer was surprised that Layla was part of this. It was totally out of character. Layla would normally be too timid for such a confrontation. Most of the time, she was so hesitant to speak that those around her barely noticed she was there.

Layla was twenty-one years old, but with her innocent manner, braided blond hair, and always anxious gray eyes, she seemed much younger. She'd been born profoundly deaf in her right ear, a condition Jennifer felt guilty about. Mainly because of this, she'd always been overly protective of her only child. And now she felt bad for turning on her.

In fact, maybe she was being too hard on them all. She changed her tone.

"Okay. So I'm having a shitty summer. Happens to everybody at some point. And you all know why. But I'll get over this. I'll survive. I always do."

"We hope you're right. But we each have something to say to you and we're not leaving until we're done."

"Good ol' Eric. CONSTABLE Eric. There you go again. Trying to take control, just like when we were married. Well, you may enjoy being the macho cop, but I'm not one of your vagrants. Even though I might look it."

Jennifer slouched back in the couch, crossed her arms, and exhaled in surrender. "I give up. It's three against one. Just go for it. All of you. And when you finish beating me up, you can let yourselves out."

Eric went first. It took much more than Jennifer's hostility to rattle him. He was accustomed to handling a lot worse on the streets and in the cells.

"Okay, I'll start . . . but before I get into it, you need to know this *isn't* an intervention. None of us want to turn this into a big deal. We thought a casual visit might be easier for everybody. So, think of this as a wake-up call from the people who care about you the most."

How much did Eric actually care about her? Jennifer wondered.

There had been no doubt about their mutual attraction when they met. It was on a sultry July evening in 2005 and John Mayall and the Bluesbreakers were on stage at Ottawa Bluesfest. Jennifer, already slightly stoned, took a deep hit from a joint that appeared out of nowhere and passed it on to the dude next to her. Then she got a good look at him. Caramel-colored skin, short dreads, and bedroom eyes. She liked what she saw and he was interested, too. Jennifer found out later he was an undercover cop five years younger than her. It didn't matter. By September, they were married. And even though they later divorced, they managed to stay on good terms for Layla's sake. As far as Jennifer was concerned, there was nothing more than friendship between them now.

"Jen, you know I've always admired the fact that you're an honest person. You call 'em as you see 'em. I think we're similar that way. That's why we got along so well in the beginning. It's also probably why we broke up. When we were first married, I never minded your drinking. How could I? I like my beers, too. And we had lots of fun, didn't we, back then? Until the booze took over. You're not a pleasant drunk, you know. Picking fights all the time. And things turned toxic fast after that. It got to a point where I couldn't take it anymore."

Before he went on, Eric looked at Rachel and Layla for some sign of support. It irked Jennifer when they nodded in agreement with him.

Eric continued. "But after we split up, you managed to pull things together. I was *so* proud of you when you made a success of the restaurant. And I'm real sorry it folded. I knew it would be tough for you and I can see you're not coping. You're in a self-destruct mode. Again. Jen, you're still young. Smart. Resourceful. It's not over for you. You can bounce back. So do yourself a favor, agree to get help. Whatever it takes. You have three people right in front of you who will support you in this."

Jennifer wasn't all that impressed. She'd heard Eric go on like this before. He deserved full marks for persistence. Or maybe he still got off on being condescending?

It was Rachel's turn. "I've written you a letter, Jen. It helped me organize what I want to say."

That was Rachel all the way. Planning things, making lists, following schedules. Her home was always spotless, with perfectly plumped cushions in her perfect winter-white living room and color-coordinated guest toiletries in the powder room.

Rachel, herself, hadn't changed much in all the years Jennifer knew her. Obsessed with maintaining her svelte figure, she'd been on the Keto diet for months and it showed. Not a hair in her blonde bob was ever out of place. And the way she dressed was too designer, too matchy-matchy, for Jennifer, who was sure her best friend had OCD. Either that, or she was trying overly hard to satisfy her millionaire husband's expectations.

Jennifer couldn't have been more different, even during her sober stretches. She fancied herself a woman of the world who didn't give a damn about home decor or hand-painted highlights. She'd always been that way. In her student years, between terms at theatre school, Jennifer backpacked solo around South America and Asia, hostel-surfing and working in fast food joints along the way. After graduation and before her restaurant venture, she'd struggled and ultimately failed as a playwright. Married and divorced twice by her early thirties, Jennifer had three tattoos in interesting places. And one recurring drinking problem.

How she and Rachel managed to stay friends for so long was a mystery to both of them.

Rachel reached into her Louis Vuitton bag. First, she brought out a tissue. Rachel was a weeper. She wouldn't get through this without crying. She knew it and so did Jennifer. Next, she pulled out and unfolded a sheet of scented paper and started to read.

"Dear Jennifer. We've known each other for more than twenty years. Over that time, we've been through a lot together. Good *and* bad. You know you've always been able to rely on me in the past, and I've relied on you, too. You have no idea how much I miss that now. When the restaurant closed in April, I wanted to give you space to mourn. But two weeks stretched to a month and now over three months. You've never answered my texts or returned my calls. That hurt a lot. Because it told me you didn't think you could count on me anymore. You might feel you're alone in this, but you're not. I miss you. And I want you to be kinder to yourself. So please stop drinking and get well again. I'm willing to take you to get help. I'll be there for you when you clean up. I promise to do this because I want my best friend back. I love you."

Rachel carefully blotted her eyes with the now bunched-up tissue, folded the letter neatly again and put it back in her bag.

Jennifer almost felt like crying, too. These guys, she thought, are actually starting to get to me. And now I have to listen to my darling Layla. This is going to get *so* much worse.

Layla was shaking. She had written something down, too, but for prolonged seconds it looked like she might not be able to get the words out after all. Jennifer wasn't sure how to react. She was torn between going over to comfort her daughter and ripping the paper out of her hands and tossing it in the garbage. Instead, she waited.

Finally, Layla was ready. "Mom, I love you so, so much, though we haven't always gotten along over the years. The truth is, I felt you never really liked me. The way I was. Different from you. Shy. Never saying much. There were times I didn't like you very much either. You bullied me, even though you probably don't recognize that's what you were doing. 'Don't be a wimp,' you used to tell me. 'Stand up for yourself.' It was hard for me to do that when I was teased all the time. Especially at school. I never fit in because the other kids made fun of my hearing problem. But it was your drinking that finally drove me away. Last fall, when I started the orderly job at Kingston General, I finally felt free. No more dramas. No more trying to live up to your expectations and failing."

Layla hesitated. Her eyes were wet and one of her tears dropped on the paper. She brushed it away and continued. "Now I'm really worried about you. I'd like us to make a new start. For us to be better together. That can't happen if you don't stop drinking. You might not feel like doing this for yourself. But if you really love me, do it for me."

Layla looked up from her notes directly at Jennifer.

"*Please,* Mom."

As her daughter was speaking, Jennifer stood up and started pacing back and forth. It was a lot to take in, what her little girl was saying. She'd never heard these things before. Had she really been that rough on her sweet Layla? And the drinking. *That's* why Layla moved away? Not just the job offer? Jesus! Even as a mother she was a failure.

Jennifer needed time to absorb this. On her own.

And then there was the half-full bottle of scotch in the bedroom. She *really* wanted a drink. *Right now.* So how could she get them to leave? Agreeing with them seemed to be the only option. Of course, they were right. She really *should* stop drinking. Only not quite as fast as they were pushing for. Not today.

"Okay. I've heard you all. And you win. I'll clean myself up. And this place, too." Jennifer gestured around the room. "I can do this. Like I said before, I'll survive . . . and once I've got things back on track, you'll be the first to know. I promise."

Eric smiled. He knew what Jennifer was doing. She was blowing them off. "Not so fast, Jen. We're not leaving until you agree to go to rehab. In fact, it's already arranged. We've contacted the Maple Tree Addiction Treatment Center. Rachel will pick you up tomorrow morning and take you there."

"Shit, guys! Is this really necessary?"

"You know the answer to that."

Jennifer finally gave up.

She went into the bedroom, picked up the bottle on the floor beside her bed and brought it out to the kitchen. Then she unscrewed the cap and dumped the contents down the sink. It was the hardest thing she'd done all summer. But the dramatic flourish, such a totally Jennifer gesture, accomplished two things. It showed the others she would go along with their plans for her. And it meant she couldn't polish off the rest of it that evening in a moment of temptation. If that happened, she'd be a mess when Rachel showed up the next morning.

Eric turned at the door before they left. "Be ready at 10 a.m. tomorrow."

And she was.

Chapter Two

"How're you doing, Jen?"

"Feeling good, Rachel. Stronger every day."

It was early October, just before Thanksgiving. Jennifer's favorite time of year. She loved how the rich glow of fall-muted sunshine bathed everything it touched in a warm golden sheen. And the weather was perfect. Still mild enough for just a sweater, with only the occasional nudge of overnight frost.

Jennifer had started taking daily walks at twilight through the nearby park, when the cool air was sometimes tinged with the sweet smoky smells from someone's fireplace. The familiar crunch of crisp dry leaves underfoot was usually the only sound at that hour, and it had a calming effect on her.

For the past ten days, ever since she'd returned home from rehab, Jennifer had eased herself into a gentle routine. Breakfast followed by meditation. A conversation with her aftercare counsellor if needed. Lunch. Exercise. Household chores, but nothing too taxing. Supper. And her twilight walks.

The timing of Rachel's call that evening was perfect. Jennifer had just come in from the park with her mind made up about two things. She was finally ready to reach out to Layla and

Eric and her friends. Would they still speak to her after she'd abandoned them for so long? Hopefully, it wasn't too late. And just as important, she had to get a job. What savings she had were almost gone and her rent was way past due. But where could she find work now? Who would hire an unsuccessful playwright and failed restaurateur, fresh out of rehab? Having her as an employee would be a risk to anyone. Still, she had to start looking. Her autumn interlude needed to come to an end.

Rachel must have been reading her mind.

"That's good to hear. I'm not sure if you're ready for this, but I'll ask just the same. You thinking of working again?"

"You bet I am. The wolves are at the door."

"Well, I may have a lead for you. Something completely different. But you're always up for a challenge, right?"

Jennifer was skeptical. She wasn't sure she could handle *too* much of a challenge at this point.

"Go on . . . "

"Okay. So last evening, I went out for drinks with some old classmates from high school. One of them is Jeff March. Maybe you've heard of him?"

The name sounded vaguely familiar.

"He's the editor of the *Ottawa Daily Chronicle.* And he told me he's putting together a special pre-Christmas insert for the paper. It'll run the first Saturday in December. There'll be the usual glitzy stuff. Recipes for entertaining. The latest party fashions. And he's looking for someone to write an article about dealing with tricky holiday social scenes. Know what I mean? Embarrassing relatives. Guests who won't leave. That kind of thing. His usual freelancer just started maternity leave. I thought of you immediately."

Jennifer found *that* hard to believe. "Me? Why me?" She figured she was the last person anybody would want to give advice on awkward situations, after what happened at *La Casita.* And how things had gone so badly for her since.

Rachel was prepared for Jennifer's reaction.

"I know what you're thinking. Why you, after . . . after, ah . . . the restaurant incident? Well, that was ages ago. And to me it was just a one-off. I know how well you handled tough customers other times, when you weren't drinking. You were a savvy hostess. I figure you know your way around dealing with people . . . "

Was she really that good a hostess? Jennifer wondered. She didn't remember much about that time, especially towards the end. Her days were such a blur back then.

" . . . and I know you're good with words, what with the plays you used to write and all."

There was a certain logic to what Rachel was saying, but she wasn't being totally candid with Jennifer. She had another reason to approach her. The real reason. Jennifer's recovery was still raw, still tentative, and Rachel was worried about a relapse. It would be better for her friend to get busy right away. Writing the article could be a lifeline. It might even be the start of something more, and if it didn't work out, it would be no big deal for Jeff. He'd likely be able to find someone else pretty fast to take it over.

"I'm not sure a play is the same thing as a newspaper article, but thanks for the vote of confidence."

Rachel persisted. "You know, Jen, writing for a paper isn't like being in the middle of a messy situation. You'd have time to think about it, then write, then think about it some more. You can fool around with it a dozen times before you submit. I'm sure you'd do a great job. What do you think?"

"I suppose I could give it a try, but would March even want me to do it? Given my past issues, I mean."

"He doesn't have to know at first . . . why not put something together as J. Carr? Or just J.C.? I can submit it to him on your behalf. You can let him know later who you are if he decides to run with it. But if you're interested, you better jump on it right away. Before he hires someone else."

Which is what Jennifer did.

Jeff March liked what she wrote and, later, so did the readers. The feedback was so good he asked her to start a daily advice column starting in early 2020. On a trial basis, of course.

Chapter Three

S*HIT HAPPENS.* That was Jennifer's deliberately cheeky suggestion for the name of her column. She wasn't entirely surprised that Jeff March didn't like it. Even though they were roughly the same age, he looked distinctly old-school conservative with his bow tie, suspenders, and horn-rimmed glasses, like some '60s reporter working the political newsbeat.

"Doesn't fit our image, Jenny," he told her. "Our readers are too mainstream. This is a government town, after all. There'd be complaints."

She didn't like Jeff—or anybody, for that matter—calling her Jenny. That's what Gary Walker, her first ex and a total bastard, called her. She hated it because it reminded her of him. But she chose not to correct her new boss.

"I get what you're saying. I suppose there *could* be some complaints. But so what? At least that would mean the column is getting folks' attention."

Jennifer tried to hide her irritation with a smile she hoped didn't look too fake. Then she looked down and pretended to flick lint off her sleeve.

"Besides, I don't plan to beat around the bush with my answers. I want to play it totally straight. No soft sell. *SHIT HAPPENS* says it perfectly."

Jennifer paused. Then she had an idea. Maybe there could be a compromise.

"What if we tone it down just a little bit? Would that work?"

"What do you mean?"

"*CRAP HAPPENS.* I could live with that. I bet the readers could too. What d'you think?"

Jeff shook his head. He didn't like that one either.

Jennifer was beginning to wonder if this whole advice column idea was going to work. If Jeff was so worried about what it was called, what other rules might he foist on her? There's no way she'd accept *anyone* editing her words to make them politically correct. She wanted her column to be punchy, with no-holds-barred responses to her readers' questions. To the confused souls looking for instant solutions to their personal tragedies, petty or otherwise, she'd offer the truth. The brutal truth, if need be. She felt they deserved it. *Get rid of the freeloader boyfriend*, she'd tell them. *Leave the two-timing wife. Don't even think about dragging your unwilling partner to couples counselling. It might patch things up temporarily, but in the long run, people usually go back to their old destructive ways, don't they? They can't help it. That's what human beings do.*

No doubt about it, hers would be a bullshit-free approach.

How else could she make her column stand out from all those traditional advice columns in rival publications? The touchy-feely ones?

But she didn't push any further. It wouldn't be a good idea to piss off the editor even before the first column had been written. She needed this contract. Desperately.

The pay would go towards the months of back rent she owed. Her long-suffering landlord was losing his patience. Jennifer's bank account was overdrawn, her VISA card maxed-out. If she didn't come up with the money soon, he'd likely kick her out. And her 2006 Corolla, its near-death rattle needing urgent attention, would have to go, too.

Getting a contract to do the column, even on a trial basis, had been a lifesaver. She didn't want to screw things up now.

So, Jennifer had to settle for *THAT'S LIFE* instead. It was Jeff's idea and he insisted. To her, it didn't have the same impact.

And the title of the column wasn't the only thing she didn't like. Jeff wanted her to use Kate Penworthy as her byline. *Really?* It didn't suit her at all. It would be perfect if she were a consumptive thirty-something romance writer, seated cat-in-lap at her dormer window, gazing wistfully out over a daisy-filled meadow. Jennifer was nothing like that.

She knew her own name wasn't right for the column, either. There were too many Jennifers around. It was one of the more common names for women of her cohort. And Carr certainly wouldn't stand out either. But that wasn't the main reason for not going with it. It would only take someone Googling her name to find out, in five seconds flat, about the *La Casita* debacle. If people knew Jennifer's past, they might question whether she should be giving other people any advice at all. Because of this, she and Jeff wanted to keep her identity a secret. At least for the first while. Other than Jeff, only Rachel and Layla would know who the person behind the byline was. Maybe Eric, too.

So, she wouldn't use Kate Penworthy and she couldn't use Jennifer Carr. She'd have to come up with something else. Something bold to capture readers' attention.

On a frigid early January evening, over pasta primavera made from scratch in Rachel's gourmet kitchen, they came up with the penname Gloria Pierce. Jennifer thought it sounded strong enough and a touch glamorous. But she waited a few days to see if it still felt right.

It did. The name Gloria Pierce resonated perfectly as the persona she wanted to project. Someone with that name would *never* be consumptive and wistful. Readers would know precisely what to expect when they wrote to her for advice: a ballsy reply from a confident woman of experience.

Almost certain that Jeff would see it her way, Jennifer marched into his office the following Monday morning, an Americano coffee in each hand. She plunked his down on the desk, settled uninvited in the chair opposite him, and proceeded to pitch her new name.

This time, she won the debate. Kate Penworthy was out. Gloria Pierce it would be.

The first column of *THAT'S LIFE—Ask Gloria Pierce* appeared in the February 14th, 2020 edition of the *Ottawa Daily Chronicle*. Valentine's Day, of course.

It certainly got a reaction. Reader feedback was swift. And divided. People either loved or hated her answers. But as long as circulation numbers didn't suffer—and they didn't, they actually went up—Jeff was happy.

Jennifer was relieved her money troubles were over, at least for the time being.

And just as she did with every other new adventure, she put all her energy into the column. It was serious business, what she was doing. Her advice could actually influence people to change the direction of their lives. Hopefully for the better. But there was always the chance—remote, she hoped, but still there—that she might get it wrong. And the consequences could potentially be disastrous.

She knew she could never let that happen.

Chapter Four

"Hi! My name is Jennifer and I'm an alcoholic."

"Hi, Jennifer!"

"It's been ages since I've come to a meeting. Ten years, actually. And for a lot of that time, I managed to stay sober. I guess that's because things were going well in my life. I owned a successful restaurant. I had a good relationship with my daughter. At least, I thought it was good . . . turns out, she didn't feel quite the same way. And I had friends. Things began to fall apart for me about two years ago. I couldn't handle the pressure at the restaurant. I started to drink again. I told myself I could stop whenever I wanted, but I was kidding myself. You know how it goes. And the more I drank, the more I neglected my work. The food, the service, everything went to shit. The restaurant finally closed last spring. And how did I deal with this? Well, I did what I always do when things get tough. I spent weeks holed up in my apartment, plastered most of the time and feeling sorry for myself. I pushed my daughter away. All my friends too. Like an idiot. I guess I come by it naturally. My mother was an alcoholic. I suspect my father was too, but he took off right after I was born."

Jennifer paused. She was growing more and more angry at herself the longer she talked. She took a deep breath before starting up again.

"Anyway, back to last summer . . . in August, my daughter and my friends came to my rescue, thank God. They took me to rehab. And in the fall, one of them used her connections to get me a job. It's a whole new career direction for me. I'm excited about it, but I'm also stressed out. It's the pressure thing again. With deadlines and shit like that. I don't want to screw up this time, but I'm struggling. A hundred times a day, I want a drink to help me get through this."

Jennifer looked around the circle.

"Just coming to this meeting makes me feel better. So you're likely going to see my face around here quite often. Thanks for listening."

The only other woman in the room spoke up.

"Thank you for sharing, Jennifer."

Then it was the next person's turn. And the next.

After the meeting, Jennifer joined five of the others for coffee at the nearby Tim Hortons. She sat next to the woman, who introduced herself.

"Hi, I'm Lizzie. Lizzie Crandall. Glad there's finally another woman."

"Jennifer Carr. Nice to meet you."

Lizzie looked to be 60ish. She had a CEO husband, successful children, and adorable grandchildren. At least, that's how she described them. Jennifer figured Lizzie was the sorority sister type. Her style was casual chic: a pastel sweater set, knife-edge pressed designer jeans, silk scarf. And lots of gold weighed down Lizzie's perfectly manicured fingers.

Years of too much time in the sun had etched fine lines around Lizzie's eyes and mouth, but otherwise she looked to be in good shape. Likely a Zumba class regular when that was the trend, Jennifer guessed. These days, it would be hot yoga instead.

Jennifer couldn't help wondering what issues dragged her out of her comfortable world to an AA meeting. She hadn't shared her story at that particular gathering. It would likely come out soon.

And it did, two meetings later. Lizzie hadn't always had a life of privilege. She was raised poor, in a house where violence was a daily sport. Both her parents had substance abuse problems. Her father also had a criminal record that spanned decades. Lizzie had been lucky to escape all that when she met her husband Bob, but she couldn't leave behind her weakness for alcohol.

Jennifer and Lizzie had more in common than it first appeared.

On their way to Tim Hortons after the first meeting in March, Jennifer took Lizzie aside as they waited at the corner for the light to change.

"Lizzie, how would you feel if I asked you to be my sponsor? I promise I'll try not to call in the middle of the night."

"Of course, I'd be happy to, Jen. And don't worry. You can call me any time you want."

"Awesome!"

The call came painfully soon.

Chapter Five

Dear Gloria,

I'm 24 years old and have been in a relationship with my boyfriend for over a year. I love him a lot and think he's the one. But lately, he seems too busy for me. In fact, it's been two weeks since we last got together. He hasn't answered my texts or my voice messages either. I'm getting frantic. Three nights ago, I drove over to his place. He wasn't home, so I waited outside. He finally appeared with some friends and it looked like they'd been partying. When I confronted him, he told me everything was cool and he'd call me the next day. I haven't heard from him since. What should I do, Gloria? Maybe he just needs a break. Should I give him his space and wait for him to come back to me? Splitting up with him is unthinkable.

—Puzzled and Missing Him

Gloria's Advice: You may be missing him, but you shouldn't be puzzled. Wake up and smell the coffee! The guy's ghosting you. He's moved on, whether or not there's someone else in his life. But he's obviously too much of a coward to do the right thing and tell you to your face. Is this really the kind of person you should think is "the one"? Time to recognize him for the d---head he is and get on with your life. Without him in it. And if he does get back in touch at some point, tell him to piss off. You can do so much better.

Send your relationship questions to:
askgloria@ottawadailychronicle.ca

Jennifer saved her work and got up from the computer for another coffee. The column was just three weeks old. Gloria's inbox was already flooded with pleas of help from people who, she was convinced, knew deep down inside how they *should* fix their problems but couldn't actually face doing it. Even if it was in their own best interests in the long run.

It's easy, Jennifer thought, to give advice to these strangers. She had no stake in the consequences. But was she really all that different from them? They were turning to her for help, and she, herself, always turned to the bottle. Fortunately, they didn't know that. To them, she was the mysterious Gloria Pierce. Someone who totally had her act together.

If they only knew.

Jennifer made final edits to the column early that day and sent it in with the latest batch.

She had other things on her mind. Layla was visiting for the first time since Christmas and was bringing her new boyfriend. They had been together for two months, and, according to Layla, it was getting serious. He'd already moved into her tiny apartment.

"Mom, this is Gil Leblanc. Gil, my mom."

"Nice to meet you, Gil. Call me Jen."

They shook hands.

He didn't look at all like Jennifer had imagined. Layla told her he was in the restaurant business, biding his time as a bartender until he could buy his own place. At 29, he'd already been married and separated and was the father of a young son.

Jennifer expected the kind of engaging demeanor most bartenders display to increase the odds of a good tip. She pictured a casual but neat appearance, too. Instead, Gil was in head-to-toe black leathers. His goatee was in need of a trim and his long dark hair was tied back in a ponytail. He looked like he'd fit right in at a Hells Angels gathering. All he was missing was a bandana and the winged skull patch.

Jennifer invited them in. They left their helmets at the door and went to the living room.

"So, can I offer you a coffee? Or—?"

"I could really use a beer. We did the ride from Kingston in one stretch. Layla'll have one too, right, babe?"

Jennifer looked at her daughter. Layla obviously hadn't told Gil about her drinking issues. And why couldn't she speak for herself?

"Sorry, no beer. No alcohol at all. There's coffee, and I've got juice and sparkling water."

"We'll have water, then."

Layla nodded her agreement.

Jennifer went to the kitchen and came back with two San Pellegrinos.

Her first impression of Gil was not a positive one, but she tried to resist reaching any premature conclusions. Besides, according to Layla, he treated her like a princess.

"I didn't know you were coming up by motorcycle. Good trip?"

"Pretty good. Right, Layla?"

Layla nodded again.

"Layla's not all that used to the bike yet. But that'll change."

So far, Layla hadn't actually said one word.

"I see . . . Layla tells me you want to open your own restaurant someday. Maybe she mentioned I used to be in the business. It's a lot of hard work, but it can be rewarding too. So tell me more. You thinking of a franchise, or are you going independent?"

It was her first rule of small talk. Ask people questions about themselves, then sit back and let them fill the air. It was a trick that worked before for Jennifer, and this time was no different.

She could tell immediately that Gil really liked Gil as a topic. She also sensed her first impression of him would be a lasting one. He was too cocky for her taste. Seriously self-absorbed. But she could live with that as long as he was good to Layla.

Gil's story was unexceptional, but he seemed to think she should be fascinated by it. He was a college dropout before heading out west to work in the Alberta oilfields. The job paid well, but he was laid off when the economy crashed. So he left his ex and their baby, came back east and started waiting tables. He moved to bartending soon after.

Thousands of other dudes did exactly the same thing, Jennifer thought. It was almost a rite of passage for twenty-somethings of a certain ilk. Good experience, no doubt, but did he have what it takes to make it with his own restaurant? She doubted it.

The three went for supper at the Bell Tower Pub down the hill from Jennifer's condo building. The topic of conversation was more of the same. All about Gil.

Jennifer paid the bill, then turned to Layla as they put on their jackets.

"It's *so* nice to see you again, love. Do you think you can stay the night? We can catch up some more." As an afterthought, Jennifer faced Gil and reluctantly added, "You too, of course. You're welcome to stay."

Layla spoke up first.

"Sure, Mom. I'm not due back at the hospital till—"

Gil cut her off. "No! I already *told* you, Layla, I have to work the lunch shift tomorrow. If we leave now, we'll make it to Kingston by nine."

"I know, Gil. So why don't you go back tonight? I could take the bus tomorrow."

Jennifer hoped that was how it would work out. She wanted time alone with Layla. She could find out how things *really* were with Gil. Jennifer didn't have a good feeling about him. Not at all.

What happened next simply reinforced her suspicions.

"I said *No*!"

Gil must have seen the startled look in Jennifer's eyes. His next words, while still firm, were less vehement. He was going to get his way. He just didn't want any push back about it from Jennifer.

"Babe, I really need the company. You know it's better if we go home together."

Layla shrugged.

They returned to Jennifer's condo, collected their helmets, and went back down together to Gil's Harley in the visitor parking lot. As they rode away, Jennifer waved until they were out of sight. She was frowning. She couldn't help it. But it was already getting dark. Gil likely didn't notice, and even if he did, she knew he wouldn't care.

"They've just left, Eric. I don't like him. Not one bit. He's a puffed-up little shit. *So* full of himself. He barely let Layla get a word in edgewise, and when she wanted to stay over so we could have more time together, he practically ordered her to leave with him."

"Just calm down, Jen. Maybe you're being too tough on him. You know Layla doesn't say much. Never did. And perhaps you're a tiny bit jealous because he's got her attention, instead of you?"

"No. Well, maybe . . . yes. Perhaps I *am* overreacting. But there's something not quite right with him. I feel like he was trying to limit her time alone with me. Makes me wonder what he's got to hide. So could you do me a favor? Could you find out if he has a criminal record?"

"I suppose I could—"

"Good. For Layla's sake, of course, not mine."

"Okay. For Layla. Just this once. What's his name?"

"Gil Leblanc. L-E-B-L-A-N-C. First name Gilbert, I think. Living in Kingston, of course, although he was in Lethbridge, Alberta for a time."

"I'll check it out and get back to you, Jen. But a word of warning. I suggest you keep your thoughts to yourself. Don't go on about him to Layla. Otherwise, you might alienate her. And if you force her to take sides, she might not choose you. You don't want to lose her again, do you?"

"No. Of course not. You're right. I'll keep my mouth shut. And you *know* how hard that'll be for me."

Ain't *that* the truth, Eric thought, as he hung up the phone.

Chapter Six

Jennifer was mystified and a little bit anxious as she parked on the street outside the brick low-rise that housed the operations of the *Ottawa Daily Chronicle*. Jeff's assistant Emma had called earlier. He wanted to see her that afternoon.

Was this going to be bad news? Jennifer wasn't really superstitious, but it *was* Friday the 13th. She thought things were going well with the column, but maybe he didn't see it that way.

On the other hand, it had been almost exactly a month since *THAT'S LIFE* was launched. Perhaps this was just Jeff's version of a routine review. There was something in Emma's voice, however, that told her the meeting wasn't going to be routine.

Even though Jennifer was ten minutes early, she didn't have to wait. Emma ushered her immediately into Jeff's office. He spoke to her without making eye contact.

"Have a seat, Jenny."

Jennifer sat down across the desk from him. He didn't smile or greet her. Not a good sign. Didn't ask how she was. Still not good. Didn't offer her a coffee. Even worse.

Instead, he picked up a section of the newspaper and tossed it across the desk so that it landed in front of her. Finally, he looked at her over the top of his glasses.

"This is your column from Tuesday."

She turned the paper around and read the first few lines. It was the letter from "Puzzled and Missing Him."

"Yes? Is there something wrong?"

"'Fraid so. We've just learned that the young woman who wrote you had some kind of breakdown after she read your response. She's now in the hospital. Her parents called us. They're beside themselves. They're talking about taking this public."

"Oh my God! She had a breakdown because of what I wrote? How could *that* be?"

"I'll tell you how. According to her mother, she was already fragile. Prone to depression. And your reply pushed her over the edge."

"But—"

"No buts, Jenny. I'm not saying your advice was wrong. What I *am* saying is there are better ways to state it. You pride yourself on your judgement and your honesty, and that's a good thing. But keep in mind the people who write to you could be troubled. Even at the end of their rope. You have to take it easier on them. Otherwise—"

Jeff didn't finish the sentence. To Jennifer, the "otherwise" sounded ominous. "I get what you're saying. Still, my reply must have seemed safe enough at the time for you to publish it word for word."

"I think we're all learning as we go. But let me make it clear. From now on, we'll be monitoring more closely what you submit. If we don't see a change in tone, we may have to cancel the column. Either that or find someone else to write it."

"I understand."

Jennifer was furious but tried to hide it. Jeff was thinking of cancelling their contract because of one slip up? Actually, it wasn't even a slip up. The response was good. The young woman just couldn't handle it. But how was Jennifer supposed to know that?

Maybe she should just quit. Right then and there. Too bad there were those damn bills to pay.

Jennifer stood up. "I'm proud of my work, Jeff. I always put one hundred percent into what I do."

"I know, Jenny. But you need a new way of expressing yourself."

"I hear you. I'll try my best."

She turned and walked out.

The whole thing sucked. Jeff was imposing his saccharin approach on her and she had no choice but to grin and bear it.

Driving home, Jennifer forced herself to focus on the traffic rather than on what Jeff had said. But she gave in to the anger as soon as she got back to her apartment.

The year had begun well enough. Despite a few wobbles, she was on the right track. She'd landed a new job. Managed to stay clean and sober. It wasn't easy, but Jennifer had been feeling good about the way things were going and hopeful for the rest of 2020.

Now, over just a few days, it was all shot to hell.

It started with Layla's new boyfriend. A textbook bully if she ever saw one. Jennifer knew the signs. Her first husband was like that. If someone in Layla's situation wrote to Gloria Pierce for help, she'd tell her to run as fast as she could in the other direction before things got worse. Because it was Layla, there was nothing Jennifer could do about it. And now, her micro-managing boss was ready to fire her in an instant. If she had her way, she'd tell him to stick their contract, and his precious newspaper, up his ass. But she couldn't.

Four days later, there was even more bad news. Not only for her, but for everybody else, too. A big deal, apparently. On March 17th, the government declared a state of emergency. Some kind of deadly virus had come to town and everybody was running for cover.

She'd have to stay home for God knows how long. Alone. It was crazy-making. All of it. With no way out.

Jennifer sat at her dining table, hunched over her second cup of coffee. It was 10:30 in the morning. She was supposed to be working on her column. The deadline to send in the next batch was that afternoon, but it had taken everything she had to get out of bed, set up the brew machine, and press the ON button.

Jennifer was just sober enough to recognize she was still a bit drunk. Not sloppy drunk like the night before, but strung-out drunk, with a stomach that threatened to erupt if she didn't take things slow. At that moment, writing a coherent Gloria Pierce-style slice of wisdom was out of the question.

Instead, she loathed herself for what she'd done. *Stupid fucking moron* played in an endless loop in her head. After months of living clean, she'd blown it in one night.

Why?

Why did she let a punk like Gil get to her? And Jeff. And the so-called coronavirus. All bad news. All in one crap of a week. And how did she react? She climbed back into the bottle, of course. Her favorite place to hide. So predictable. So pathetic.

After her third coffee, Jennifer felt marginally better. She forced her thoughts to move on.

Wallowing in self-disgust and mental lashings wouldn't make things any better. Focusing on her priorities would. Layla came first. Then her job. If she let herself go, like she did the previous summer, she'd lose both. And there'd be nobody knocking at her door to drag her to rehab and help her patch up her life for the umpteenth time. Because of the pandemic, everybody she knew was isolating.

There was only one thing she could do. She called Lizzie.

"I've been a bad girl, Lizzie. I slipped up last night. Big time. And boy, do I feel like a piece of shit this morning."

"Want to tell me about it?"

"I guess so. I'm feeling overwhelmed. There's too much on my mind. None of it good."

For ten minutes, Jennifer vented and Lizzie listened.

"Yup. Sounds like things are really bad for you right now. But don't let last night erase all the progress you've made. You might disagree, but I think you're a strong woman when you put your mind to it. You can handle this. So do it for your daughter, of course. And most of all, do it for yourself."

"It feels harder this time, Lizzie. This COVID thing, or whatever they're calling it, it's really messing up my support system."

"What do you mean?"

"I've just checked the AA meeting schedule and they've been suspended. I can't see Eric or Rachel or anybody else, even if I wanted to tell them about this. Which I don't. You're my only lifeline right now. And I don't want to lean on you too much."

"Don't worry about that, Jen. That's what I'm here for. Besides, I'm stuck at home, too. I won't get to see the kids and the grandkids for God knows how long. So, I have lots of time to talk with you."

"Thanks, Lizzie."

"Tonight, if the urge comes back, call me right away. I promise I'll drop everything to listen. You'll be my priority. We can work through this together."

Chapter Seven

She was Layla's first COVID death. Sofia Esposito was her name. A sweet little Italian lady, not even five feet tall. The chart said she was 72 years old. Layla didn't know much else about her and had no way of finding out because Sofia couldn't speak English. Later, after they jammed the ventilator tube down her throat, she couldn't speak at all.

She'd been brought to Kingston General Hospital feverish and barely breathing, and Layla had helped settle her in. Sofia was moved to the ICU the next morning when her symptoms got even worse. The prognosis was bleak.

There was something about Sofia that compelled Layla to visit her later that evening near the end of her shift. Maybe it was because Sofia had clasped her hand so desperately when she first arrived, as if Layla were family. Her own family wasn't allowed in the hospital, of course. Only patients and staff.

Layla had just reached her bedside when Sofia's eyes fluttered open. She looked up, clearly confused, before she finally focused on Layla. Then the confusion turned to fear. No wonder, Layla thought. Maybe Sofia somehow knew she was nearing the end, and the only other person there with her was a stranger. A shapeless featureless stranger, fully concealed by protective equipment like a mad scientist conducting some sinister experiment.

None of her loved ones could be there to comfort her. Nobody she knew could hold her hand and pray, or whisper a gentle goodbye with warm, caring words in a language she understood.

Sofia didn't deserve to go this way.

She shut her eyes again. Layla, in tears, leaned close to her. "You are *so* loved, Mrs. Sofia."

It was all she could think of to say.

Sofia slipped away later that evening.

Layla had been working as an orderly for more than a year. She'd seen death a number of times. But, for her, Sofia's lonely passing was the most difficult.

Layla was still upset the next morning when she called Jennifer. "It's *so* sad, Mom. She was all alone. I can still see the frightened look in her eyes. I'll never forget it."

"I'm so sorry, love. I wish I could be there to help you get through it."

"Thanks, but don't worry. Gil's here for me. And you wouldn't see much of me anyway. I'm working extra shifts with all the COVID cases."

"Will you have a break soon? I don't want you to get sick yourself."

"I've got next Monday off. And I plan to stay in bed all day."

"Good! You deserve the rest. Please be careful, love. I'll be in touch soon."

There was absolutely nothing reassuring to Jennifer about what Layla said. Her sweet girl was an essential worker, exhausted from long hours at the hospital in the middle of a pandemic, with a boyfriend who was likely too focused on himself to offer her much support. And she was *so* far away.

After their call, it took only thirty seconds for Jennifer to make up her mind.

She was going to Kingston.

"Hi, love. I thought I'd pay you a quick visit on your day off. I'm downstairs in front." It was a typically brisk late-March morning. Decayed mounds of dirty snow still resisted the spring melt, and in places where the ground did poke through, the soggy debris that had accumulated over the winter gave off a rotting odor.

Jennifer had left Ottawa at eight and arrived in Kingston a little over two hours later. She hadn't told her daughter in advance she was coming. She was worried Layla, under Gil's influence, might make some excuse not to see her.

"Mom! This is a surprise!"

"I know I shouldn't come up, Layla. Social distancing and all that. But I thought you might come down and we could sit and chat at one of the picnic tables in the back. Six feet apart, of course. And I've brought us coffees and doughnuts to help keep us warm."

Social distancing was a convenient excuse. It was more about seeing Layla on her own.

"Sure, Mom. I'll be right down. Gil's in the shower. I'll see if he wants to join us after."

I'd like it better if he didn't, Jennifer thought.

When Layla emerged from the main entrance and came closer, Jennifer didn't like what she saw. There were dark circles of exhaustion under Layla's eyes and her cheeks were chapped. Jennifer had seen frontline medical staff on TV with similar red marks caused by the N95 masks they wore all day long.

"How're you feeling today, love? You're looking a little worse for the wear."

Layla shrugged. "I know, Mom. I can't do much about it. Goes with the job."

The two walked in single file around the side of the high-rise to the back where they sat at opposite corners of one of the tables. They were alone except for a bundled-up elderly woman who shuffled by them with her Shih Tzu.

Jennifer reached as far as she could across the table to give Layla the brown paper bag holding her doughnut. Then she took Layla's coffee cup out of its cardboard carrier and passed it to her. Layla took off her mitten to pick up the coffee. That's when Jennifer saw it. A dark purple bruise circling Layla's wrist like a grotesque tattoo.

"What happened there, Layla?" Jennifer pointed to the bruise. "Surely you didn't get that at the hospital?"

Layla pulled down her jacket sleeve until it almost covered her whole hand. "It's nothing. I honestly don't remember how I got it."

"You don't remember? It looks too painful not to know where it came from."

"Forget it, Mom. No big deal."

At that moment, Layla looked up and past Jennifer. Gil was approaching from the front of the building. He greeted them when he got close.

"Hey, babe. Hey, Jen."

He sat down next to Layla and put his arm around her. His hair was still wet from the shower. It looked to Jennifer like he wanted to join them as fast as possible. She doubted it was because he was anxious to see his girlfriend's mother.

"How're you doing, Gil?"

"I'm good. You?"

"I'm fine, thanks. But I'm concerned about Layla. I think she's working too hard. She'll make herself sick. That's why I've come down today."

"Don't worry. I'll take care of her." Gil looked at Layla. "Right, babe?"

Layla nodded.

He turned back to Jennifer. "I'm around pretty much all day if she needs me. I got laid off last week when the bar closed. Just like all the other bars in town . . . goddamn COVID rules—"

"Sorry to hear that, but I'm glad Layla won't be alone."

Except Jennifer *wasn't* glad. Not in the slightest. It was bad enough he was a bully. What if he was violent with Layla, too? The bruising around her wrist, did he do that? Were there bruises in other places too, hidden under her winter clothing?

There he was, hanging around their apartment all day, doing fuck all, while her daughter worked her butt off on the pandemic frontline. And he was free to inflict whatever injury he wanted on her under cover of the lockdown.

Jennifer sat quietly as Gil took over the conversation, going on about how he was applying for the government's new COVID relief benefits. How he'd use his free time to work out in the exercise room, mask on of course, and cook Layla nice meals for when she got home from the hospital.

After five minutes of hearing Gil talk but not registering one word, Jennifer had enough. She stood up abruptly and turned to go. There couldn't be any hugs this time.

"Okay . . . well . . . I just thought I'd check in to see how you two were doing. I should be off and let you enjoy the rest of your day. I'll call you later, Layla, okay? Love you."

Leaving her daughter with Gil was the last thing Jennifer wanted to do. But what choice did she have? She had to act as if she had no issues whatsoever with this asshole. Otherwise, things might go badly for Layla.

It was a long drive back to Ottawa.

Chapter Eight

Eric decided to give Jennifer the details in person, even though it would have been easier over the phone. He wasn't exactly sure what her reaction would be, but he knew from experience she didn't always think rationally when it came to bad news about Layla. What's more, when he spoke to her earlier to invite himself over, she was already upset about something. If he were with her, just this one time bending COVID isolation rules, he might be able to stop her from doing things she would regret later.

When he called up from the lobby, Jennifer buzzed him in right away. Stepping out of the elevator, he heard "Enter Sandman" playing from the direction of her unit. He knew what that meant. She was in a Metallica mood again. For sure, there was going to be drama.

As he walked down the hall, the music got so loud he could feel vibrations from the bass guitar traveling along the worn carpet. It was a wonder the neighbors hadn't complained. Or maybe they had, and Jennifer just ignored them. He had to pound on the door twice before she turned down the volume and let him in. Eric paused just inside the entrance while she finished looping her facemask elastics behind her ears. The mask covered everything except her eyes, but Eric didn't need to see more. Jennifer was obviously agitated as hell.

"Jesus, girl, take it easy on the eardrums!"

"Your eardrums are the least of my worries."

"Okay, I *get* it. You have issues. And I have information. But before we start, can I have a coffee? It was a tough day at the courthouse. Child porn case. You know how I feel about them."

Jennifer, impatient with the request, went to the kitchen and poured cold coffee from breakfast into a mug. After reheating it in the microwave, she automatically added two sugars, no cream. She didn't need to ask. She'd made his coffee every morning for years.

In the living room, she barely managed to hold back until Eric pulled down his mask and took a sip.

"Okay, Jen. You want to go first?"

"I certainly *do.* And this time, when I'm done, don't tell me I should mind my own business. Because I know I'm right."

"Right about what?"

"Right about Layla's loser boyfriend. And he's a *dangerous* loser at that."

"What's he done now?"

Eric took another sip. He had no intention of debating the point. Given what he'd learned about Gil Leblanc, he was hardly going to disagree with Jennifer's assessment.

"Well, I drove to Kingston yesterday—"

Eric didn't speak, but he shot her a look that said *Are you crazy? Were you looking for trouble or what?*

"I know, I know, I'm a helicopter mom, but I'm really worried about Layla and how hard she's been working at the hospital. I'm absolutely *terrified* she'll catch COVID."

"So, how was she? When I spoke to her last week, she seemed tired but otherwise okay."

"That's how she was yesterday, too. Except for one thing. I noticed she had bruising on her arm, just above her wrist. And it wasn't your garden variety kind of bruising. It was dark, almost black, and it went all the way around. I asked Layla about it, but she brushed me off."

Jennifer glared at Eric. Her eyes glistened and her mask swelled and collapsed with each fierce breath. "I'm sure Gil did it!"

Eric sat forward, instantly on edge. He didn't really want to agree with her, but he'd worked on too many domestic violence cases to ignore the signs.

"I know what you're going to say, Eric, in that totally *irritating* way you have. You're going to say don't jump to conclusions."

Eric didn't respond. He just looked away, shaking his head.

"But tell me, what other possible explanation is there?"

Finally, he answered. "You'll be surprised to hear I think you may be right."

"Really?"

"Well, I won't go so far as to say it *has* to be the boyfriend. There's a slight chance something or someone else did it. But it very well could be him. Especially given what I've found out."

"What you've found out? So you checked his criminal record?"

"Yes. I got it yesterday. At first, I wasn't sure I should say anything. I was worried what you might do. Like, try to butt in somehow. And then she might cut you off, maybe even for good."

"Goddamn it, Eric! Don't fucking censor what you tell me! She's my DAUGHTER for Christ's sake . . . so, what's he done?"

"Two convictions for possession of a controlled substance. Theft under $5,000. And one conviction for domestic assault. The charges are old ones. They come from seven years ago in Alberta. He did his time, Jen. People change. And there've been no charges since. So I was willing to give him the benefit of the doubt. But now, with what you've just told me, I'm not so sure."

"Sounds like you'd made up a pretty little speech to convince me to back off. But the guy's trouble. BIG trouble. We've got to do something about it!"

"I'm not sure we *can* do anything, Jen. You're telling me Layla won't admit Gil did it. *If* he did it. And I doubt there are other witnesses. So, we have no evidence. Even if charges are filed at some point, there'd be no reasonable prospect of conviction unless Layla decides to cooperate. And that doesn't seem likely right now."

"But we've got to get her away from him!"

"She's an adult, Jen. She's her own person. Look, even though I'm her stepdad, I love her like she's my own. You know that, don't you? And if it turns out he *is* beating her up, I'd be the first one to kick his fucking ass to hell and back. But right now, our hands are tied. The best I can do is to keep in close touch with her. How about I go to Kingston myself to check out the situation? Maybe if he realizes I'm watching, he'll think twice about doing her harm."

"Yes. Please go, Eric. And let me know how it turns out. If only there was some way I could convince her to break up with him—"

"Be careful with that, Jen. It could turn out badly. For everyone."

After Eric left, Jennifer went to the fridge and pulled out a chilled bottle of Sauvignon Blanc. She hesitated only a few seconds before unscrewing the cap and pouring a full glass. To calm herself, of course.

Just one wouldn't do any harm, would it? After all, it was only wine, not the hard stuff like the last time. Besides, a glass of wine in the evening was supposed to be good for one's health. Of course, she was in total control this time. She could stop whenever she wanted. She definitely wasn't going to have more. Not that night, anyway.

Jennifer screwed the cap back on and put the bottle back in the fridge. Then she took her glass to the living room, sat on the couch, and called Rachel.

"Jen, so good to hear from you. How're you doing?"

"I'm busy with the column, but I have to admit I'm spooked about this pandemic thing. I suppose I should be grateful I still have my job. Lots of people don't."

"I'm glad that worked out for you, Jen. And speaking about jobs, how is Layla? I was thinking about her the other day. I guess she's in the thick of things at that hospital."

"Yes. I'm *so* worried about her."

"I'm not surprised. But she's young and healthy. And the frontline workers . . . they're taking all the precautions, aren't they? They have those special uniforms. What do they call them? PPE?"

"Yes. PPE. But her work isn't the only thing that's bothering me. She has a new boyfriend. In fact, he's moved in with her. And I don't like him at all."

"Oh? Why not?"

"Well, I won't go into too much detail. Let's just say he's older than her and seems to get off on bossing her around."

"That's not good—"

"No, it's not. And Eric tells me he has a criminal record."

"Holy shit! Does Layla know?"

"I have no idea. It gets even worse. I went to Kingston a

few days ago to see how she was doing, and there were signs he's been physical with her. I saw bruises."

"That's *terrible*!"

"I wish I could get her to kick him out, but Eric says I should stay out of it. He thinks she might choose to keep the boyfriend and stop speaking to me. He could be right."

Jennifer swallowed half the wine in her glass in one go.

"You must be beside yourself, Jen."

"I am . . . if only I could warn her in a way that wouldn't make her turn her back on me."

They both went quiet, thinking. Then Rachel had an idea.

"Well, maybe you can. She knows you're the real Gloria Pierce, right?"

"Right."

"And she reads your columns?"

"She tells me she does. Every day."

"So, here's a suggestion. You get lots of emails looking for help. There's bound to be one that describes a situation like the one she's in. Bad relationship. Isolating because of the virus. Wondering what to do."

"Actually, I received one something like that a week ago."

"Okay. So, why don't you publish it with your answer? Perhaps not your usual abrupt kind of answer. But sympathetic. Understanding. Find a tone that will resonate with Layla. It might make her realize she needs to dump this guy. What do you think?"

"Sounds good in theory, Rachel. I'm not sure it'll work. Still, I guess it's worth a try."

They spoke for a few more minutes, mainly about Rachel's charity activities and how her foundation had to use Zoom now for their meetings. How she missed the weekly facials and the restaurants and the social life. Instead, she had her gourmet meals delivered. She was catching up on her Book Club list and binge-watching all twenty-one seasons of *Midsomer Murders*. To Jennifer, it sounded like the pandemic was treating her pretty well. No surprise there. Things always seemed to turn out right for Rachel.

"Can I say one more thing before we hang up, Jen? You must be feeling good about how you're doing these days, staying dry and all. I know it hasn't been easy. But now you're back on top again. I'm proud of you for that. You must be proud, too."

Jennifer wasn't feeling proud at all. She was feeling uncomfortable.

"Of course. Thanks for that, Rachel. Talk to you soon."

After the call ended, Jennifer finished the rest of her glass and went back to the fridge for more.

Chapter Nine

Dear Gloria,

My sister and her boyfriend of several months are now isolating together because of the COVID-19 pandemic. They live in another city, so I have only seen them together a couple of times. My impression is that he's a controlling bully. My sister is shy and vulnerable by nature, and even more so when she is with him. He does all the talking, and he likes to make all the decisions for both of them. What's worse, the last time I saw her I noticed signs she had been injured. I think he did it to her, but when I asked what happened she said she didn't remember. I have since found out he had several criminal convictions in the past, including for domestic assault. Gloria, I fear for her safety. What can I do to get her away from him?

—Feeling Helpless

Gloria's Advice: From the way you are describing your sister's situation, you clearly believe her new relationship is abusive. I understand why you feel this way. There is indeed a strong possibility she is in danger. Your sister may not recognize what is happening and, given what you say about her, may allow it to continue or get even worse. For her own good, she needs to be aware of the warning signs. The abuse can start with one partner behaving in a controlling way that wears down the other partner's sense of self-worth. It sounds to me like this may already be happening in your sister's case. Attacks that begin as verbal can lead to physical violence and, in extreme cases, to death. She should know that she does not need to stay in an abusive relationship. If she feels frightened or confused about how things are with her boyfriend, she should reach out for help. She can call 9-1-1 for the police if criminal behavior such as assault occurs. She can seek refuge in the local women's shelter. Family and friends may be willing to help her escape to a secure place. I encourage you to show her this column so she can be made aware of her options. Please know that I wish your sister a safe outcome. There are many people willing to help her achieve this.

Send your relationship questions to:
askgloria@ottawadailychronicle.ca

All the words were Jennifer's. She had decided to start the whole column from scratch. None of the emails Gloria Pierce received since *THAT'S LIFE* started was exactly right for the message she wanted to give Layla.

It wasn't easy. What she wrote had to be specific enough for Layla to see it could apply to her, but vague enough so she didn't feel Jennifer was attacking Gil personally. So, it was "sister" instead of "daughter." And the tone was gentle, not blunt. Rachel was right about that.

Jennifer finished the column by noon the next day and sent it in with the next batch.

"Here we go again," Jennifer grumbled into her cell phone after she was put on hold by Emma, who explained there wouldn't be a face-to-face meeting with Jeff this time. COVID rules, of course.

"What's his problem *now*?"

She waited a full five minutes. Finally, Jeff came on the line.

"Hi, Jenny. I wanted to touch base with you to find out if everything is okay?"

"Everything's fine, Jeff. Why do you ask?"

His tone changed instantly from curious to critical.

"Well, to be honest with you, I'm not happy about your missed deadlines. It's happened a couple of times lately. We can't hold up the layout work just because of you. You know that, right?"

This was a surprise. Sure, she'd been distracted by what was happening with Layla. She'd cut it close a few times. Was she ever actually late? She hoped not. But she wasn't exactly sure.

"What do you mean, missed deadlines? I thought I'd been sending my stuff to you on time. Not only that, but I'm actually ahead of the game. This week, I've written a few extra columns in advance. I can pull them out of my back pocket anytime, if need be."

It wasn't true. There was no full back pocket.

"Think again, Jenny. You were late last week, and the week before that, too. I want more discipline from you. This has to stop."

Deadlines were Jennifer's enemy. Discipline was not one of her strong points. In fact, she was perversely proud of her disordered existence. She always thought she got her best work done in the midst of chaos. That is, when she was sober. But these days, she had to admit she'd slipped a bit—just a tiny little bit—on the drinking front. Had she slipped on getting her columns in, too? Maybe. But if she had, it certainly wasn't on purpose.

"Sorry, Jeff. I've got a lot on my mind. This won't happen again, I promise."

"It better not. Listen, Jenny, I took you on because I thought you had a talent for clever writing. And, frankly, because you're Rachel's good friend. The last thing I want to do is let you go. But this is the second time I've had trouble with you. Three strikes and you're out. Got it?"

Jennifer sighed. "Yes, Jeff. Got it."

"Okay, then. Let's get things back on track. And maybe you can send me those columns you've set aside, just in case something else happens."

Something else meaning *I screw up again and you fire me*, Jennifer thought. Threats again. It's always threats with this guy. And now she'd have to work overtime to write the extra columns for him. Fuck!

Jennifer called Lizzie on Skype. It was the only way they

could see each other. Everybody from the Prime Minister on down was still telling people to stay home.

To Jennifer, Lizzie looked pretty much the same as she did before the COVID lockdown began, although her hair was a bit shaggy. All the salons were closed, of course. But her eye makeup was flawless and her Versace fleece top looked *so* much classier than the ratty housecoat Jennifer had on.

"You're looking great, Lizzie, for this obscene time of day."

"I've just come back from the grocery store," Lizzie explained. "I go early for seniors' hour. I'm always running into someone I know there, so I have to keep up appearances. But you don't see any lipstick, do you? I figure why bother when it'll just be hidden under my mask anyway."

Why bother with any makeup at all? Jennifer thought. She hadn't worn any since COVID first hit.

"Can we get serious, Lizzie?"

"Of course."

"Well, I might as well come right out and say it. I'm drinking. And I have been ever since the last time we spoke. I need to stop before I fuck up my life. I can't afford to do *that* again. But I can't seem to find the strength."

"Oh, Jen! I'm *so* sorry. What's going on now?"

"Well, it's like I told you before. My boss is *that* close to firing me. This time, he gave me shit for missing deadlines."

"And did you?"

"I must have. But not intentionally. I guess I just lost track of time, which is way too easy to do. With the damn lockdown, each day's the same as the day before. And then there's my daughter's boyfriend. The story keeps getting worse on that front, too. They're isolating together and I think he beats her up."

Jennifer was surprised when tears came to her eyes. Embarrassed too. She wiped them with the back of her hand and continued.

"I feel totally helpless, alone in this apartment, waiting out this goddamn pandemic. It's almost too much to take, Lizzie. I figured a glass of wine every now and then would help calm my nerves. I can handle this, I thought. How stupid is *that*?"

"I know. I've been there, Jen. Lots of little problems piling up into one big mess. That's why I started going to AA. Too bad the meetings are still suspended. But you and I could go over the steps together on our own. We could take it fast or slow. However you want. You up for that?"

Jennifer knew all the AA steps. They worked for a lot of people. But she had trouble with some of them.

"I'm not sure. I never really got into the religious thing. All that *handing myself over to God* stuff. I just went to the meetings to be with people who have the same problem I do. Misery loves company, I guess."

"So you prefer we just talk? That's fine with me. How about I Skype you tomorrow morning?"

"Can I call you sometime instead?"

"Okay. But—" Lizzie was puzzled. The classic *don't call me, I'll call you* brush off. Why did Jen Skype her if she didn't want her help to get clean? Obviously, she hasn't hit rock bottom yet. But it's coming.

"So nice to chat today, Lizzie."

Jennifer hung up. I'm glad Lizzie's my sponsor, she thought. I really do want to stop. I'm sure she gets that. It'll happen soon. And when I'm ready, it's good to know she'll be there for me.

For lunch, Jennifer made herself a grilled cheese sandwich and washed it down with a glass of Beaujolais-Villages. And then another. By 4:00, she had finished the entire bottle.

It was the first truly warm day of spring. Finally, the bulky jackets and salt-stained winter boots could be put away until the fall.

Because there were no sidewalks on Jennifer's street, she and Eric strolled along the side of the pavement. It seemed like everyone else in the neighborhood was doing the same thing, all of them desperate to escape the confines of their homes. Thanks to the lockdown, there were few places to go in the city except out on the streets.

In other years, an April day like this would bring out throngs of folks energized by the end of the dreary winter months. This year, the scene was strangely quiet. Solemn, even. Walkers passed each other with exaggerated care, shuffling awkwardly to the middle of the road when others approached from the opposite direction. Always keeping their distance. To Jennifer, it was like the milling mob in a zombie movie, minus the moaning.

When Eric spoke about his visit with Layla, he kept his voice low so the pedestrians in front of them couldn't listen in.

"What can I say, Jen? You were right. That Gil guy's got a big mouth on him. Almost as big as his ego. I could tell he was nervous, maybe because he knows I'm a cop. And that's not a bad thing. Anyway, I think he was trying to impress me with his grandiose restaurant plans. It didn't work."

"And how was Layla?"

"She looked tired. Beyond that, I just don't know. I didn't have the chance to speak with her on her own. Gil was with her the whole time. And she was totally covered from head to toe. There was no way to tell if there were any signs of assault."

"So where does that leave us, then?"

"I admit I'm worried. The way I see it, she's overwhelmed by him and we know he's no angel. Whether or not he's getting physical with her, it's not a healthy relationship. If we lived closer to her, we might be able to keep better track of what's really going on. But we're not. So, we'll just have to be there for her when she calls for help. And she will."

Jennifer stopped walking suddenly, making Eric stop, too.

"I wasn't going to tell you this, Eric, but I guess you should know. And please don't go all ballistic on me. I wrote one of my columns about Layla's situation. It's going to be published next week."

"You *what*?"

"Don't worry. I didn't use names. I didn't give specifics about injuries. Nothing like that. Just general advice on how to get away from an abuser. I'm pretty sure she'll read it. She tells me she reads all my columns."

"And you did that because?"

"It was Rachel's idea. It was the only way I could try to get through to her. I can't just sit by, waiting for something awful to happen to her. I *had* to do it."

"Let's hope this doesn't blow up in your face."

"I don't know how it possibly could."

Chapter Ten

Layla could hardly wait to get home. She was coming off a long shift and was exhausted. Maybe Gil had a nice supper waiting for her. He did that at least once a week. She was such a lucky girl. She was *so* looking forward to snuggling up on the couch beside him and falling asleep watching TV.

Because of the pandemic, Layla always followed a strict routine when she came back from the hospital. Just inside the front door, she would strip everything off. Her scrubs, her Crocs, her underwear. Everything. The clothes would go in the laundry. Next, she would go straight to the bathroom to shower, not touching anything and not going anywhere near Gil. Only after ten minutes under hot, almost scalding, water, would she emerge from the bathroom, ready for the usual evening activities.

Unfortunately, what happened that evening was not routine.

Layla opened the door to her apartment, stepped in and turned to lock the deadbolt behind her.

That's when Gil pounced.

Layla screamed, but the sound was cut off when he slammed her up against the wall and covered her mouth and nose with his hand. She could hardly breathe.

"What the fuck is going on, Layla? You bitchin' to your parents about me? You tryin' to get me in trouble again?"

Layla reached up and tried to pull his hand away, but she wasn't strong enough.

Gil glared at her with furious eyes until she gave up. Then he grabbed her wrist, the same wrist that still had traces of bruising, and dragged her behind him into the living room. He pushed her onto the couch and dropped down beside her.

"ANSWER me! Have you been talking to your parents behind my back? Have you?"

Layla's voice was shaky. "No, Gil." She couldn't get out more words, struggling to regain her breath.

Gil grabbed her shoulders and yanked her closer to him. When his face was six inches from hers, he started yelling again. Spit came out with the words.

"YOU'RE LYING! First, your crazy mother shows up here to check us out. Then that cop who calls himself your father. Did they think they could scare me off? NO FUCKIN' WAY! Oh, but that's not all . . . the next thing I know, your mother is writing SHIT about me in the paper!"

Now she understood what made him so angry.

Layla had read the Gloria Pierce column online before rushing to work that morning. That poor girl's situation with the controlling boyfriend sounded a little bit like what was happening between Gil and her. But things were different for them. Gil didn't have a criminal record. And he really loved her. Didn't he always apologize after one of his blowouts? Then things would get better, at least for a while. That's just the way it worked with him.

So Gil had read the column, too. Layla didn't like it, but she was pretty sure he checked out her emails and browsing history when she was working. He knew Jennifer was the real Gloria Pierce, Layla told him weeks ago. And when Gil saw what she wrote, he must have taken it personally.

"I've *never* said anything to them, Gil! I swear!"

"Then why are they sticking their goddamn noses in our business? It's gotta stop. Or else—"

"I don't care what they think, Gil. I know you love me. And I love you. Just ignore them."

Gil scowled at her. Then, apparently deciding she was telling the truth, he let go of her shoulders and sat back.

"Okay. But they better not try to interfere again. They'll be sorry if they do. I'll fucking make sure of that!"

Then, as if the confrontation had never happened, he turned on the TV and clicked through the sports channels to a rerun of the 2008 Stanley Cup playoff final. Layla sat quietly until she was sure he'd calmed down. Then she got up, went straight to the bathroom, and showered.

Gil hadn't made supper, so it was up to her. As she waited for the macaroni to finish boiling, she wondered what he meant when he asked if she was trying to get him in trouble *again*.

Jennifer received Gil's WhatsApp text just before midnight on the day her domestic abuse column was published. She forwarded it to Eric right away but waited until the next morning to call him.

WTF. First u come then your ex. Spying on us. AND NOW THE FUCKING ARTICLE.
U THINK I WOULDN'T SEE IT?
I know u wrote it, GLORIA. Try to get rid of me. Won't work.
STAY AWAY. U don't want me to pay u a visit.

"It scares the hell out of me, Eric. He's dangerous for Layla. Now he's threatening me, too. How can we stop this?"

"Like I keep saying, Jen, we can't do much about Layla. But there is something you can do to make sure he doesn't hurt you."

"Like what? A restraining order?"

"Restraining order . . . peace bond. Whatever you want to call it. Just go to a Justice of the Peace. Explain the situation. Ask for a peace bond. If it's granted, it'll mean he has to keep a certain distance away from you and not contact you. If he breaches, it could result in a criminal charge against him. I bet he'd do just about *anything* to avoid that, given his past convictions."

"Let's say I do go for a peace bond. What if he takes it out on Layla?"

"I suppose it's possible. But if he knows what's good for him, he won't risk it. Just take things one step at a time, Jen, okay? And right now, it's the only thing you can do."

"So where do I go for this?"

"Go to the Elgin Street courthouse. Make your case to one of the JPs there. See what happens."

"Thanks, Eric. I hope this works."

It was too early in the day for a drink. But if she needed a good reason to have one, Gil's threat was it.

Six ounces and seven hours later, Jennifer woke up. With a pounding headache and jelly legs, she was in no condition to speak to anyone about a peace bond. Who would believe her? She'd have to go to the courthouse the next day.

Jennifer sat in the waiting area in front of the intake court, filling in the blanks of the multiple-page peace bond application she'd printed off from the website. She'd already added her name to the list of people wanting to see the JP. It was a busy afternoon. There were five names ahead of her on the list.

Forty minutes later, it was her turn. The JP appeared, called her name, and led her back to the intake courtroom. It wasn't as fancy as it sounded. Just a small stuffy box-shaped space, more like the utilitarian office of a low-level manager, with no windows to the outside and no discernable air circulation. There were three visitor chairs in front of a beat-up oak desk that looked like it had been resurrected from surplus storage. The JP motioned for her to take a seat and walked around the desk to the chair on the other side of a plexiglass screen. A woman in her fifties, with coke-bottle-thick glasses and a severe Prince Valiant haircut, the JP spoke with a voice just short of yelling to be heard through her mask and the screen.

"Before we start, you should know that we are being recorded."

Jennifer nodded.

"Your name for the record, please?"

"Jennifer Carr, Your Honor."

"That's Your Worship, not Your Honor. I'm not a judge."

"Sorry . . . Your Worship."

"Do you have identification with you?"

Jennifer opened her bag, pulled out her driver's licence and placed it on the desk facing the JP, who glanced at it and carried on.

"Please state why you are here today."

Jennifer paced her words slowly at first, but heard herself speaking louder and faster as her emotions took over. She described Gil's controlling relationship with Layla and her own encounters with him. How he had a criminal record and how she felt threatened by the text message he sent. But before she had the chance to pull out her cellphone and show it, the JP stopped her.

"So, you're here for a peace bond?"

"Yes, Your Worship. I already have the form filled out."

Jennifer put the application on the desk, but the JP ignored it.

"Unfortunately, your matter won't be proceeding any further at this time."

"Why not?"

Jennifer was shocked. Hadn't she made it totally clear that Gil was dangerous? That he might come after her?

"A lot of people think they can walk out of here with a peace bond that takes immediate effect. It doesn't work like that, even when there is no virus to worry about. The process involves scheduling a court hearing. In normal times, that can take up to two months."

That's way too slow, Jennifer thought. I could be dead by then.

"But we're not in normal times. Because of the pandemic, most courts have been shut down to be refitted for safety precautions. Peace bond matters will not be proceeding for the foreseeable future. If this person actually does confront you, my advice is to call the police."

Jennifer was horrified.

She had no protection. Gil might show up at her door at any time looking to pick a fight. Not only that, but until he was out of the picture, she wouldn't dare try to get in touch with Layla for fear it might provoke him, no matter how harmless their communication was.

She never felt so vulnerable. What the hell kind of a justice system lets this happen?

Chapter Eleven

Jennifer sat in front of her laptop, staring at the monitor. Her fingers were in position on the keyboard. She'd selected a question from the handful of emails Gloria Pierce had received the day before. It was about a woman in a long-term relationship with a divorced man who refused to tell his teenage son about her.

Now all she needed to do was type the answer. She knew what she wanted Gloria to say. She'd even made a few half-hearted attempts at it, but the prose wasn't working for her. Just pedestrian words cobbled together in flabby sentences. With each draft, she decided the answer sucked and immediately deleted it again.

It was a focus problem. She couldn't focus enough to write one of her usual sharp, provocative responses. She picked up her coffee mug. It was almost empty, and the little that was left in the bottom was stone cold. That gave her an excuse to get up, go to the kitchen, and make another pot. It was classic work avoidance, and she knew it. After that, she forced herself to sit down at her laptop to try again. But it was no use. All she could think about was Gil. The sadistic grip he held over Layla and the fact that she was now his target, too.

Jennifer struggled for another hour. The frustration turned into panic. She was late. Very late. She was supposed to have delivered her latest batch to the paper two days earlier, but she had to finish this column first. What made it worse was that she still hadn't sent in the extra columns she told Jeff she'd already completed. They didn't exist then and they didn't exist now.

She half expected Jeff would call at any minute to fire her.

The phone rang but it wasn't Jeff.

"Lizzie! So nice to hear from you!"

Jennifer was embarrassed. She hadn't called or Skyped with Lizzie for days.

"You okay, Jen? I haven't heard from you lately. I'm worried about you."

"I'm fine. It's just that I'm up to my eyeballs in work—"

"Is that the only reason?"

It wasn't. But it was the only one Jennifer wanted to give. What was the point of telling her sponsor she was still drinking and couldn't face stopping just then? Besides, she sensed from the way Lizzie asked the question she already knew the truth. The next words confirmed this.

"Let me guess. It's still out of control, isn't it? Your drinking, I mean. Please don't insult me by trying to deny it. So, here's some tough love from me, Jen. You've been through this before. You know what happens next. It'll drag you down and destroy you. You'll lose *everything . . . again*. How many times do you want to do this to yourself? GET A GRIP, JEN!"

Jennifer felt like a kid caught shoplifting. She could hardly wait to get off the phone.

"You're right. I'm sorry, Lizzie!"

"Don't apologize to me. You're only hurting yourself. And your daughter. And your friends."

"I know. I know I need to stop. But it's tough for me right now, alone in this fucking COVID isolation. In fact, it's overwhelming."

It was Lizzie's turn to feel bad. Jen was right. The pandemic wasn't making things easy for anybody, and especially for people who lived alone. *Alcoholics* who lived alone. Her tone softened.

"Why don't you join the Zoom AA meetings? They've just started up. It's most of the same gang as before, and I want us to stay in touch. Anything I can do, just let me know. I promise I'll take it easier on you next time. Talk to you soon?"

"Of course, Lizzie. Thanks. Thanks for caring."

The whole exchange took less than two minutes.

Zoom meetings. Sponsor calls. They seemed like too much effort. Jennifer already had more than enough to deal with. She turned to stare at the blank monitor screen again.

The call from Jeff came a day later. "Should I give up on you, Jenny?"

"I don't know what to say, Jeff. I'm dealing with some heavy personal shit right now. It's making it difficult for me to concentrate on the column. I'm really, really sorry."

"So, I'll repeat my question. Should I give up on you?"

"I hope not—"

"Listen, Jenny. I like you. I like your writing. But you've pushed things too far. If you were anybody else, I'd drop you in a second. The main thing holding me back is that your column is so popular. We're still getting lots of feedback from readers. Gloria's got a big following. I'd hate for us to lose that. Plus, I've been talking with Rachel. She tells me you're going through a rough time with your daughter."

"Yes."

"Well, I'm not a total bastard, you know. I *do* sympathize. Life hasn't always been easy with my kids, either. So, I'm going to give you one more chance. This time I'm suggesting a different approach. We can tell readers Gloria Pierce is taking a short break. Let's call it a sabbatical. Then, when you're ready, we can start the column again. How does this sound?"

Did she have any choice?

"Sounds good, Jeff. Thanks."

"Okay. Let's do it. But I have two conditions. The first is that your sabbatical can't be indefinite. It's got to be a short one, or we really *will* part ways. The second is that you need to send me those extra columns you said you wrote. If, in fact, you actually wrote them?"

Jennifer didn't answer the question directly. He probably figured out she hadn't.

"Okay, Jeff, you'll get them soon."

After they hung up, Jennifer felt marginally better. So Jeff didn't want to fire her after all. He and his damn deadlines were going away, at least for a little while. It would be hell on her finances, of course. Maybe she'd have to break down and ask Eric for help with the rent. But it was better than being dumped completely.

Jennifer went back to her laptop and the question about the divorced boyfriend. Finally, the words started to flow. Later that afternoon, so did the scotch.

Chapter Twelve

When Layla left to go to work that morning, it was just like every other day. Gil, still in his underwear, was in the kitchen making himself bacon and eggs. As far as she could tell, he had no hint of a fever. He wasn't coughing. He didn't complain of a sore throat. There was nothing to indicate he was anything but healthy.

It was a different story when she got home that evening.

Layla opened the front door to silence instead of the sounds of cheering sports fans on television. As she undressed in the front hallway, she called Gil's name, but he didn't answer right away. Maybe he's out, Layla thought, although *that* didn't happen often. He was terrified of getting COVID. Occasionally, he'd go for a walk, but that was it. Layla did all the grocery shopping. And there was nowhere else he could have gone anyway. The authorities had closed everything down. Restaurants. Bars. Cinemas. Everything.

So, where was he?

Finally, Gil croaked at her from the bedroom. "I think I've got it."

She could barely hear him. Layla stopped at the bedroom door on her way to the shower. Gil, still not dressed, was lying on the bed with his eyes closed and a pained look on his face.

"Got what, babe?"

"What d'you think? COVID, of course."

He started coughing.

Layla didn't think he had COVID. How could he? He hadn't been close to anybody but her, and she always took precautions. She thought it might just be a cold. Besides, when Gil wasn't feeling well in the past, he'd make a big deal of even his mildest symptoms. More than once, she found it humorous, the way he carried on, but she was careful not to laugh when that happened. Maybe this was like those other times.

"I'll shower first, then I'll come in to see you."

Gil groaned as he rolled over on his stomach and continued coughing into his pillow.

Layla went to the bathroom and turned on the shower. Then she stepped into the tub and pulled the plastic curtain closed behind her.

As she shampooed, she thought back over the past weeks. She always made sure to wash away any germs from the hospital as soon as she came in, just like she was doing today. She laundered her soiled clothes each evening. She wiped down all the groceries she brought into the apartment. She did everything right.

It just couldn't happen. It *must* be a cold. He'd get over it.

Layla finished rinsing her hair and reached for the soap. She lathered herself all over with it, taking care to go easy on the bruised parts. Then she stopped and stood motionless. She remembered the horrible fight they had the week before. And that one time, she hadn't had the chance to shower first.

Now she was worried.

"It *can't* be COVID, it just *can't* . . . " she murmered over and over to herself as she turned the water off, stepped out of the tub, and wrapped a towel around her body.

Gil's coughing got louder. Layla went to her backpack, pulled out a mask and put it on. Then, she rushed to the bedroom, sat beside him on the bed and placed her hand on his forehead.

There was no fever. That was a good sign.

She tried to reassure him.

"You feel normal, babe. It might not be COVID. If it's just a sore throat and coughing, it could be something else. A cold, maybe. Or some other kind of infection. But the only way to know for sure is for you to get tested."

Gil, his coughing paused, sat up in bed. He grabbed Layla's arm and squeezed hard.

"STOP it, Gil. That HURTS!"

He tightened his grip instead. "I don't GIVE a shit. You don't believe me, do you? You think I'm FAKING it!?"

"No, Gil, I don't think that. All I'm saying is you should check it out. It might not be that bad."

"Well, *I* think it's COVID. And that means you gave it to me! Thanks a lot, BITCH!"

Still holding on to her arm, he made a fist with his other hand and swung it at her head, striking her left ear. The ear she needed to hear. Then he let her arm go and shoved her away.

Layla fell off the bed and onto the floor.

She lay there, dizzy from the blow. Her ear was ringing, and she cupped her hand over it. Then she closed her eyes, hoping that was the end of the attack. It seemed to be, at least for the moment.

Most of the other times Gil was violent with her, she was at least partly to blame. That's what he told her, anyway. She'd messed up somehow and had to suffer the consequences.

But not this time. This time was different. How could he hit her *there*? He *knew* it was her only good ear. He knew she was super-sensitive about protecting it. Was he trying to make some sick point? And if he *did* have COVID, how was it her fault? That one occasion, the evening of the fight . . . well . . . *he* was the one who started it before she had the chance to shower. Not her.

For the first time, Layla was furious with him. But she kept it to herself. It was safer that way. The state he was in, it wouldn't take much to provoke him again.

What was it her mother wrote in the *Gloria* column last week? Don't stay in a bad relationship. Get out. Get help.

Gil went too far this time. It was clear what she had to do. She had to escape as soon as possible.

Early the next morning, Layla got ready for work at the exact same time she did every day. She wore her scrubs. Made her lunch and put it in her backpack. Gil decided to stay in bed and didn't notice the backpack was bulging with extra clothing and toiletries. He didn't know she had no intention of going to the hospital. She would have at least eight hours' head start before he realized she wasn't coming back.

Instead, she went to the bus station. Before boarding the bus to Ottawa, she called her supervisor and explained she might have been exposed to COVID and would need to be tested before returning. That part was true. What she didn't say was that she was leaving Kingston and wasn't sure when she'd be back.

Next, she called Jennifer.

"Hi, Mom. I'm coming to Ottawa. The bus is leaving in ten minutes."

"Layla, you sound terrible. What's going on?"

"I'm breaking up with Gil. No time to talk about it now. The reason I'm calling is I'll need a place to stay. I might have been exposed to COVID and I don't want to give it to you or Dad, so I'll have to go somewhere else. Somewhere Gil won't find me."

"Oh my God, Layla! I hope you don't have it—"

"I feel fine so far. I don't have any symptoms. And it might not be COVID at all. But I'll have to isolate until I can get tested, just to be sure."

"Of course, love. I'm *so* glad you're coming back. I'll find a safe place for you. Call me again when you get here."

"Thanks, Mom. I love you."

"Love you, too. Talk to you soon."

Jennifer had mixed feelings. She was relieved her daughter was coming back to Ottawa. But she was afraid Layla was still a target. For Gil. For COVID. Or for both.

"Hi, Rachel."

"Jen! This is a surprise! I haven't heard from you in a while. Jeff tells me you're on a sabbatical from the paper. Hope you're okay?"

Jennifer knew what Rachel really meant when she said, *Hope you're okay.* It was code for *Hope you're still on the wagon.*

She wasn't okay. She wasn't still on the wagon. But she was in slightly better shape this time around. So far, she'd been able to balance the drinking and the basic motions of daily living. The further descent into days-long oblivion might be inevitable, but she hadn't quite reached that point. Yet.

That made the little white lie more convincing.

"I'm okay. *Really* I am. And I'm sorry I haven't been in touch. It's just that I've been feeling a little overwhelmed lately. Jeff and I agreed I needed a little break, that's all. I plan to get back to work soon. You know how it is."

Actually, Rachel probably *didn't* know how it was. Her life was always so tidy, so safe. Even with the pandemic, nothing really bad had happened to her. Jennifer hoped that wouldn't change with the request she was about to make.

"Rachel, I need a huge favor. I'll understand if you say no."

"What is it, Jen?"

"You have a guest suite in your basement, right? I wonder if Layla could stay there a few days? She's leaving that dickhead boyfriend of hers, thank God, and coming back to Ottawa. She tells me she might have been exposed to COVID. Until she can get tested, she'll need to isolate."

There was a long silence. Jennifer knew it was a lot to ask. The virus had arrived only six weeks earlier. Nobody, not even the doctors, understood it completely. Not how it was passed on, not the full damage it could do to peoples' bodies. The growing casualty count every night on the news fed the miasma of fear spreading everywhere. And, despite this, Jennifer was asking Rachel to risk having Layla, a possible victim, stay in her home.

But Rachel came through. "Oh my God! Yes, of course, she can stay here. She can use the separate entrance in the back. I'll leave the key under the doormat."

"Thanks a million, Rachel. You're the best! She's on the bus right now. She'll be arriving in a couple of hours. In the meantime, I'll pick up some groceries for her and drop them off. I owe you *big* time for this."

"So what's the story, Layla? What happened with Gil?"

Jennifer sat at the patio table in Rachel's back garden, facing the door leading down to the guest suite. Layla stood in the open doorway. They were careful to keep their distance, but it was close enough that Jennifer could see Layla had lost weight. Not that she had any to spare. And she still had dark circles under her sad eyes.

"We had a big fight last night. He punched me in my good ear."

"He did *that*? Oh my God!"

"That's when I finally realized I had to get away. There were other times when . . . you know . . . he was mad at me. But this time, it was too much."

"I'm glad you finally see that, Layla. I never had a good feeling about him. It seemed to me he was always trying to control you. And that time I came down, when I saw the bruising on your wrist . . . I was *so* worried—"

"Is that why Dad came a few days later?"

"Yes. That and the fact I'd asked him to check if Gil had a criminal record. He found out he does. So, we were both anxious."

"Gil has a *criminal record*?"

"Yes. I'm not surprised he didn't tell you. A number of offenses, including assault. Domestic assault."

Layla leaned against the door frame to steady herself. Jennifer saw tears in her eyes.

"I still love him, Mom. I can't help it. But I know he's not good for me. The things he does . . . the fights keep getting worse and worse. He scares me now."

"Promise me you won't go back to him?"

"But what if he changes? What if he says he'll never hit me again?"

"How could you actually believe him? First you say he's getting worse, then you hope he might change. Don't count on it. He obviously didn't learn anything from his past convictions."

"I feel so stupid, Mom—"

"Don't. We all make mistakes, Layla. I'm far from perfect. You've seen that. But we can learn from our experiences, right?"

She heard herself doing it again. Giving advice to her daughter. Giving advice was how she made a living these days, but learning from her own mistakes? She still hadn't learned to stay away from alcohol. She was such a hypocrite. "Let's change the topic. You say you might have been exposed to COVID?"

"Yes. Gil thinks he has it. He says he got it from me. That I brought it home from the hospital. I think he's just got a cold, but I suppose there's a chance he could be right. I don't have any symptoms other than a headache. And that might be stress. Anyway, I should probably get tested. I'll go to the Brewer Park Assessment Center first thing tomorrow."

"Good. Rachel tells me you can stay here until you get the results. I understand it takes a few days. We can talk later about what happens after that."

As soon as she got home, Jennifer poured herself a double and called Eric.

"Layla's back, Eric. She's staying at Rachel's place in the guest suite."

"I'm glad to hear that, but why isn't she with you?"

Eric sounded more and more agitated as Jennifer filled him in.

"Good thing he's a couple hours' drive away. Otherwise, I'd go beat the crap out of him. And that wouldn't be good for my career advancement."

Eric had seen more than one of his fellow officers exposed in the media for bad behavior. He had no intention of joining them.

"So Layla leaving him is one problem solved. Now we have a bunch more to deal with."

"What do you mean . . . a bunch more, Eric?"

"Well, first off, there's Layla's COVID test. Where will she go if the result is positive? Who knows if Rachel would let her stay there? And if the results are negative, I guess she'll want to move in with you?"

"I hadn't thought that far ahead." Jennifer didn't like that idea. Up to now, she'd managed to hide her latest little drinking indulgences from everybody. She wouldn't be able to do that if Layla stayed with her. She'd have to stop.

"And whether she's with you or not, Jen, it's possible Gil might wind up on your doorstep looking for her. Maybe even tonight, when he realizes she's taken off."

"Fuck! You're scaring me, Eric! What do I do if he does show up here?"

"He can't get in, can he? Unless he has the keys—"

"I gave Layla a set. If she left them at her apartment, I suppose he might."

"Well, one way or the other, call 9-1-1 immediately. You can call me, too. In fact, would you like me to come over and sleep on your couch tonight? Would that make you feel safer?"

That was the *last* thing Jennifer wanted. She was halfway through her drink and was already thinking about the next one.

"Thanks, Eric, I'll be okay. No need to come over."

"All right, then. We can arrange to get your lock changed tomorrow, just in case."

"Before you go, there's something else I need to ask you. Can you lend me some money? Things are really tight since I took a break from the paper. I'll pay you back as soon as I start working again."

"Sure, Jen. I'll transfer the funds tonight. How much do you want?"

"Eight hundred? Is that too much?"

"It's a lot, but I can handle it. Call me if you need anything else."

Chapter Thirteen

Jennifer spent the evening in front of her TV, struggling to stay alert through the remnants of her afternoon buzz. For once, she'd made the decision not to have her usual nightcap. She needed to stay relatively sober in case Gil made an appearance.

She tried to focus on the finale of *Homeland*, the volume turned up irritatingly high to make it harder for her to drift off. Her cast-iron frying pan was within easy reach on the coffee table if Gil did show up with fighting on his mind.

But there was no sign of him, not even a phone call to ask if Layla was with her. Jennifer started doubting herself. Maybe she was overreacting. Would he really bother riding all the way to Ottawa just because he thought Layla was late coming home from work?

By midnight, she was more asleep than awake. She gave up and decided to go to bed. Easing herself up off the couch, she moved with slow, deliberate steps to her bedroom, grabbing a chair back and then the doorframe to steady herself on the way.

So far, so good, she thought, just before tripping on the bedside rug and pitching forward. The mattress broke the fall, but her legs didn't quite make it. They dangled in mid-air until she was able to crawl forward and settle herself fully on top of the duvet.

"How graceful was that?" she mumbled. She was glad nobody else was there. Anyone witnessing her acrobatics would find them either hilarious or pitiful.

"Where IS she?"

The growl cut through Jennifer's heavy slumber and pulled her part way back to consciousness. She opened one eye. It was still dark and she wasn't sure if the voice came from the dream side or the awake side.

"I SAID, WHERE THE FUCK *IS* SHE?"

It was Gil's voice. He'd raised the decibels. And it definitely came from the awake side.

Jennifer opened both eyes wide.

All she could see in the dark was his silhouette hovering over her from the right. She started to roll left to get out of his reach, but she didn't make it. His arms shot out, gripped her shoulders, and pushed her back down on the bed. Then he grabbed her jaw with one hand and twisted her head around to face him.

"Nice try. But not fast enough."

He started coughing. He had no mask. If he had COVID, Jennifer thought, then he didn't mind sharing it with her.

Jennifer surprised herself. She had been dreading any kind of confrontation with Gil. But now that it was actually happening, she wasn't afraid after all. Instead, she was angry.

Who did he think he was, this insignificant little jerk who thought he could force the information out of her? No way *that* was going to happen.

"I figured she was already here. But even if she didn't come running home to mommy, you know where she's at."

"Why should I tell you? You'd only hurt her again."

He slapped her face with the back of his other hand.

It stung like hell.

Shit! Why didn't she bring that frying pan with her when she came to bed? At least she had her cell phone beside her, under the duvet. She'd call Eric the second she had the chance.

"Go ahead, beat me up. It won't work. I'm not going to tell you."

Another slap. Harder this time. "Fine. Have it your way. I can wait all fuckin' night."

More coughing.

Gil turned on the bedside lamp, looked around the room and found what he wanted. Something to tie up Jennifer's hands. "STAY WHERE YOU ARE!" He went to the chair in the corner and pulled the belt out of her bathrobe. She thought about reaching for her phone, but he'd likely grab it from her before she could turn it on.

He looped the belt through one of the headboard spindles and tied her wrists together with it.

"Comfy?" He laughed. He thought he was funny. "I'm feeling a little thirsty after the long ride—" Gil swaggered to the kitchen and opened the fridge door. Jennifer's view of him was partly obscured, but it didn't take any imagination to know what he was up to. First, he pulled out a milk carton and dropped it on the floor. Three eggs, all she had left, followed one by one. Then he unscrewed the top of a jug of orange juice, poured its contents over the smashed eggs, and heaved the jug into the living room where it hit a window and fell.

The half-empty bottle of wine that he fished out of the back of the fridge was more appealing to him. Gil returned to the bedroom doorway and held up the bottle.

"Drinking again, are we? And here Layla thought you kicked the habit. She'll be *so* disappointed. Don't mind if I help myself. I'll be in the living room if you need anything."

Gil laughed again as he turned away.

She glanced over at her clock-radio. It was 5:00 in the morning. Jennifer could hear him turn on the TV and surf through the channels till he found a football game. After that came the occasional belch and, finally, snoring.

She had plenty of time to think. And to try to free herself.

So, he thought tying her up and trashing her place would make her tell him where Layla was. Really? She'd done some major damage here herself during her binges. No big deal cleaning up another mess. And didn't he think far enough ahead to realize she'd report the assault to the police? Obviously not. How fucking stupid can a lowlife get?

It took almost an hour, using her teeth to loosen the knot,

to free one hand. Leaving her other hand in place, she reached under the duvet for her cellphone and speed-dialled Eric's number. By that point, dawn had broken. Eric would already be out of bed and making breakfast for himself.

"Eric!"

"Jen! I can hardly hear you! What's up?"

"Gil's here. Tied me to the bed. He's asleep in the living room."

"There in ten. Don't move."

Jennifer turned her phone off and shoved it back under the duvet. She slid her free hand in place and looped the belt around it.

Unless he got close, it looked like she was still tied up.

But Gil hadn't heard anything. He was still snoring on the couch.

It wasn't a dramatic, break-down-the-door kind of entry.

Instead, Eric quietly unlocked the door and pushed it forward a few inches. Before stepping in, he listened for any sound that would tell him Gil was awake. All he heard was a TV commentator talking about draft picks and Gil's slow heavy breathing.

Eric pulled out his zip-tie restraints and entered the apartment. He walked cautiously to the couch and leaned over to grab Gil's wrist.

Gil wasn't sleeping after all. He leaped to his feet and

raised his fists.

"Come and GET me, asshole!"

Eric dropped the restraints and got ready to defend himself.

"STOP, Gil! I've called for backup. They'll be here any minute. Don't make things worse for yourself."

Gil lowered his fists. But he wasn't giving up.

He lunged forward and punched Eric with a right uppercut to the jaw.

Eric went down.

Gil started kicking him. His first target was Eric's stomach.

Behind him, Jennifer slipped quietly from the bedroom into the living room. He didn't notice.

"Not such a tough cop after all, ARE you, motherfucker!"

With both hands, Jennifer grabbed the cast-iron pan off the coffee table.

Gil heard the noise and turned toward it, but it was too late. The pan arced through the air and crashed into the side of his head. He fell unconscious to the floor.

Jennifer stepped over him to reach Eric. She knew Gil wouldn't hear her words but she couldn't resist saying them anyway.

"Nice try. But not fast enough."

"Jesus, Jen. That was a wicked knockout. Remind me never to get on your bad side when culinary weapons are nearby."

Eric sat on Jennifer's couch, holding a plastic sandwich bag filled with ice cubes against his swollen jaw. As far as he could tell, nothing was broken. He still had all his teeth. But he'd be feeling pain there and in his stomach for days to come.

Jennifer brought a coffee into the living room and sat beside him. It was for her. Eric's mouth was too sore to handle the heat.

"I *had* to do it, Eric. You'd be in way worse shape if I hadn't."

"I know. And I'm grateful. It might have been me they carted off to the hospital instead. And who knows what might have happened to you—"

"It makes me shudder to think what he's been doing to Layla all these months."

"Well, he won't be bothering *any* of us for a while. After they have his head checked out, he'll be taken to the detention center. There'll be criminal charges. He'll likely stay behind bars unless he's released on bail."

"Let's hope to God *that* doesn't happen."

Chapter Fourteen

Layla got the call as she stood in line at the COVID assessment center. She'd already been there an hour, and it looked like it might take at least another hour before she could get tested. She didn't mind. She actually enjoyed passing the time chatting with the elderly gentleman standing behind her. At a safe distance, of course. Just like everybody else in the lineup that, as a result, trailed all the way around the perimeter of the sports field where the center was located.

As usual, Layla didn't say all that much and was happy just to listen. The retired professor had been a world traveller in his younger days, and his stories reminded her of ones she'd heard about her mother's backpacking experiences when she was Layla's age.

The woman ahead of her was something else entirely. Complaining to everybody within earshot about the long wait. The closed shops. The ridiculous run on toilet paper. It turned out she was a recent widow. Poor lady, Layla thought. Life has suddenly become so overwhelmingly difficult for her. In a way she, too, reminded Layla of Jennifer, and how they both had to cope with isolating alone. She felt sorry for them.

The line shuffled ahead. Then her cellphone buzzed.

"Hi, Mom. I was just thinking about you. You good?"

"I'm okay, love. But there's something I need to tell you. Are you alone?"

"Not really. I'm in line for my COVID test."

"Should I call you back later?"

This sounded like bad news to Layla. But how could it possibly be worse than what she'd been through the past few days?

"No. Tell me now. I can take it."

"If you're sure—"

"I'm *sure*, Mom."

"Gil showed up at my place early this morning looking for you."

"He did?!"

"Yes. And it wasn't a warm and cuddly visit."

"Oh my God! What happened? Are you okay?"

The woman in front of her had stopped complaining and started listening in. Layla brought her cellphone closer to her mouth and lowered her voice.

"I mean, he didn't hurt you or anything, did he?"

"I'm fine."

Fine, other than being tied up, slapped, and having her condo vandalized. But Jennifer thought the news would be hard enough for Layla to hear without giving her all the details.

"Unfortunately, Eric got the worst of it. There was a fight."

"Oh no! Is he okay?"

"He's feeling it today. Nothing too serious, though. No broken bones or anything like that."

"Where's Gil now?"

"Likely in jail. First, though, he was taken to the hospital. I knocked him out with my frying pan."

It wasn't funny when it happened, but it sounded funny now. Jennifer couldn't help smiling.

"Really? You did that?"

"Please don't be mad at me, love. I had to stop the fight somehow."

"How can I be mad, Mom. I mean, it's my fault. He was *my* boyfriend—"

"It's nobody's fault but his own, Layla. But let's just focus on what's important now. Your COVID test. And now that we've been exposed to Gil, I guess Eric and I should get tested, too, if we start showing symptoms. Fingers crossed it's a false alarm for all of us."

Layla had to wait three days to get her test results. Three long, lonely days isolating not in her own home, but in someone else's guest suite. A suite so pristine, so precisely staged, it looked like it belonged in some five-star hotel featured in a high-end travel review. The lavender-scented bedsheets were satin and when she touched the wallpaper, it felt smooth as silk. A robe laid out for her on the bed was the same plush Turkish cotton as the towels displayed just so in the marble bathroom. Layla appreciated having a nice place to stay, but it was impossible to feel comfortable for fear of messing things up.

While she was there, she played endless games of Candy Crush and binge-watched the last two seasons of *Game of Thrones*. After that, she read all the back issues of *Hello!* magazine she found in a neat stack on the bedside table, flipping fast through photos of palatial homes of minor European aristocrats. She wasn't the slightest bit interested in their glamorous lives but the magazines helped pass the time. Besides, how else could she stop thinking about Gil?

Sometimes the distractions didn't work.

The nights were the hardest, when she lay in bed trying, but failing, to sleep. Instead, she remembered how he'd been *so* good to her at the beginning. It had been almost like a dream, those first couple of months. He didn't care that she was hard of hearing. He was okay that she didn't say much, either. Just the opposite. He was quite happy to spend their time together doing all the talking himself. And when he came over to her place, he brought all sorts of wonderful gourmet ingredients he whipped up into awesome meals.

No guy had ever been that interested in her before. Not to mention how gorgeous he was.

Why didn't she notice the change after he moved in? It started with the yelling. Every couple has disagreements, she said to herself at the time. And making up again afterwards was *so* nice.

Then he wanted her to cut down on seeing her few friends. Perhaps that should have been some kind of warning. Back then, she just figured he wanted her all to himself. And when COVID hit, getting together with her friends became impossible anyway. The physical stuff came later. The hitting. The rough handling. But every time he was so sorry about it afterwards she always forgave him. She was desperate for his affection and fooled herself into thinking things would get better. She could see now that was never going to happen.

She'd wanted to be with him forever. But not the way he was toward the end. And certainly not after what he did to her parents.

Each night, she cried. It was like someone close to her had died.

Finally, Layla got the news: her COVID test results were negative.

So, Gil didn't catch the virus from her, and that meant she could go home to Kingston and return to work at the hospital. According to texts she received from her coworkers there, the situation was a nightmare. The ICU was full beyond capacity. They needed her back on the job as soon as possible.

But Layla was worried. Jennifer had heard from Eric that Gil's bail hearing would take place any day. What if he got released? Would he come after her? Would she have to stay in hiding? Until she knew where he was, going back to her Kingston apartment was out of the question. She decided to wait for the bail decision at her mother's place.

Layla stuffed all her belongings in her backpack, left a thank you note for Rachel and took an Uber ride to Jennifer's condo.

"Mom, are you okay?"

Jennifer didn't look at all well. She was lying on her couch, wrapped in the duvet from her bed even though it was an unusually warm day. Despite this, she was shivering.

"I've got a bug, love. I hope to God it isn't COVID. Don't get too close. And keep your mask on."

"Sorry you're feeling bad, Mom. How can I help? Can I get you anything?"

"I really need a coffee, please."

Jennifer started coughing and couldn't stop.

Layla went to the kitchen and washed her hands. Then she set up the coffee maker, turned it on and waited.

For Jennifer, there was more on her mind than being sick. It had been a week since she'd gone to the liquor store. She hadn't had a drink in two days and, boy, could she use one now.

Layla brought a mug of hot coffee to the living room and set it down on the table beside Jennifer. Then she backed away to a chair on the opposite side of the room and waited for her mother's coughing to stop. When it did, Jennifer propped herself up on one elbow, pulled down her mask, and reached for the mug.

After the first sip, she started coughing again. She pulled the mask back up immediately.

What Layla saw disturbed her. The coughing. The shivering. *Especially* the shivering. This looked worse than a cold. Even if Gil didn't get out on bail, she'd postpone going home until Jennifer was better.

"I'm not sure how much I can do for you, Mom, but think I should stay here for a while. I've brought all my stuff and can sleep on the couch. And I'm not contagious. My COVID test results came back negatve."

Minutes later, they both got the same WhatsApp text message from Eric.

> *Just heard from courthouse. Gil's*
> *bail hearing on docket this aft. Will*
> *keep you posted.*

Chapter Fifteen

"Blah blah blah . . . "

So much noise.

The words didn't matter to Gil. Standing in the prisoner's box, he tuned out as the presiding JP started to give her decision.

Why pay any attention when she recited the charges against him? Assault times two. Damage to property under five thousand dollars. And more. Big fuckin' deal.

Then she described in detail the events of that night at the bitch's apartment. Did he really need to listen to this shit? He already knew what happened. He was there.

There was only one thing Gil wanted to hear. Was she going to let him out or not?

It could have gone either way. He was fully aware of that. The plan his defense lawyer presented to the court wasn't all that great. He had no sureties, no reliable relatives or friends to supervise him while he waited for his trial. Instead, the John Howard Society had stepped in for more limited monitoring. Not ideal, but better than nothing. And the criminal record thing? That didn't work in his favor either. But he'd managed to stay out of trouble for seven years since his last convictions. Maybe the JP would think he could do it again.

Finally, she got to the part he was waiting for.

"Mr. Leblanc, I share the Crown's concern that any repeat of your alleged violent behavior could have dire consequences."

Damn! This wasn't sounding good.

"However, I believe the plan put together for your release sufficiently mitigates this risk and you may be released today. But I *am* imposing strict conditions—"

Fuck, yes! He was getting out!

"Your conditions are as follows. There will be a five-thousand-dollar bond. It is not payable immediately, but it could become payable if you breach any other conditions. Your bail supervision will be by the John Howard Society, with weekly reporting. You must remain in Ontario. You are to have no contact or communication whatsoever with Eric Nash or Jennifer Carr, and you must stay 200 meters away from where they live or work. You are not to possess any weapons—"

On and on she went. Gil nodded at each condition. Anything to get the hell out of there. She could have told him to kiss her ass a thousand times and he would have done it willingly, with a "thank you, ma'am" and a big, sucky smile.

Gil walked out of the courthouse after retrieving his belongings and signing the release documents. He wasn't due to report to the John Howard Society for a week. Right now, there was only once place for him to go—back to the apartment in Kingston.

But where the hell was Layla?

"Hello?"

"I'm afraid I've got bad news." The last thing Layla needed was more bad news, but she put Eric on speakerphone so both she and Jennifer could hear it anyway.

"Gil had his bail hearing. He's being released."

"No! How could they *do* that?"

Only Layla responded. Jennifer was starting to have trouble breathing. For her, speaking was out of the question.

"Layla, is that you? How come you're with Mom? I thought you were isolating?"

"I was. Until my test results came back this morning. I don't have COVID."

"Thank God for that! I was pretty worried about you, kiddo. The answer to your question is simple. His lawyer convinced the JP it was safe to let him out. I understand he has a lot of conditions, including staying away from Jen and me."

"But what if he doesn't? Stay away, I mean?"

"He'll be arrested again. And likely detained until his trial."

"Where is he now?"

"Who knows? All I know is he's out."

"Shit, Dad! Maybe he's gone back to my apartment."

"Why don't you stay with Jennifer for a while? Or with me?"

"I've already decided to stay with Mom. She's not feeling so good. I can take care of her here."

"Oh? Sorry to hear that. At least it's not COVID, right?"

Layla didn't answer. She wasn't so sure.

"Anything I can do to help?"

"I don't think so, but I'll let you know."

Layla kept busy tidying up the apartment and bringing liquids to Jennifer. There wasn't much else she could do.

And Jennifer wasn't getting any better. In fact, by early evening, she got worse. Much worse. The tortured sounds of her broken breathing could be heard all over the condo and she was barely conscious.

Layla called 9-1-1.

Chapter Sixteen

Layla already figured visitors weren't allowed at the Civic Hospital. That's the way it was where she worked in Kingston. The hospital's website simply confirmed it:

NOTICE: The hospital is in full visitor restrictions as part of our ongoing response to COVID-19.

She was going anyway.

For sure, her Mom had COVID. She just *knew* it. She'd been around lots of COVID cases and Jennifer's symptoms, after her rapid decline the night before, were just like the ones she saw in the other patients.

Layla's mind went where she didn't want it to go. She tried hard not to think about how Jennifer's condition might deteriorate after she was admitted but found it impossible to clear her thoughts. She was an orderly, after all, and knew too much. It wasn't that long ago she stood helpless at the bedside of Mrs. Sofia before she slipped away.

What happened to Mrs. Sofia wasn't going to happen to her mother. Jennifer was *not* going to go through this on her own.

And if Layla didn't go to the hospital, she might never see her alive again.

Just before noon, the hospital confirmed Layla's suspicions. Jennifer's test had come back positive. Minutes later, Layla gave Eric an update over the phone.

"I'm so scared, Dad. The hospital just called. Mom's got COVID."

"Oh Jesus! Poor Jen. How is she doing now? Did they tell you?"

"They said she's about the same as when she left here last night. They've got her on oxygen . . . Dad, I'm really worried. I saw so many awful cases in Kingston."

"I'm sure you did, Layla. Let's try to be positive. She's exactly where she should be. They'll take the best possible care of her there."

"I know, Dad. And I want to help, too. At least be with her. But visitors aren't allowed."

"For good reason. Don't do anything crazy, Layla. Stay away from the hospital. I wouldn't want you to risk it, and I'm sure Jen wouldn't either."

"But Dad—"

Layla didn't care what he said. It was no use repeating to him how deeply she felt and what she knew she needed to do. If she wore her scrubs and an N95 mask, they might think she was staff and let her pass. It was worth a try.

Maybe it was just her imagination, but the hospital, an austere red brick Victorian edifice, appeared particularly hostile to Layla that afternoon. Hoping she looked like any other orderly starting a shift, she strode through the automatic doors at the front entrance with a show of confidence she didn't really feel. As it turned out, getting inside was easy. Just a polite inquiry by a hospital volunteer as to her destination. Layla had already thought of an answer. "The Orthopedic Unit," she mumbled and kept on going.

Still, even though she might look like a hospital worker, there was no guarantee she would make it all the way to Jennifer's bedside.

After checking the directory, she followed the signs to the General Surgery Ward, which according to the newspaper, had been converted into the COVID Unit. She didn't waste any time getting there, moving fast past the Tim Hortons on the left and gift shops on the right. They were all closed. There were no lineups for double-double coffees. No anxious visitors buying arrangements from flower shop volunteers. Unlike Layla, the fast-food staff, the volunteers, the relatives and friends all stayed away, just as they were instructed.

Layla stopped at the COVID Unit nursing station.

"Excuse me, could you tell me which room Jennifer Carr is in?"

The nurse, busy at a computer behind the counter, glanced up at Layla. She seemed puzzled, likely wondering why some young orderly, wearing a mask and gloves but no ID and no other PPE, was bothering her about a specific patient. Then she shrugged and pointed to a semi-private room along a corridor on the left.

"She's in 4218. Don't disturb her. I just checked and she's resting. And, anyway, you'd need full PPE first."

"How is she?"

"Not good. The doctor's talking ventilator. Odds get even worse once that happens."

Layla flinched. The nurse noticed.

"You'll get used to it."

Then she turned back to her computer.

Layla walked down the corridor and stopped outside the room. The curtains were pulled back and she could see Jennifer lying in the bed closest to the window, her eyes closed and her face partially covered by a clear oxygen mask. She was so pale and limp, she almost disappeared into the folds of the sheets.

Just like Mrs. Sofia.

Layla felt sick.

All she wanted to do was sit with her mother for a few moments. Hold her hand. And, most important of all, tell her how much she loved her.

Layla looked back at the nurse. She was pounding away at her computer keyboard.

Now was her chance.

Layla slipped quickly into the room and moved to the side

of Jennifer's bed.

"HEY! DON'T GO IN THERE!"

Layla ignored the nurse's barking from down the hall.

She leaned close to her mother and whispered, through her mask, in her ear.

"Mom, it's me. I can't stay long. They won't let me. But I know you'll be better soon."

Layla knew no such thing, but saying it out loud was comforting to her and might be to Jennifer too, if the words filtered through somehow.

"I can't wait till you get out of here. And when you come home, I'll take such good care of you. I love you, Mom. I love you so much."

Layla stroked Jennifer's forehead with her gloved hand.

As she stepped back, Jennifer's eyes opened and Layla thought she could see a faint smile underneath the oxygen mask.

By then, the nurse had reached Room 4218.

Layla moved away from the bed.

"I know, I know. I'm going."

The nurse marched her to the elevator. It didn't take any more scolding for Layla to leave the hospital fast. Just outside the entrance, she paused to take a deep breath of fresh spring air, something her mother could not do. Then she turned and started walking along the side of the building toward the bus shelter. She didn't get far. Her legs felt like they couldn't hold her up anymore.

She thought she was going to faint. Layla leaned against the hard brick wall and wept.

Back at the condo, Layla tried to calm herself before calling Eric. She wasn't entirely successful.

"I have a confession to make, Dad. I just came back from the hospital."

"Layla! You went! Was that wise? Did they actually let you in?"

"Well, nobody stopped me. I know I shouldn't have gone. But I just *had* to."

"I guess I'm not really surprised. How's she doing?"

"She looked terrible, Dad. She's on oxygen. The nurse said she was getting worse. I'm *so* afraid."

Eric could tell Layla was crying.

"Easy, girl! I know this is tough. Let's try to stay calm."

Layla sobbed into the phone.

"I think I'm going to lose her, Dad. I think she's going to *die*!"

Chapter Seventeen

Rachel shivered and pulled up the collar of her cashmere jacket. Then she fished the key fob out of her Kate Spade bag, unlocked the door of her BMW and climbed in. It was supposed to be warmer than this by now. Much warmer. She pressed the button on the dashboard to heat her leather seat.

In another week, leaf buds on the old-growth trees would unfurl, creating an emerald-green canopy over her Rockcliffe Park home lasting until October. Yellow and orange and pink tulips, their bulbs planted along the front pathway by her gardener the previous fall, would burst into full bloom any day now. So why the blast of raw weather three days in a row? It felt more like March than May.

At least the sun was shining when she backed out of the driveway and started the short drive to pick up Layla at the condo. From there, the two would go to the hospital to get Jennifer, who was now well enough to come home. By the time she arrived, the sun was gone. Angry slate-gray clouds scudded fast across the morning sky, threatening a cold rain.

Rachel parked as close to the front entrance as she could get. She was a few minutes early. So was Layla, who was waiting for her just outside the door. Rachel was about to roll down the window and call out for her when she saw a man approach from the visitor parking area. Layla saw him, too, and took a half-step back when he got close. This didn't seem right to Rachel. Not only did the guy look like some B movie thug, dressed all in black and wearing sunglasses despite the darkening skies, but Layla was clearly not happy to see him. Rachel pulled her cellphone out of her bag. She was ready to call the police if it looked like he was going to cause trouble.

"Hey, babe! Great to see you. I've missed you a lot, you know."

Gil spoke with the smooth, oily version of his voice he thought sounded seductive. Layla told him once when they first met she liked it when he talked like that.

"Gil! What are you doing here?"

Layla was confused. She was afraid of him and what he might do to her if things turned ugly, and at the same time, she had the impulse to embrace him, to feel his arms around her again. She didn't know where this urge came from. It surprised her. And it didn't last long.

Gil tilted his head to one side and smiled with the puppy-dog gaze that had charmed her in the past. Maybe it would work this time, too. "I want to be with you so bad, babe. Can we talk?"

"How did you find me?"

He wasn't expecting this question. Maybe this wasn't going to be so easy.

"I figured you might visit your mother's place at some point. I've been hanging out nearby. Waiting for the chance to see you again."

"You mean you were stalking me!"

This was definitely headed in the wrong direction for Gil.

"Ah, shit, Layla! Don't talk like that! I don't mean you any harm, babe. I'm here because I really want us to think about getting back together again."

"You can't be serious! After what you did to me? And to my mom and dad?"

The puppy-dog tilt disappeared. It was replaced by his downtrodden look. He really needed to connect with her again. He'd gone back to her place after he was released. All his stuff was there. So why not try to convince her he should stay? Otherwise, he'd wind up living in some crappy rooming house.

"But isn't it supposed to be just the two of us, babe? We're so good together . . . I thought you were on my side, not your parents'. I can see they've been poisoning you against me."

Gil stepped forward and gripped Layla's shoulder.

"LET ME GO!"

"NO! Not until—"

"NOT UNTIL WHAT?" Layla recognized Rachel's voice. She'd never heard her shout like that before. She was *so* relieved. Gil would probably back off now that there was a witness.

Gil turned to see Rachel walking towards them. His hand dropped away from Layla's shoulder.

"Who the fuck are YOU?" he said.

"Never mind who I am. You're Gil, right? Jennifer told me *all* about you."

He didn't answer.

"And Gil, or whoever you are, can't you see you're not wanted here?"

"Why don't you just fuck off and leave us alone."

"I'm not going anywhere. And you should know I've already called the police. They're on their way right now."

She wasn't bluffing. They heard the faint sound of a siren getting closer and louder.

Gil started to run. But it was too late.

Rachel and Layla sat in the lobby of the condo building, warming themselves after speaking to the police. Once the officers were gone, Layla pulled out her cellphone and called Eric.

"Hi, Dad. First thing I need to tell you is we're okay. Rachel and me, that is."

"Why? What happened?"

"Gil showed up here at the condo building. He wanted me to get back together with him."

"Seriously? What the hell was he thinking? But you say you're okay?"

"Yes, thanks to Rachel. She came to pick me up. Things started to get tense and she called the police. They took him away. It all happened pretty quick."

"What do you mean things were tense? Did he get physical?"

"He grabbed my shoulder. But that's all. He didn't hurt me."

"Thank God for that."

"The police want us to go to the station and make a statement. Dad . . . I'm worried if they let him out again, he'll come looking for me."

"I doubt that'll happen, Layla. Even if he wasn't violent with you, he's breached one of his bail conditions."

"Really?"

"Yes. He's supposed to stay at least 200 meters away from where your mother or I live. He was breaching that just by showing up there today. Which means there's a good chance he won't be let out this time."

"That's a relief! Got to leave now, Dad. I'll call you when we get back."

Rachel and Layla were an hour late when they finally reached the hospital.

Jennifer, just a little impatient at the delay, was wheeled out to Rachel's car. Even though she was still weak, she was one of the lucky ones. She'd beaten COVID. The nurses said it was a miracle.

Chapter Eighteen

"Dad called while you were sleeping, Mom. He says he can't come over after all. He just got his test result back and it's positive. He's isolating."

Jennifer sat up abruptly on the couch and immediately regretted doing so. She'd been home a week but was still suffering. Sore all over and barely able to move. So exhausted, she didn't want to move anyway. The sudden motion sent an even stronger jolt of pain up her back. She didn't dare try to lie down again. It would hurt too much.

How long was this damn virus supposed to last anyway? There was no answer to that question. It was so new, nobody—not the researchers, not the frontline doctors and nurses—had any idea. Still, despite all the lingering after effects, at least she was out of danger.

"You mean he has *COVID*?"

"Yes. But he told me he doesn't have any symptoms. Not one."

"That's a relief. I wonder who gave it to him?"

"He says there's an outbreak at the detention center. He thinks he got it there."

Layla helped ease Jennifer back on the pillows.

"The other thing he told me was that Gil won't be getting out of jail before his trial."

"Couldn't happen to a more deserving person."

Jennifer noticed the sudden frown on Layla's face.

"Sorry, Layla. I shouldn't be so flippant. I know you're still feeling upset about him."

"It's okay, Mom. I'll get over it. I hope you do, too."

The first time Jennifer and Layla went for a walk, it lasted all of five minutes. It wasn't the weather that cut it short. The sun was shining and it was a perfect day to be outside. But even twelve whole days after returning home, five minutes was all Jennifer could manage. She was starting to think she was one of the "long haulers" the medical experts were beginning to talk about. The ravages of COVID seemed to drag on forever in those cases.

Her arm was looped through Layla's for support as they slowly made their way to the corner and back. She felt a hundred years old but she was happy. Here she was, walking with her darling Layla on a beautiful spring day. Fortunate just to be alive. So many others didn't make it.

After they returned to the apartment, Layla made sure Jennifer was comfortable and left again for a longer walk by herself. Neither Jennifer nor Layla had much chance to be on their own for almost two weeks. They needed a break from each other.

After Layla was gone, Jennifer reached for her cellphone. She had an overdue call to make.

"Lizzie?"

"Jennifer! How *are* you? It's been ages since we talked. I've been worried about you!"

"I know. And I'm sorry. A lot has happened lately . . . I'm feeling better now."

"Great, I'd love to hear about it."

Jennifer filled Lizzie in on everything. Her sabbatical. Layla's escape from Gil. The confrontation when he showed up looking for her. Her battle with COVID. And now, her slow recovery.

"Holy shit, Jen! That's wild! My life is so boring by comparison. I'm either staying at home or doing the grocery run. Too much Netflix and too much food."

"Sometimes boring is a good thing. But Lizzie, what I really want to tell you is I've totally stopped drinking. And, fingers crossed, I never will again."

"Wow! That's *such* good news."

"To be honest, it wasn't my choice at first. I was forced into it because of COVID. When you're lying semi-conscious in a hospital bed for days and days on end, not knowing if you'll live or die . . . well . . . I can tell you it's a unique form of rehab. Layla's been taking care of me ever since I was discharged. So, there's no way for me to get my hands on alcohol anyway. And you know what? I don't even want to. Maybe I've finally had my come-to-Jesus moment. A near-death experience will do that, I guess. And now that I have a second chance, I don't want to blow it."

"Good girl."

"Not to mention, I'm getting to spend some wonderful time with Layla . . . . Before we go, Lizzie, I want to thank you for hanging in. You've been so patient with me."

"Well, if you want, we can still have our calls. With this damn pandemic dragging on, both of us can use the extra encouragement. You okay with that?"

"Sure. And I think I'll join in the Zoom meetings, too."

After they hung up, Jennifer had just enough energy to make herself a coffee. And she began to think nice things about the future.

"Layla, love, there's something I want to ask you."

"Sure, go ahead."

"I feel I'm just about ready to start writing the column again. I don't know if my editor will agree, but I have something different in mind for the first one. Sort of a new beginning. I'd like to re-introduce myself to my readers. Not as Gloria Pierce, but as *me*, Jennifer Carr. Then I want to fill them in on all the things that've happened to me since I went on my little sabbatical. And what I've learned that I can pass along to them. Turn all this negative shit into a positive."

"Awesome, Mom! And you want to ask me—?"

"I wonder if I could mention our experience with Gil? Or would that upset you?"

Layla thought about it for a moment, staring off into the distance. "No. I guess not. Not if you do it without using our real names."

"Of course."

"Okay, then. And if you're writing about the good outcomes, I want you to include us."

Jennifer liked the sound of that.

"Us? Go on."

"Well, Mom. I've been doing some thinking. And I've decided to move back to Ottawa. I'm sure I can get an orderly job right away at one of the hospitals here. It would mean I can be closer to you. I can help you get better."

Was she really hearing this? It was almost too much for Jennifer to hope for.

"Layla, that would be fantastic! Are you telling your pain-in-the-ass mother that she's not so bad after all?"

"I don't want to dig up old stuff, Mom, but you know that I used to feel overwhelmed by you. I guess I needed to get away for a bit and try things on my own. And now that I have . . . well . . . I see things a little differently. You were just trying to protect me, right? I understand that now."

"I'm sorry if I came on too strong, love."

"I know. And once I'm back in Ottawa, I want you to give me some space. Let me do my thing. If I make mistakes, let me fix them myself. Then we'll be cool. Deal?"

Jennifer pulled an already twice-used tissue out of her sleeve and dried her eyes. She was giggling and crying a few happy tears at the same time. Maybe, she thought, I didn't screw up with my sweet Layla after all. She loves me. And she's coming back.

"Deal!"

Chapter Nineteen

THAT'S LIFE
Ask Jennifer Carr

Dear Readers,

I'm back, after months of sabbatical. And you have no idea how glad I am to be writing to you again. Today's column is a special one. I have a lot to tell you, dear readers, so grab your beverage of choice. Find a comfortable seat. And settle in for a long read. But first things first. Let me introduce you to the real me. It's certainly time I did. You know me as Gloria Pierce, the advice columnist. My real name is Jennifer Carr. I'm sure you already noticed the name change in the byline above. And my email address at the end of this column has changed, too. Go ahead, Google my name. You will likely see a few reviews of my now-closed restaurant, La Casita. The early ones are pretty good. The later ones, not so much. You may also see a somewhat obscure newspaper article about an unfortunate incident with a customer there. I won't go into the details in this column, but I might as well come right out and say it: what happened was my fault. And it was part of the downward spiral that led to La Casita's closing slightly more than a year ago. I didn't handle it well, dear readers. I went into seclusion, separating myself from those closest to me. I drank too much. Alcohol took over my life and the lives of those who love me. I did all the things an advice columnist, THIS advice columnist, would tell you not to do. But I was a different person back then. Ultimately, with the help of friends and family, I recovered and moved on. I learned a lot from that experience. And this wouldn't be an advice column if I didn't share my learning, would it? So, here goes:

Life lesson #1: Nobody is perfect. Shit happens. And when you stumble and fall, your loved ones, the ones who truly love you back, may offer to help you stand up again. Let them.

Starting the THAT'S LIFE column earlier this year was a godsend. I am eternally grateful to the editor for having confidence in me. Nevertheless, because of doubts that might have been raised by the restaurant experience, we decided not to use my real name. Now that I am returning to "active duty," we also agreed it was time to reveal who the real Gloria is. So that, dear readers, is all you need to know about my checkered past. I turn now to my sabbatical, which was considerably more eventful than anticipated.

Since March, we have all endured a pandemic that has forced us into hiding. For some, the isolation is more difficult than for others. I'll give you two examples.

First, there are many of us who live alone. Being shut in, without another human being to talk to, to touch, to simply be with, can be the worst kind of torture. A phone call, a Facetime or Skype conversation, even a small care package, could make a big difference.

Life lesson #2: If you know anybody living alone in this scary time, reach out to them. Communicate by whatever means you can.

Do it on a regular basis. It will make you both feel good.

And second, we have all started to hear about the increase in domestic violence, with more incidents of abuse by intimate partners due to increased health and financial pressures and prolonged exposure. I had the sad experience of observing such a situation with a close relative. Fortunately, she has managed to leave her violent partner, who has been brought to justice.

Life lesson #3: If you experience unacceptable and demeaning behavior, do not make excuses for the perpetrator. It is not your fault. It never is. Leave. If you have no family or friends to provide safe haven, check out the available community resources.

Life lesson #4: If you witness unacceptable and demeaning behavior, do not stand by. Make it clear you are ready to help the victim.

And speaking of the pandemic, I can tell you now that I am a COVID survivor. I first felt the symptoms six weeks ago. I have never gone through anything like this virus and I almost didn't make it. But I am one of the lucky ones. With the expert care of frontline staff, I recovered. I owe my life to them. There is a silver lining to my COVID experience. It has brought my daughter and me much closer together. Since my release from the hospital, she has devoted herself to my care. In fact, she has decided to move back to this city after a period of living away. My relationship with my daughter is the most important thing in the world to me. I will make every effort to maintain it. And that includes my promise to recognize she is now an adult with her own path to follow.

Life lesson #5: Relationships need mutual respect to flourish. They need time and space and energy. They can be hard work, but the good ones are always worth it.

So there you have it, dear readers. A rather fulsome introduction to the real me and a few life lessons I can share with you. And now that you know me, I hope I can continue to enjoy

your confidence. Write to me. I promise I will always give you my honest, unvarnished advice. That's all I have ever done and all I will ever do. Until the next time, stay safe.
—Jennifer

Send your relationship questions to:
askjennifer@ottawadailychronicle.ca

About the Author

Anna Blauveldt was born and raised in Fredericton, New Brunswick, Canada and graduated with an Honours B.A. degree from the University of New Brunswick. She moved to Ottawa, Canada to pursue a career with the federal government, culminating in her appointment as Canada's Ambassador to Iceland. She subsequently completed the Post-Graduate Creative Writing Program of Humber College in Toronto and obtained a Masters' degree with Merit in Creative and Critical Writing from the University of Gloucestershire, UK in 2019.

Her children's picture book, *Kat and the Meanies,* was published in 2016 by Under the Maple Tree Books. Her short story *Irma* appeared in the 2019 anthology "A Two-Four of Tales," and her story *Released* appeared in the 2020 anthology "Short Stories for a Long Year," both published by Ottawa Independent Writers.

Acknowledgments

Thanks go to Nicole and Greig for making room in their busy schedules to share clear recollections of, and astute observations on, their fertility clinic experiences. These stories have greatly benefitted from the insights of my husband John and the example set by our daughter Katya, a truly creative spirit whose work has been performed at the Edinburgh Fringe Festival. One of my lifelong goals is to make her as proud of me as I am of her. Finally, I appreciate the incisive feedback of Dr. Martin Randall, University of Gloucestershire, who helped me immeasurably in the gestation of *To Play at God.*